A WOMAN UNBECOMING

A WOMAN UNBECOMING

EDITED BY

RACHEL A. BRUNE AND CAROL GYZANDER

"A Woman Unbecoming" by CM Harris originally appeared in *Coppice & Brake,* 2020, Crone Girls Press.

"Failed Love Lessons" by Linda D. Addison originally appeared in *The Place of Broken Things* (Crystal Lake Publishing, 2019), HWA Bram Stoker Award®.

"How Does Your Garden Grow?" by Samantha Bryant originally appeared in "The Fantastic Other," February 2022.

"To Thine Self Be True" by Alp Beck originally appeared in *Hell's Grannies: Kickass Tales of the Crone,* 2016, Lafcadio Press.

"The Fall of the Ho-Man's Empire" by Paige L. Christie originally appeared in THE WYRD Student Literary Magazine, 1993, Saint Lawrence University.

"Colossal" by Tara Laskowski originally appeared in F(r)iction, Volume 16, 2020.

"Tom Roan's Widow" by Darin Kennedy originally appeared in *Ghost Anthology,* 2013, Dark Hall Press.

"Patron Saint" by Steven Van Patten originally appeared in *Tales from the Canyons of the Damned* 38, 2020, Holt Smith Limited.

ISBN: 978-1-952388-12-5(print)
978-1-952388-11-8 (ebook)

Original Cover Art & Design by
Lynne Hansen
https://lynnehansen.zenfolio.com

Published by
Crone Girls Press
Crone Girls Press Trade Paperback Edition August 2022
Printed in the USA

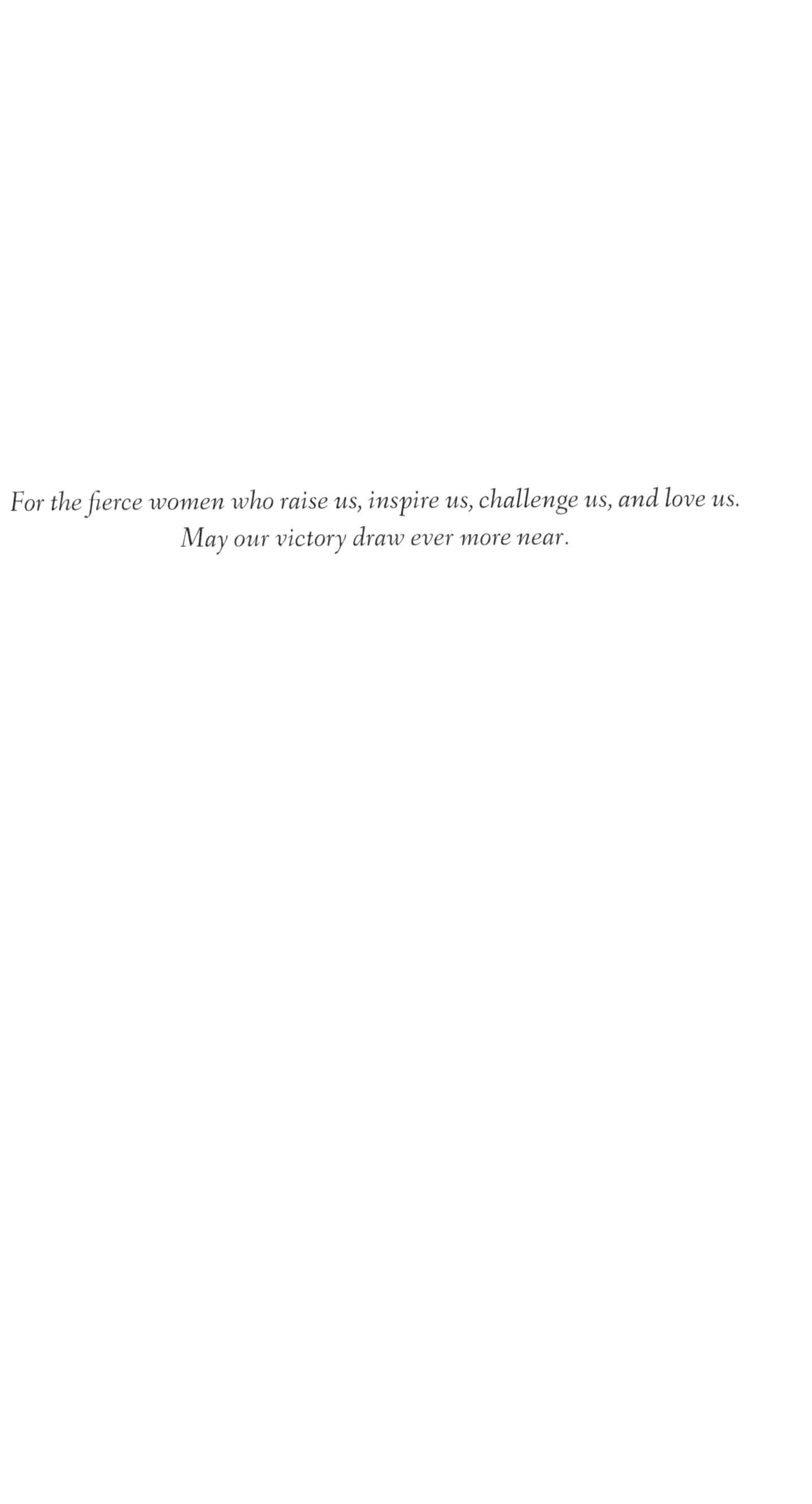

*For the fierce women who raise us, inspire us, challenge us, and love us.
May our victory draw ever more near.*

CONTENTS

PREFACE

RACHEL A. BRUNE

I was born into a world where (most) women who looked like me were able to get credit cards, bank accounts, and own property in their own name, where reproductive health rights were guaranteed, where sure, the ERA hadn't been passed, but was it really necessary? Look at all the progress we had made...perhaps it was obsolete now? I was the world's most complacent feminist. In fact, when I was younger, I wouldn't even have applied that label to myself. Why would I need to?

Yeah, I was a dumbass when I was younger, and that complacency came home to roost. But as I got older, I read more widely, met more people, had more life experience. I learned more about my own history, and that of people—women—who *didn't* look like me. I learned more about my own body, and how it works, and I learned that there were more things on earth than dreamt of in anyone's philosophy. And I went from a complacent feminist to a raging one.

When I began Crone Girls Press, I was specifically inspired to include stories that embraced the wide range of authors and perspectives that the horror genre offers. We've published some amazing tales that have crawled into my mind, nestled down, hibernated, and then exploded outwards, leaving my conceptions in little bloody gunks all over the previously calm assumptions of my worldview. And I LOVE it. This anthology is an opportunity to share stories that celebrate rage of all flavors—anti-patriarchal, primal, queer, feminist—and to do so in a way that contributes directly to organizations that have been working all along to support access to reproductive healthcare rights.

Thank you for choosing to pick up this volume and for your support of reproductive healthcare rights access. We hope you enjoy the exquisite terrors that await!

Rachel A. Brune, Editor
August 2022

PREFACE
CAROL GYZANDER

I was in my junior year of high school when the original Roe ruling was issued, supporting a fundamental right to privacy and protecting a pregnant person's right to have an abortion. We were the young women following on the heels of Gloria Steinem and the initial women's rights movement, and we moved into some new freedoms and roles because of Roe v. Wade. As one can imagine, the recent Supreme Court decision overruling Roe has stirred up a lot of emotion and memories.

However, even though we had fifty years of abortion rights, for the last five decades the intersections between financial, social, racial, and gender oppression have raised barriers to accessing abortion and reproductive healthcare and services. People already needed support.

With the Supreme Court reversal of Roe v. Wade last month, it just got so much worse.

I feel betrayed, undercut, and discounted—and now is the time to act on these feelings.

We asked some of our fellow authors to contribute pieces to this horror anthology celebrating women's rage, power, and agency. Rachel and I found ourselves overwhelmed with the power and strength that these stories and poems carry, and yes, the rage against situations where women have been victimized or powerless. It's intense.

This anthology is not meant to espouse violence as a means to resolve a situation. However, there is a normalized level of violence against women in many areas of fiction; one of the benefits of horror is that we can express our rage and get it out in the open where it can become productive rather than keeping it bottled up inside.

Once we experience this catharsis, we can channel that energy and use it to face many of the issues that must be addressed for everyone targeted by these attacks against reproductive rights, especially women. Profits from our anthology will be donated to support reproductive healthcare rights and candidates in the upcoming midterm elections who will fight for reproductive healthcare access measures.

So, read on! Feel their power. These women are going to cut the world and let it bleed.

Carol Gyzander, Editor
August 2022

INTRODUCTION
GWENDOLYN KISTE

I'm at once incredibly happy as well as unbelievably dismayed that this book exists.

I'm happy that we have this anthology in the world because this is an amazing group of authors telling an amazing group of horror stories. The mere existence of a powerful work of literature like this one is a reminder of all the strength and goodness that's alive and well in the horror genre today. And that's something worth celebrating.

However, I'm also so very grief-stricken that we live in a country where we need to have a charity anthology like this one to benefit reproductive rights. Access to abortion is a human right, plain and simple. There's no reason to deny any pregnant person the right to control their own body. Full stop. It's always been far too difficult to get an abortion in America. Now, in many swathes of the country, it's downright impossible and even illegal. The fall of Roe vs. Wade has utterly decimated our country in many ways that we already understand and in some ways we're yet to fully fathom. Because even though we don't want to imagine it, the worst is yet to come as we grapple with the fallout of the Dobbs ruling.

But since we're already living in a post-Roe world, I'm beyond grateful that Crone Girls Press has truly knocked it out of the park with this charity anthology. I'm fortunate to count many of the authors included in the table of contents as friends, and that makes me feel so proud to know so many wonderful writers who are willing to donate their time and their fiction to benefit human rights in America.

And let's talk about that cover. There's no possible way to take your eyes off it. The bright colors, the striking imagery—everything about it draws you in. Artist Lynne Hansen never disappoints, and this artwork in particular is so gorgeous and unforgettable and absolutely perfect for this thought-provoking book.

While I will never stop reeling from the loss of Roe, there's comfort in the fact that charity anthologies like this one exist. It reminds me of the kindness and compassion in the world, and how that will help to guide us out of this moment. And when I read the stories contained in these pages, it reminds me of our rage and grief and power, and how that will help to guide us out of this moment as well.

We have a long way to go before we have a chance of escaping the darkness that's descended on American life. But so long as we stick together and keep moving forward in support of each other, then I have at least a little hope for a better tomorrow.

Enjoy this fabulous and terrifying book. I have no doubt that when you turn the last page, you'll be changed for the better.

major, a set-back—
incubators are failing
on *Humanity*…

the project's other facets
proceeding as planned:
habitat and climate good

our sole vexation
is these damned incubators
vital for phase two

they still pulse yellow fluid
through ectopic ports,
they transfer blood and gas

and their outer skins
riddled red with thready veins
reveal the usual swelling

they're operational, yet
they're non-productive
for reasons undetermined

we've undertaken
invasive clinical tests
to find the error

results are inconclusive
we don't understand
the men's morale is falling

and existing crew
lack the coding expertise
to reboot the tech

as for the Lysistrata
when we forced the ports
the units self-destructed

though some will still blink
their viability is
poor in the long-term

the context just doesn't suit
we're lost without them
sir, for *Humanity*'s sake

we ask permission
to abort the colony

—await your response

About the Author

LEE MURRAY is a multi-award-winning writer and poet from Aotearoa-New Zealand, and a four-time Bram Stoker Award® winner, including for poetry for *Tortured Willows*. Lee is a Grimshaw-Sargeson Fellow, an NZSA Honorary Fellow, and an Elgin-, Rhysling-, Dwarf Star-, and Pushcart-nominated poet. Her poem "cheongsam" won her the Australian Shadows Award for 2021. Read more at leemurray.info.

"I'm not mad." The woman laughs. "I bet you hear that a lot, right? But I'm really not."

I smile and lean forward in my chair, enough to seem interested without being intimidating. Her posture is relaxed, her tone conversational. The table between us looks sturdy enough, and besides, her hands are cuffed. The guards tell me the alarm clipped to my belt will bring help within six seconds. I wonder how long the murder took. It was probably over a lot quicker than that.

The unit's busy tonight. I can hear doors opening and closing, someone wailing at the far end of the corridor. I'm doing this assessment as a favour for a colleague, covering her on-call for a few hours so she can get home to her kid's birthday party. No good deed goes unpunished, at least not when you're swapping a shift.

"Do you want to tell me what happened?" I ask. Under normal circumstances I'd be taking notes, but pens aren't allowed in the secure unit. Neither are pencils, mobile phones, laptops, or any other potentially lethal weapons.

"What's your name?" she asks.

"Doctor Ferguson," I tell her.

She repeats my name, rolling the words around her mouth like they have an interesting taste. "I'm Cynthia. But you knew that already, didn't you?"

She nods to the folder on the table. There's plenty of detail in there. Cynthia is forty-one, a barrister, and married—as is the way of these things—to another lawyer. Her two daughters are seven and three, and she's the proud owner of a house with a south-facing garden just outside Edinburgh. Not the usual sort you get in a place like this, but as we're fond of pointing out in the world of forensic psychiatry, high social status is no barrier to criminal intent.

"You want to know how it happened." She sits back, as if this is her office and I'm a prospective client. "Then you'll decide whether I'm mad, or bad, or a combination of the two, and they'll put me in prison or Carstairs for the rest of my life. Is that your plan?"

"My job's to write a report detailing my findings and a recommendation. Then it's up to the court what they do with it."

None of this is unfamiliar territory to her. She's a specialist in criminal law, and by all accounts she's world-class. "Don't worry. I don't mind talking to you. It won't matter soon anyway."

"Why do you say that?"

"Because everything's about to change."

I get the feeling she'd stand up if her hands weren't cuffed to the arms of her chair. According to her notes, she teaches 'Women and the Criminal Justice System' at the University.

Her eyes flick up to the fluorescent strip lighting on the ceiling, a tiny gesture I almost miss.

I rest my hand on her notes. "When the police picked you up, you said you weren't in control of your actions. Do you still think that's true?"

For the first time, she looks uncertain. "I don't know. Maybe." She rubs her right eye against her shoulder. "I killed him. You know that, don't you?"

"Why did you do it?"

She sighs. "I'd spent months preparing the case, going over what Oscar Ryan had done to her. What he did to her body afterwards. I knew it inside out, until it felt like I was the one he'd done it to, but he was going to jail for the rest of his life, and it was me that was going to put him there." The cuffs jangle as she tries to move her hands. "Except the police went and screwed it all up. Some moron got sloppy and forgot how to file his paperwork, so one bit of evidence suddenly wasn't admissible, and the prosecution managed to convince the jury that if *that* was in doubt, they couldn't believe the rest of it either."

I glance down at the notes. "The verdict was not proven, wasn't it?"

"Might as well have been not guilty. And just as he was leaving the court—like he had a right to be alive after what he'd done, after he'd raped her and killed her and dumped her body to rot in Ratho Quarry —he looked straight at me and smiled. He was letting me know he was going to do it all over again."

"So you killed him."

She nods her head. "I used to be really good, you know. One of those hobbies you always think you'll go back to, some day when the kids are bigger. I went home and got my kit, I waited for him outside his house, and when he showed up, I shot him."

The arrows had hit Ryan with such force that two had passed clean through his neck and out the other side. The third—the one the Procurator Fiscal had listed as the official cause of death—had lodged in his right eye socket.

"Not a bad grouping under the circumstances." She smiles, pleased. "Nice to know I'm still a half-decent shot."

"And you waited there for the police to arrest you."

Her face takes on a thoughtful expression. "I suppose I did. It didn't really occur to me to do anything else at that point."

"How did it make you feel?"

"Good. I felt good." Then she pauses and corrects herself. "No, that's not it. I felt *righteous*. Like I'd done a difficult, important job, and I'd done it well. I've met plenty of criminals who said God told them to do it. I used to think they were *mental*. Now I understand."

"Is that what you're saying? God made you do it?"

Her eyes make that little upward flick again. "It won't be the last, you know."

"The last what?"

"The last death. It's a shame it has to be this way, but it's clear that as a species we've run out of other options. Sometimes you need to clear the dead wood so the forest can grow."

"Dead wood?"

"Yes, that's right." She sounds happy, like she's talking to a bright student who's picked up a concept without needing it explained in detail. "Don't worry, you'll probably be fine."

"Why'd you say that?" I wonder if she's starting to include me in her delusion.

"She doesn't mind your lot." Her voice is low, as if we're sharing secrets, which in a way we are.

"My lot?"

"Sorry. I'm not trying to be rude. She just won't care. She doesn't mind what you do to each other. That's not her thing."

"Plenty of straight men don't abuse women." I decide not to worry about how she's correctly guessed my sexuality. She's a perceptive woman, and it's not something Peter and I keep secret anyway.

"They've had their chance." She laughs, a dry, sharp sound. "She's waking up, and everything's going to have to change. It's like birth. It's long and hard and bloody, and not everyone survives it." Her voice holds utter conviction, her mouth curved into the beatific smile of an oracle. "Our children will live in a better world."

A shiver creeps down my spine. The heating's always on in these places, even in the depths of winter, but tonight the air seems cold. Outside the barred window the sky is grey, the light with that peculiar silver intensity that presages a storm. I stand up and rap the door sharply. "I'm done in here," I say.

The door opens, and the prison officers take her back to her room. I tell the Police Surgeon I'll have the report finished by Friday.

It feels like a promise I have no ability to keep.

Back at the car I dial Peter's mobile, but don't hit the call button.

Instead, I light a cigarette and sit with my hands clenched around the steering wheel to stop them from shaking. The full face of the moon is casting deep shadows onto tarmac. I'd have sworn blind it was a crescent when I arrived. Now the silver disc is reflecting back at me from every surface—mirrors, windscreens, puddles, broken glass.

The State Hospital's siren, silent for the last thirty years, begins a thin, drawn-out wail, and in the distance, I hear the baying of Actaeon's hounds.

About the Author

JUDE REID lives in Glasgow and writes short horror stories in the narrow gaps between full time work as a surgeon, wrangling her kids, and trying to wear out a border collie. At the moment she's stressed out of her mind trying to finish her current novel. You can find her on Twitter @squintywitch.

A WOMAN UNBECOMING

CM HARRIS

"On your left," he snarls.

Though there's plenty of room on the trail, Alice swerves right, jerked from her reverie of watching asphalt blur beneath her knobby front tire.

The guy buzzes by on a mint-green Bianchi, wearing less-than-opaque white Lycra shorts. His ragged breath confirms he is riding for blood and glory.

A roadie announcing the obvious. *Great.* He's probably incredulous that she's riding her mountain bike on a paved trail on this perfect summer day. Probably thinking, *Ooo, how extreme!*

No. Calm down, or it will happen again.

Alice didn't require clairvoyance to know the trail would be crowded on a blue-skied Sunday. The Greenway had been so cluttered in Uptown she chose not to turn on her music and carefully wove through the walkers, rollerbladers, families puttering along. Once the pavement cleared out in the Minneapolis suburbs, the hot summer wind rumbling pleasantly past her earbuds, the occasional cricket, the siren call of a cardinal, Alice found she didn't really need the songs for inspiration.

She was content, felt good again. Even her new knee, though

tender, felt strong. If she could keep feeling like this, she might even be able to get along with her co-workers at the agency, maybe not tank another performance review.

Alice exhales, pushing out old toxins. But it only serves to wake up the new ones.

Another roadie echoes, "On your left." This one's a bit more winded and takes longer to pass. He wears a purple T-shirt and, thankfully, black Lycra shorts. His paint-chipped Peugeot squeaks with every revolution.

And then it starts, though she tries to fight it.

The two guys are co-workers. Gary. And, David? No, Dan. They work for 3M Office Products. Drones out of the hive for the weekend. Letting loose. And it's imperative that they put a woman on a slower bike well behind them.

She can see it, hear it as if she were there: earlier that week at 3M Office Supplies Division, Gary explaining *Le Tour de France* to Dan, trying to coax him out for a ride, trying to establish dominance.

Then, just an hour ago at Gary's house, the two men stuffed their Taco Bell midsections into tights. As Gary mixed endurance drinks (they would be riding thirteen miles after all) he informed Dan where to get the best price on a steel Bianchi. It wouldn't be as tricked out as his own carbon fiber frame but a nice starter that could be upgraded.

Dan insisted he was just fine on his old Peugeot.

The other man sighed. "You at least need a real jersey."

Dan did not argue, though he did not agree. Sure, his baggy T increased his drag coefficient but it also made a convenient tent when his junk got all jumbled up in the bike shorts. He wasn't about to tell his manager that those white shorts were as transparent as a negligee. That would mean admitting he'd seen the man's butt-crack in all its bushy glory. And you didn't embarrass this guy.

After everyone is clear on the fact that the road bikers have indeed passed in the left lane of an abundantly wide trail, they fall into line in front of Alice.

And then they slow down.

Alice triggers a short burst of the Jekyll's brakes, and the discs screech against the pads.

Gary points at the ground to his side, indicating a right turn, which unfortunately, is the same direction Alice is headed. All three exit the trail and speed toward an industrial park intersection. The roadies slow, bikes wobbling as they gape at road construction signs.

Alice knows where the detour is. She veers into the grass, then bunny hops off the curb, free of the roadies and their sloppy thoughts invading her head.

"Hey," Dan says, "she didn't call it."

"What?" Gary says as she speeds away. "She passed on the *right* and didn't call it?"

"Nope."

The other man growls.

Gooseflesh rises on Alice's arms. She understands that grunt from way down inside her. She blinks rapidly. If she closes her eyes for too long she'll absorb too much of their anger and then the ebony strands in her mind will get too sticky to untangle.

Should she slow and take their dressing down? Or turn and head home? This is the most remote part of the trail. Even on the weekend, the prairie by the interstate is often deserted.

Alice can't afford a run-in right now. She's too skittish. It's only been a few months since a surgeon replaced her knee ligament with the Achilles tendon of a cadaver. She's still trying to gather strength and courage before venturing back onto the sketchier dirt trails.

She could pull out her phone. Make a show of dialing 911. Film whatever shenanigans they're going to pull. She does have that multi-purpose tool, the one with the serrated blade, in her Camelbak, but she'll look like an idiot fumbling around with it.

Okay, okay. Settle down. It's not going to go that far. Just let them have their say.

This new paranoid side is exactly what her boss had been complaining about. But there was something un-right planted inside her now. Forget the metal pins in her shin, never mind the sutures. You can't get away from a dead man's flesh, once it's threaded into you, your vascular network giving it new life. The surgeon had scoffed at her fears. We hit it with a good deal of radiation, he'd said, I doubt your body will reject it.

But what if it rejects me?

The roadies pull up behind Alice, their rear wheel hubs like a swarm of hornets.

She gives in, closes her eyes, and slides open her new invisible window into the mind.

Gary is trying to will her to look at him, staring at her with his melting glare.

Dan shakes his head. "Just leave it." He prefers to watch the pulse of her buttocks.

Gary snorts and speeds up. He pulls into the left lane and begins to pass, but then slows and turns to her.

"On your left!"

Alice opens her eyes and stares forward, nods to music that's not playing in her earbuds.

"I said, on your left!" Gary screams. "ON YOUR LEFT, YOU FUCKING CUNT!"

He passes laughing, as does Dan. They pedal off, shaking their heads, lesson taught.

Alice glowers. Why should she have announced passing when she wasn't even near them? It's not that she's opposed to politeness. She must have said "on your left" a dozen times in Uptown.

She does have to admit his statement has a certain cadence; like something a particularly foul-mouthed drum corps would chant as they marched onto the football field:

On your left, you fucking cunt! On your left, you fucking cunt!

And now she's chanting it too, panting it out.

The roadies aren't fast. She's reeling them in at a worrying pace. They are all over their bikes, torsos wagging, arms yanking the handlebars to get up the slightest incline. They rock and bounce on their saddles with every stroke, seat posts set too high.

She'll catch them soon. *Crap.* But, damn it, why is she supposed to cower? If she was a guy, they wouldn't have said a word.

At the far end of the loop, where the trail runs parallel to a retirement home, Alice focuses her energy. She can't pass them going full bore; she must take them at ninety percent. A racer once told her, *never pass if you can't stay ahead.* Pull up with the quads. Push out with the hamstrings and glutes. Round out every corner of the stroke with the calves, ankles and toes as if you're removing dogshit from your clipless shoes. Spin. Spin. Make like an eggbeater and spin!

Ahead, an elderly woman with long white hair hunches over a motorized scooter and putters toward them in the left lane.

Alice slows and nods a smile at her. *Stay human, girl, stay human.*

The crone leers back with crooked yellow teeth, her eyes dark and hollow. She raises a big-knuckled forefinger as she passes, her mouth agape—black inside.

Rip their legs off.

Bile rises in Alice's throat. She looks over her shoulder.

The old woman is gone. No scooter. Nothing.

Alice kicks it, a chill tickling at her back like fingertips. She passes the roadies and veers back into the lane a few bike lengths ahead.

"What the hell," Gary yelps. "Can you believe this shit?"

Dan chews his lip. There's no going back when Gary gets the scent. This is how the guy dogs 3M underlings, even a few lateral execs. It never ends well for anyone. He wishes he had begged off this stupid ride. But as ordered, he falls in behind Gary's rear wheel, drafting to conserve energy.

The three turn toward the city, west wind pressing their backs, and sail at thirty miles per hour on the downdraft. Great white clouds have piled up in the early evening sky. The moon hangs above the

Minneapolis skyline, nearly as orange as the sun's own reflection off the glass-plated towers. Shadows lengthen along the Cedar Lake trail, sprigs of yarrow and mustard grass bend to the will of the breeze. The bogs are cooling down.

Alice and the roadies rage across the asphalt, which runs parallel to the Burlington Northern train tracks. Tires howl and mouths pant in a *ménage à trois* of anger and fear and glee like hounds on a rabbit. On a downhill sprint, the men catch her, Gary yelling again and again: *on your left on your left on your left.*

There are millions of guys like this. Why can't she just ignore the furious voice rising inside like other women do? Could she make it to the off-road section, where skinny tires fear to tread, and just remove herself from this mess?

Who cares! Your knee is fine.

The wet voice is that of the cadaver in the U of M holding tank. It slowly bobs, an eye donor with dark pits in its orbital sockets. But the pits go infinitely deep into an abyss, far into nothingness until stars twinkle into view.

So just fuck it. Fuck it all.

Alice. Oh, Alice?

Let's see what these maggots have got.

They race by the Vonartis building, a fortress of pharmaceutical laboratories, which pumps out a sickeningly sweet steam reminiscent of Franken Berry cereal. Thick power lines buzz above them, and Alice's left leg tingles in response. Deep inside the knee, something gives way, not with the firecracker pain of her original injury, but with a sloughing of materials no longer needed, materials repurposed.

Dancing on her pedals, she flies up the next hill and gloms onto Dan's rear wheel. She nudges his tire with the Jekyll's front knobby, creating a whirring hiss. He pumps harder, adding a couple inches of distance.

"Here she comes again!" Gary says with a rasp. "Goddamn."

Goddamn, indeed.

Alice glances down in shock. The new knee is working smooth as silk. In fact, the post-op quadriceps bulge and pump larger than those on her right leg. The skin on the left side of her torso stretches and stings hot, just as her forearms once did when bullies on the playground handed out those snakebite skin twisters. But this time, instead of wincing, she swoons, eyelids fluttering. *So nice.*

Alice hammers past Dan and then Gary. It would be so easy to veer over and push him into the fence, into the cattails or that pond—her balance on the Jekyll steadier than his stranglehold on his expensive thoroughbred—and so delicious to see that fabric torn to strips. She sweated out any semblance of meek miles back. The only reminder of the gentler sex is her hourglass figure that tricked at least two of them into assuming she might be managed.

Another mile ticks off without them catching her. Maybe they're right on her tail. She refuses to look. But she sees the sparkling green pain behind their eyes and feels their hearts flubbering in their chests. Both are beginning to devise ways out of this situation with egos intact.

On the prairie straightaway, Alice eases up.

TRAIL CLOSED FOR REPAIRS

It's over. No way are they going to follow her into gravel. They probably turned off the trail to their posh homes in the Cedar Lake neighborhood. Her lungs rake in hard gasps of dense, pollen-filled air. Rotten disappointment rises in her throat and her leg begins to twitch and twang like a strike to the funny bone. Sparks dance in her vision, as furiously as spermatozoa under a microscope.

The wind carries up a sharp gust of male pheromone. Alice's nostrils flare and her mouth begins to salivate. It smells wonderful, feral.

She passes the sign and sees that the trail construction is nearly finished. No rock, just an onyx ribbon of fresh asphalt for another hundred yards. Without the yellow stripes, it's anybody's road.

Gary pulls up beside her, pushing into her space, his snarling face inches from hers. His body odor activates something in her even deeper down than his first grunt.

Her stomach growls.

"I know you can hear me, *bitch*! ON YOUR L—"

His face lengthens and he falters.

For an endless moment as they roll along, she sees what he sees, the growing hugeness of her, the veins snaking black down her leg, up her arms and forking across her neck.

He shakes off his hesitation. "On your—"

Her right hand secure on her own handlebar, Alice's left hand shoots out and grabs the man's helmet strap and mirrored sunglasses. She yanks down hard and swerves into the grass to avoid his flailing arms.

Dan catches Gary's pedal in his front spokes and they both go down in a twisted, skidding heap.

Alice taps her brakes and coasts, arms quivering, legs spinning backwards. Everything is green. So green. And black, but not. Black like nothingness. The nothing hungers for something.

Gary cries after her through furious tears. "You goddamn bitch!"

She slows, glances back, her left cheek drawn over her teeth in a sneer she hadn't planned. Half her face is numb, and drool runs down her chin. She rips off her glasses to force more light into the consuming green and black.

Dan groans but his weathered face, wild-eyed and hurting, falls silent when he meets her awe-filled gaze.

Alice turns her bike around. She can't leave the poor things like this.

The hunger is too great.

She rolls up on them, dismounts, and lays the Jekyll down in a thatch of milkweed. Her metal cleats click the asphalt like talons. She limps toward them, a syncopation no longer from injury but from limb disproportion, like wearing stilettos with one broken heel. A mosquito, sated with her blood, takes flight from her arm and pops midair with a barely audible *snick*. Dark matter fizzes in the air.

Dan desperately tries to untangle his flesh from the bike.

Gary refuses to look at what she is becoming. "Bitch! You fu—"

Her post-op leg swings and smashes his nose up into his skull.

She cocks her head and peers at the comical way one of his eyes has rolled up further than the other. The brass cleats ripped off a good deal of his upper lip.

"Oh my god," Dan murmurs. "Are you cr—please, calm down. He's just an ass. You never called left, it's the rules." After wincing at her, he averts his eyes from her elongating limbs and fights the sagging weight of Gary and the Bianchi. One of his legs splays out from the wreck, an angry red swathe of road rash striping his thigh. His other leg twists backwards, the foot still clipped into a pedal.

Alice leans over Dan.

He trembles. "Please."

His genitals are bunched up sideways in the Lycra shorts. Though it's a classic target, Alice leaves them alone; he can't walk home on those. She chooses his ankle instead. When she stomps, it pops like turkey gristle on Thanksgiving.

His bellow becomes a wet gurgle as he clutches at his calf.

She feeds Dan her shoe with half the force she fed it to Gary.

He slumps back. All is silent.

Alice shakes her head, amazed. With every thump of her pounding heart, black veins stretch across her leg like worms. The skin on her left side is losing opacity, like the Visible Woman educational doll in the Christmas catalog that her parents refused to buy because one could see all the way through to the rectum.

This new knee is going to last forever. She'll have to start training her right leg alone to maintain balance. No, it will catch up. She feels like a new woman. So unbecoming for a woman. A woman un-becoming. She can't help but chuckle. There are others like her; she can hear their whispers, others who have been darkly blessed by the donor.

Alice searches the roadies' jersey pockets. She finds Gary's cellphone and stomps it into black shards. She shrugs off her Camelbak and rummages around in the pouch. Though she's ravenous, she flings the banana PowerBar into the brush. Void flesh demands living flesh; it won't be assuaged with colorful packaging or sensible nutritional information. Ah, the multitool.

Gary stirs and dislodges himself from Dan. He whimpers and crawls toward the brush.

Alice allows him time to choose a more secluded spot amongst the chirping frogs and buzzing dragonflies. She picks through the attachments on the multi-tool until she finds the serrated blade.

The train tracks beyond begin to hiss. But there is no locomotive in sight. High above, a Delta flight drops its landing gear. Inside, three first time flyers clutch the armrests.

Alice crouches over Gary as he sputters blood. A bleached white incisor hangs by a thread of gums from the side of his oozing mouth.

Her elongating fingers pat her lips. "You have something there." Her voice is low and hollow, reverberating like a gong that can speak.

He reaches up to numbly smack a hand at the wrong side of his mouth.

"No, there," Alice says. "On your left."

About the Author

CM HARRIS is the author of novels *She Never Left*, *Maiden Leap*, *The Children of Mother Glory*, and *Enter Oblivion*. Her short stories and essays appear in Oprah Winfrey's *O Magazine*, Escape Artists' *Pseudopod* podcast, *Coppice & Brake: A Dark Fiction Anthology*, *Meniscus Literary Journal*, *SALiT Magazine*, *Harrington Literary Quarterly*, and the anthology *Queer Voices: Poetry, Prose, and Pride*. Her screenplay "The Cost of Glory" received a Gold award for Best Concept Script and a Silver award for Best Feature Script from the Queen Palm Film Festival.

IN THE DREAM, a woman prostrated herself while holding out a wooden offering bowl filled with tissue and blood.

We were in no temple, but standing upon an altar made of red sandstone. The sky was orange and the clouds were heavy, bulging, a thousand breasts dripping with an incipient storm.

A puddle of blood spread on the rock under her, growing by the second. She wore a white robe, the kind they drape on Greek statues. The soft linen fabric sopped up the blood, turning red as it eagerly drew up the heavy liquid.

In a rasping, tight voice, she cried:

"I pray to you, o Goddess!"

Lightning tore across the sky. I appeared in front of her, towering over her and radiating an uncanny light. I was a giantess. It all seemed perfectly natural.

In the dream I said, in a deep, steady voice that could not have been my own, "I receive your prayers, my sister. But I cannot save you."

The woman turned her face toward me, her face twisted, red-splotched, and ugly. "I've had salvation and it was cheap. I want justice."

A stabbing pain hit my chest, hooked onto something, and stayed there.

I reached down and placed an enormous hand upon her shoulder. My wings closed around her, as if to protect her. "I can't bring you justice, child. I'm not strong enough for that."

She turned her face downward again and wept bitterly but silently, mouthing hateful words under her breath and out of sight. I soaked them up like prayers.—But it was cruel to make her wait, so I put a finger under her chin and made her raise her face again to me.

"I can't bring you justice, child, but I can bring you other things. If you truly desire them."

The pool of blood spread wider underneath her. She was losing her color. Her skin felt cool against my fingers. Her breath shuddered.

Tears rolled down her face and she turned her head to the side. "I cannot. My daughters—"

Her body shook and the bowl fell from her limp fingers. The front of her white robes were splashed with it.

I picked up the bowl. It still held a little of the blood. I lifted her in my arms and put the bowl in front of her lips. "Drink."

"No!"

"Drink, and you will forget all of this, and they will be forgiven. That's the only mercy I can give you, the mercy of another god."

She closed her eyes and leaned forward, touching her lips to the bowl. Then she gagged, swung an arm, and knocked the bowl back down on the stone. "No! I won't! I won't drink it! *Fuck* justice! Fuck salvation! Fuck that whole family! Fuck them all! Give me revenge!"

With one last shudder, she fell at my feet, eyes blank, mouth empty of breath. The hook buried in my heart was set now, and the threads between us pulled hard. I stepped over the woman's body, feeling something hot rise up in my chest.

I had been summoned.

I woke up to the sound of a low voice murmuring from the other side of the room. I turned over and reached out a hand to touch my husband, Mike, but the other side of the bed was empty. The sheets were still slightly warm.

The bathroom light was on. Mike stood in the doorway with his phone at his ear. When I sat up, he waved at me: *down, down.*

His voice sounded rough, tense. "What time did she...? Why didn't you...? You said she had a fever, didn't she?" He rubbed the back of his neck. "Oh. Yes, she did. In high school. Yes. I understand. God's will."

He beeped off the phone with his thumb, then tossed it onto a dresser. "Leah had to go into the hospital just now, Erin. They're saying she's going to lose the baby."

Mike's sister Leah had two other children, young girls, and she had gotten pregnant again almost immediately. She had had some bleeding recently.

I rubbed my eyes. "Are you going to the hospital? Should I get dressed? I'll thaw something from the freezer."

"Nothing we can do about it now but pray." He reached behind him and turned out the bathroom light. "Come on. Let's go back to sleep."

He lay down in bed and turned away from me, his muscles quivering with tension. I knew he expected me to reach out to him, to soothe him.

But I couldn't. I waited until he was asleep, then slipped out of bed, put on some clothes and a jacket, and drove to the hospital.

An aide at the hospital front desk told me that visiting hours were over, but that Leah was sleeping peacefully. I knew she was lying. If she had been telling me the truth, she would have told me that she couldn't release patient information.

I found a chair in the waiting area that wasn't too uncomfortable and curled up in it to wait. The aide's eyes stayed on me as if magnetized. I wasn't sure why. I am a diminutive, middle-aged woman with mouse-colored hair and a soft, gentle voice that is often drowned out by others' conversations.

It was July so the sun rose early, leaving still a long time to wait. I got a cup of coffee at the café, which was technically only open for staff breakfast at the time, but they kindly let me have a cup. I read tattered copies of Christian magazines from the waiting area.

At 9 a.m., I asked to see Leah again; they told me a nurse was with her, but that I'd be able to see her soon.

A few minutes later, Mike walked into the waiting room, wearing a dark suit.

"Erin! What are you doing here?"

I uncurled my legs from underneath me. "I'm here to see Leah. She must have had a rough night and I wanted to offer my company."

"She doesn't want to see anyone," Mike snapped. "She just lost a baby. Go home and take a shower. They need you at the bookstore today."

His words stung. I had the feeling he was trying to drive me out of the hospital for some reason. *Don't look...don't see...don't know.* The hook embedded in my heart twitched, as another thread fastened to it, fastening Mike to me.

I didn't want to say words in anger and be mistaken. I got up, heaving my purse over my shoulder. "Okay. But tell Mother to let me know if she wants me."

"I will," he promised.

Outside, the hospital parking lot was buzzing with cars. The big double doors opened and closed. It smelled like dry grass and heated asphalt. The day was already starting to swelter.

Mike kissed me on the top of my head as I got into my twenty-year-old little Volkswagen. "I'm sorry I used such strong words inside. Just be a good girl, Erin. Nobody needs any more stress today."

My face turned red. I climbed into the car and closed the door.

Mike tapped on the window until I rolled it down.

"Aren't you forgetting something?" He pointed to his cheek.

I stared at him. A hundred different times that he'd made me kiss him on the cheek—in the middle of an argument, after he teased me and made me cry, after sex that left me sore and angry—sprang to mind.

Did I have the strength to leave him? I asked myself that after every fight that went nowhere, every time I sobbed myself to sleep, every time I begged for the money to do something frivolous. I had no money, no place to sleep, no friends that would let me stay with them for more than a night or two. A car that would probably break down if I drove it out of city limits.

I shook my head. "I...I just keep thinking about Leah. I feel sick to my stomach, the thought of her losing the baby."

"Maybe she won't." Mike straightened up. "I know you've always wanted kids, Erin. So pray for the baby. Pray for a miracle."

"I will." My eyes had filled with tears that made my eyes burn. I wiped them away so I could drive. "With all my heart."

I took a shower, changed clothes, and drove to the bookstore. Mike had already called his parents to let them know I'd be late. Fortunately it was a slow morning, with only a few customers browsing the aisles. Mother Parker, Mike's mother, sat at the register, greeting customers with her friendly smile and waving off my apologies.

I changed the coffee in the coffee pot, cleaned out the break room, walked the store to look for anything out of place, cleaned a sticky spot off one of the reading tables, and emptied the trash bins. I boxed up the shipping orders for that afternoon, tucking a bookmark with a gold-embossed bible inside the front cover of the top book in every shipment.

Parker's Christian Bookstore—Old Colorado City's #1 Christian Bookstore and Homeschool Curriculum Resource—Rare Books, Best-sellers, Reader's Digest Editions!

When I was done, I ate a peanut-butter sandwich in the break room and drank another cup of coffee. I felt both better and worse. My nerves and mind had settled. Leah wasn't dead; I had just awakened suddenly from a nightmare. If she lost the baby, it would be a shame but not the end of the world. They could always try again. My stomach was upset, though, churning from the acid in the coffee. I brushed up my crumbs from the counter and went back to work.

At the front counter, Mother Parker was speaking to our pastor, Bryan Meyer. He had a hand on her shoulder. They both glanced at me, eyes narrowing, and my steps faltered.

"Erin..." Mother Parker said. "We have some terrible news for you. Leah didn't lose the baby, but she's had to be put into a medical coma. There was terrible bleeding last—this morning, and the doctors almost lost them both."

Pastor Meyer added, "Mike tells me that you've been praying for your sister in Christ, Erin. Your prayers will be needed more than ever for baby and mother."

I dropped to my knees, skinning one of them on the tough carpet. I saw the woman pushing the bowl of blood and tissue toward me.

"What—what about Emma and Elise?"

Pastor Meyer helped me up to my feet. He smelled fresh, like soap.

Mother Parker wrung her hands together. "Oh, I thought you knew! They were already with their other grandmother since Leah wasn't feeling well. They're fine."

The threads running through the bookstore felt so tangled about me that I wasn't sure that I'd be able to stand without Pastor Meyer's hand on my shoulder.

"That's—that's good," I said.

"It'll be better if you stay busy." Pastor Meyer squeezed my shoulder. "Don't worry too much. Just put your faith in God's love. He will save the child and the mother, too."

He squeezed my shoulder again. "It's a son."

After the bookstore closed, I called the hospital about Leah; they told me that she was asleep. I bit my tongue. It was so hard to know what to believe.

I should have gone home afterwards, but I didn't. I was hungry and craving something different. I stopped at a grocery and wandered the aisles. Whatever I was looking for, I couldn't find it. I settled on a plastic container of hot shredded pork barbecue from the deli counter with some Ritz crackers and a bottle of the spiciest hot sauce I could find. I didn't want to eat at home, so I stopped in a big park between the bookstore and the house, a place in the foothills called Garden of the Gods.—It was named back in the day. I'm sure the name would be different now.

I drove along the roads through the park. Joggers ran along the paths under the red sandstone formations towering above us, golden retrievers trotting alongside them on leashes. Buses and families filled the parking lots. Tourists pulled out on the overlooks to take photos of the gigantic, knifelike rock formations against the wide blue sky.

My little car struggled up the inclines and puttered around the winding curves until I spotted a familiar black SUV parked beside the road near a big, flat sandstone formation. The SUV had a bookstore bumper sticker and a window decal of a stick figure family kneeling before a cross in the back window—a father, a mother, and two stick girls in triangle dresses. I pulled over and got out.

Even though it had been cloudy all day, the afternoon heat was stifling. The sky was the orange of a waiting storm, covered with bulging mammatus clouds. I kicked off my flats and took the plastic grocery bag of barbecue with me.

I scrambled up the big slab of sandstone until I was above the road, above the cars. I started to settle down on a clean piece of stone to eat.—Someone was crying.

The sound led me further up the rock formation, then along the thin line of an animal trail along a nearby ridge. Rocks and pine needles dug into the callouses of my feet.

The trail led to a vertical sandstone formation like an enormous stack of pebbles. My brother-in-law James, Leah's husband, was a small thing curled underneath, his knees pulled up to his chest. I walked up beside him and put my hand on his shoulder.

He leaned against my leg. I knelt down. He buried his head in my shoulder.

"James, it's me, Erin. It's going to storm. You should go home."

He rubbed his tears on the fabric of my dress. "What will I do now? What about the girls? Why did she have to do that in high school? Why did she have to kill our child? She knew that God would have his vengeance onto her. Why did she have to sin back then? I told her I would marry her. Why did she sin?"

I pushed away from him. "What are you talking about?"

He reached out for me and crushed me to him. "God killed my wife to punish her for murdering our unborn child in high school. She was called to bear my child. And now God has claimed her. *And* my son."

I struggled to get away from him but his grip on me tightened. "I don't understand, James. What happened? I thought she was in a coma."

He turned his tear-stained face up to me. "They're just saying that to help with the legal stuff. She had an ectopic pregnancy, Erin. My seed planted itself in her tubes because her womb was warped...there wasn't enough room. The doctors told us that the only way to save her was to kill the baby, and they couldn't. It was God's will. God's will."

My grip on the grocery bag went limp. The glass bottle of hot sauce rolled along the rock, clinking.

"Is she dead?"

The hook in my heart quivered.

"She died last night. What am I going to do? What if her grandparents try to take the children? They need a mother!" His arms locked around me. "You and Mike will have to take them. Say you'll take them. You don't have children of your own."

His words wound themselves around my throat, trying to choke out my breath. All I had to do was nod. I fought to get out of his embrace.

He clung to me. Then his hand touched my breast and he flinched away.

I scrambled free and got to my feet. "Leah was my sister."

"It's what she would have wanted."

He did not know what Leah would have wanted. I put my hand to my breast where he had touched it. The hook came free, trailing threads so thick they were like strips of leather.

James looked up at me, his eyes widening. He seemed to shrink, becoming small as a child before me, as small as a dog. An insect.

He knelt on his hands and knees in front of me, shaking. The smell of piss rose from him. "An angel from Heaven! O God, I pray to you—give me back my son!"

I smiled, and took what was sometimes granted to the powerless.

Wrong god.

In the old days, three goddesses were said to punish patricides and oath-breakers—but those were tales told by men of power with disobedient sons. They called us ugly and gave us bat wings. They mocked our rage, yet feared it.—At least they got the whips right.

Darkness fell and thunder raged. The winds rose, howling. Leaves and branches were torn away from trees. The sky twisted and lashed. Power lines lashed along the roadsides like poisonous snakes. Men and women alike were torn limb from limb—bookstores, churches, and hospitals also.

By dawn my divinity had abandoned me, although my fury had not faded. The freak storm had left many dead, but also many survivors.

My sister's daughters went with their grandparents. I cleaned up the legalities, sold the bookstore to an erotic press, and left Colorado for good. I was a diminutive, middle-aged woman with mouse-colored hair and a soft, gentle voice that is often drowned out by others' conversations.

But I remained marked by the goddess. And you don't want to see me smile.

About the Author

DEANNA KNIPPLING writes atmospheric gothic horror, mystery, suspense, and twisted tales from the edge of space & time. Her hobbies are cooking, taking long walks on Florida beaches, digging into the realm of open-source intelligence, fangirling over history, science, and psychology—and reading lots of fiction, graphic novels, and web comics while her tea goes cold. Author of *The House Without a Summer* and *A Murder of Crows,* you can find her at WonderlandPress.com.

THE TAPPING

CAROL GYZANDER

THE DENTED OLD Volvo wheezed up the circular driveway and stalled out in front of the pink gingerbread-encrusted Victorian mansion outside Newport, Rhode Island. Set back from the road, it was the only one in the neighborhood without Halloween jack-o-lanterns.

"We made it! Wow, it's huge." John leaned over his wife, April, to peer at the wraparound porch and the third-floor turret. Massive trees towered overhead, fallen leaves covered the lawn, and thick ivy partially obscured most windows. "Needs a bit of landscaping work, though."

April sighed. "Great-Aunt Gertrude is a bit old to do gardening. She's been doing everything else around here since her husband Henry's heart attack decades ago." She wrung her hands together. "I really hope it's not an imposition for us to move here now that he's passed away. She's all the family I have left now. I mean, except for you."

John leaned over and brushed one of the blonde curls off her face. "Darling, we've talked about this. You said she's getting old, and we're here to help her. The best thing she can do is transfer the house to us, and then she can stay here until she kicks the bucket. It's the least we can do, right?"

"I haven't seen her since my family moved to Manhattan when I was ten. I hope she doesn't think we're getting back in touch now just because we've lost the business." She shrugged. "Her letter said the front door would be open."

April slipped from the car and trotted up the front steps onto the porch.

John stepped out and stood with his arms crossed. After a moment, he cleared his throat. "April? Aren't you forgetting something?" When she turned toward him with a frown, he said, "The *bags*?"

The young woman ran back down the steps. "Of course, I'm sorry."

He pulled out their two ratty suitcases. Leaning over her, he hissed, "What have I told you about apologizing all the time?"

"Oh. I'm sorry." She gulped. "I mean...I'll try not to do that." She lugged her suitcase toward the front steps.

He shook his head and followed her, easily carrying the other bag. He paused at the incongruity of the weathered black cat cutout tacked on the grand front door.

April knocked twice, then swung the door open. "Hello?"

He followed her inside and shook his head to dispel the feeling that the cat's eyes followed him. The couple looked around the grand foyer, the lofty ceiling, and the walls lined with intricate mahogany paneling. His gaze traveled from the carved newel post of the grand staircase to the landing with its stained-glass window and then to the second floor.

"You know, they say that places aren't as big as you remember, but this is huge!" She spun around in the vast space. "Great-Aunt Gertrude said she spends afternoons in the parlor. This way, to the left."

The couple passed through the ornately carved archway. Gertrude sat on a tufted horsehair-stuffed sofa framed with glistening mahogany. Her spine was ramrod straight despite her frailness, and her gray hair was arranged in intricate curls.

"Auntie!" April ran to the older woman, gently embraced her around the shoulders, and kissed her cheek. "It's so wonderful to see you! Thank you for letting us stay with you. This is my husband, John Wojcik. John, this is Great-Aunt Gertrude."

The older woman sat erectly on the stuffed sofa, hands folded in her lap. Her blue eyes showed bright and piercing despite her wrinkled face, and she squinted for just a moment as she looked up and down at his rumpled clothes.

"How do you do, Aunt Gertrude?" He reached out a hand, and she delicately placed her palm in his, then withdrew it.

"As well as can be expected at my age, young man. Please, both of you have a seat." She gestured at the pair of chairs facing the sofa, then turned toward April, who immediately perched on the chair's edge. "I was sad to hear when you lost your parents last summer, dear. So close to my Henry's passing. But I'm glad you're here now because Halloween was his favorite holiday."

She smiled for a moment. "I understand that you two got married right after you finished Vassar, April? You may recall I attended Smith College."

"Yes, John and I met while I was in school. I hardly ever saw my parents because they were so busy these last ten years, but he's really filled the gap."

John sat on the arm of his wife's chair. He slid his arm around April's waist, pulling her over sideways and kissing the top of her head while he looked around the enormous room filled with antiques. "My debutante wife certainly helped me get some clients."

The older woman raised her eyebrows. "Well, April dear, your mother was always...quite a strong-minded individual; may she rest in peace. May I pour you some tea? Or perhaps something stronger? Dinner will be ready soon. I have some stew on the stove and hope you can help me with it."

"Now you're talking. I could certainly go for a drink." John stood and moved around the room, looking at the ornately framed oil paintings and delicate bric-a-brac covered with dust.

"Of course. You've had a long journey. What will you have, John?"

"Oh, bourbon on the rocks would be terrific." He watched the two women exchange glances. "Or...wine?"

Gertrude nodded and gestured to the tray on a side table bearing a bottle of wine and several glasses. April gathered herself to stand up.

John waved her off. "I've got it. You always mess up the cork." He opened the bottle of wine and poured it, passing a glass to April without even asking if she wanted one.

"Here's to...family." He raised his glass to the two women. "I think we're all going to get along fine."

April smiled meekly and sipped her wine. They exchanged pleasantries until the older woman asked for April's assistance to stand. She took them on a tour of the main floor of the house, walking slowly and leaning on April's arm as they went across the foyer, through the large living room, then into the library—lined from floor to ceiling with massive bookshelves that were crammed full of leather-bound books.

"These were Henry's pride and joy. He would work here many a night, pouring over the old books at the desk or sitting in his favorite chair here by the fireplace." Gertrude gestured to an ample wing chair, covered in burgundy leather, with a side table and Tiffany lamp next to it. "If there's anything in here that you'd like to read, please feel free. Just take care because many of these are old; some are first editions, including an early volume of Poe."

John had been feeling himself shrink smaller and smaller as they toured the sprawling mansion. But at her words, he stepped into the middle of the room and threw his shoulders back as he turned around. "Now, this is the kind of room I could get used to."

Gertrude fixed him with a steady gaze. "Yes, I can see that it appeals to you. Anyway, I believe that the stew must be ready. Can you help me, dear?" She turned and headed toward the door, drawing April with her.

John paused and trailed his fingers across a shelf of books with a smile before following them. "I could sell these for a fortune."

Entering the dining room, he stopped short at the large family portraits lining the vast, high-ceilinged space. No matter where he moved in the room, they all seemed to be looking directly at him. An inlaid table with a dozen chairs dominated the room. The flickering flames in the elaborate fireplace gave a warm glow and softened the room's formal appearance.

Three places were set at the table. The two women came in from what must be the kitchen area, April carrying a tray of dishes. Gertrude sank into her chair, and April served the stew, then helped her aunt slide the massive chair closer.

"April, sit on my left, and John, please take the seat here on my right. That way, you can see Henry while we eat." Gertrude gestured at the life-size oil painting of a robust, red-bearded man that hung over the carved marble mantle. "He's the one who built up our fortune, which has enabled us to keep this beautiful home that's been in the family for generations. I miss him so much."

John took his seat, glanced up at the painting, and froze. Gertrude's husband was a powerfully strong man, sitting in the same burgundy leather chair that John already coveted, one hand resting on the large knob of his wooden walking stick. A giant, carved jack-o-lantern sat on the table beside him; candlelight made the eyes glow. The man's expression was erudite, compelling, and slightly mocking as he looked down at the viewer. John felt himself shrink again under that steady gaze, as if he were being judged, and quickly looked away.

April beamed as she slid into the opposite chair. "Oh, Auntie! Isn't this where you taught me to use the Ouija board? I remember these beautiful candlesticks."

Gertrude nodded. "Yes, my dear, and I recall that you had a natural aptitude for it."

"Oh, I'm sorry. I wasn't looking for compliments."

Her aunt patted her hand. "You never need to apologize to me, my dear."

April smiled and blushed.

As usual, John thought the opinions of others boring and found himself having to lead the conversation during dinner. He had to override April when she tried to sidetrack the conversation into discussing some obscure literature book he'd never heard of. By the time Gertrude asked her to bring in the dessert, he had shared that the two of them had lived in the city since their marriage, had no children, and that, while he had not attended college, John had established his own entertainment management business—which had recently fallen into bankruptcy. Of course, through no fault of his own.

Gertrude had precisely three bites of her dessert and then leaned back in her chair. "Well, with all that the two of you have been through, I must say I'm delighted that you took me up on the offer of moving here for help."

April leaned forward and squeezed her hand. "Oh, of course, Auntie. And I must say that your offer came at a perfect time for us as well since—"

John cleared his throat and spoke loudly. "We're happy to come and help *you*. And if you need any assistance with financial affairs, rest assured that I know all about business and will be happy to handle anything you need. Family is so very important. Isn't that right, honey?"

His wife looked at her plate. "Yes, of course, John. Whatever you say."

Gertrude raised her eyebrows but said nothing. After April cleared the table, the older woman leaned forward and invited them to head upstairs.

"I hope you won't mind if I don't take you to your room myself. Henry and I always limited ourselves to one trip up and down the stairs each day after his stroke; walking was so difficult, even using his cane. I usually spend my evenings in here to be close to him." She looked up at the portrait. "We fell in love because we used to have the most stimulating intellectual discussions. He made me feel like a valued human being."

Her lips trembling, Gertrude looked back at the couple. "Anyway, you two are lucky to have each other. The first door on the right, dear; the master bedroom is farther down on the left. I'll be up later."

The pair dragged their suitcases upstairs. April dashed around the spacious room, exclaiming over the carved walnut dresser and bed. She ran into the en suite bathroom and immediately laid all their personal items out on the marble vanity.

"Oh, John! It makes me feel so wonderful to be here. Like I've come home!"

John scowled. "Well, she can't keep this place going forever. And I could indeed get used to using that library as my office once it's ours."

She ran to him and put her hands on his shoulders. "Don't be grumpy. You're right. I sense that Gertrude needs some stimulating conversating; she seemed to enjoy talking about books. It sounds like she still misses Henry."

His frown eased as he grabbed her waist and pulled her to him, ignoring her startled cry. "Well, we're just the ones to help her, then. I was always the best on my high school debate team." He started to kiss her neck roughly. "Once she sees how much I can help her, I'm sure I can convince her to rewrite her will."

When she started to protest his words, he smothered her with a kiss. "In the meantime, I know just how to make use of that giant bed."

April pulled back and gave him a tiny smile, one hand on his chest. "I'm sorry, John. It's been such a crazy day. Let's just go to sleep."

He stared at her with wide eyes, then opened his mouth to speak—but she touched her fingertips to his lips.

"Shhh! Let's not make noise and bother Aunt Gertrude," she whispered, then turned and slid into bed facing the edge.

John lay on his back in the middle of the four-poster bed, glaring up at the ceiling in the darkness. It was a comfortable bed, but he hadn't been able to get to sleep. It wasn't just the surprise of his wife turning down his advances. The old house creaked and made noises, and he was utterly unused to hearing nature outside, having lived in Brooklyn his entire life. As usual, April was sleeping on the very edge of the bed since he always needed a lot of room to be comfortable.

The wind blew, rattling the large-paned window and scraping the ivy across the glass. He twitched. He was just starting to relax when he heard a peculiar ticking sound that repeated every few seconds. Like someone was tapping on a table with their fingertips.

Once, and again. A pause. Once, then again.

He turned his head in the darkness, trying to determine the origin of the sound. It came from somewhere near the door, as best he could figure. It stopped, and his eyes closed as he finally started to drift into sleep. He was so tired.

Tap. Then again. Pause.

Tap, then again.

He sat upright in bed, reaching over to shake April by her shoulder.

"Wha—? What is it? You okay?" She rubbed her eyes.

"Can't you hear that noise? *The tapping!*"

She paused, sitting halfway up in bed, and listened. "I don't hear anything. Didn't you take one of your anxiety pills? You want me to get you one?" She started to slide out of bed.

"No, no!" He waved his hand in her direction. "There's nothing wrong with *me*. There's something wrong with this house. I tell you there's a tapping sound, and you think it's *me*?"

She yawned. "I'm sorry. It's just that you woke me and—"

"Oh, right. You're sorry. Go back to sleep. You're useless."

She laid back down and closed her eyes, and with his heightened focus, he could tell when her breathing slipped into the regular, deep rhythm of sleep.

John didn't sleep. He got out of bed and went to the door. Opening it, he ventured a few steps into the hallway's darkness. The tapping sound approached him from the moonlight-filled window at the far end of the hall. A wave of frigid air enveloped his torso, and when he breathed in, his lungs felt pierced by chattering cold. The sound invaded his ears so that he could no longer tell if what he heard was the tapping or the hammering of his own heart.

The sound passed by him. He gasped, then scrambled back into the bedroom, shut the door, and lay on the bed until morning came.

At breakfast, he mentioned the tapping sound. Gertrude did not appear surprised—she explained that it was likely the sound of the deathwatch beetle that commonly infests old homes where it feeds on the ancient hardwood used in the beams. The male tapped, and the female answered in a mating ritual. She pointed out with a frown, however, that it usually mated in the late spring, not the fall.

John stared at her. "You mean it's a real bug? I'll have to research that later."

Gertrude gave a gentle smile. "Yes, Henry and I have talked about this recently. Did you know that the tapping sound was likely the inspiration for Edgar Allan Poe? In 'The Tell-Tale Heart,' the man clearly has a mental disorder and is hyper-focused on sound. He hears something like the deathwatch tapping and extrapolates it to be the old man's beating heart. Interesting, because the idea of the beetle came from Thoreau."

The couple looked at each other. John mouthed the word, "Recently?"

April frowned and shook her head slightly, then turned back to Gertrude. "I remember the deathwatch beetle, Auntie. I studied Thoreau at Vassar. In one of his essays, he challenged people to become in tune with nature by aligning themselves with the beetle's tapping as it tries to attract a mate."

Gertrude's face lit up. "Yes, exactly! But it has a darker interpretation as well. It is frequently taken to mean that someone is going to die." She looked directly at her grandniece. "Henry died here in the house, and I remember hearing that sound before his last stroke. I haven't heard it since."

John pushed his chair back and threw his napkin down on the table. "Well. Not the most appetizing conversation, ladies. I do believe I'll do some research and then look around the house to see if I can find these pests. Clearly, you need my help because they *must* be eradicated. This house will lose value if the beams are weakened." As he stormed out of the dining room, he heard the two relatives resume their conversation over the different approaches to life presented by Thoreau and Poe.

"Damn college women. Think they're so smart." Fists clenched, he charged into the library, crossed the thick Persian carpet, and dropped into the burgundy leather wing chair. It seemed to fit his body perfectly, and John's shoulders started to relax. He pulled out his phone to search about the beetles, then put it away and found a book on the shelves about entomology instead.

John showed up filthy at dinner after climbing through the dirt-floored basement all day, checking massive support beams for signs of beetle infestation. He saw no indications of any bugs eating the old wood, even after heading up to the third floor to check the beams in the dusty attic. While he found no explanation for the tapping sound, he discovered many crates full of expensive items that he was sure he could sell.

The meal started well enough, but he found himself opening a second bottle of wine when he could barely manage to get a word in edgewise. The conversation left him fuming, mostly because it didn't seem to take him into account at all. Gertrude droned on about all the family members whose portraits lined the room and what she remembered about them. April seemed to hang on her aunt's every word, laughing gaily at the stories. By the end of the meal, he'd had enough and slammed his empty wineglass down on the table.

"Right, then. While you two have been gabbing all day, I've been working hard and checking out the house. No sign of those beetles that you mentioned." He crossed his arms and stared at the two women.

"Thank you, John. I do appreciate the effort that you put in today." Gertrude laced her fingers together in her lap. "I'm sure it must have been exhausting."

"Well, yes, I have to say it was hard work. Plus, I'm tired after not sleeping last night." He turned to April. "What do you say we make it an early evening, honey?"

"Oh, well, since it's Halloween Eve, Auntie and I were going to try the Ouija—" She looked up at him and stopped short. "Of course, dear, you must be exhausted. Whatever you say. Will you excuse us, Auntie?"

"Of course, dear. We can continue...later."

April fussed about when they reached their bedroom, laying her bathrobe on a side chair. Although he was losing his balance as they undressed, she insisted that he take one of his sleeping pills. "You deserve a good night's rest now that you've worked so hard to show there aren't any deathwatch beetles. I'm sure it was just the ivy tapping on the window last night."

He swallowed the pill and climbed into bed, feeling exhaustion overtake him as the room spun. She lay down at his side, and soon he was sound asleep.

Something woke John in the middle of the night. Groggy, he reached out for his wife but found the bed empty. He rubbed his face with his hand, shaking his head to try and clear it. "April?" He checked the bathroom, then stumbled to the door when he realized her bathrobe was missing.

He paused as he heard faint noises. Tap, then again. Pause. Tap, then again. He shuddered and held his hands to his ears, then made himself open the door.

This time there was light in the hall, coming from downstairs. He fumbled his way down to the dining room, holding onto the wall to keep himself upright and feeling a slight chill on the back of his neck. The tapping sound followed him, growing louder as he stepped into the dining room and paused just inside the doorway.

He stared at the candlelit table. All the chairs were filled except the head chair. People in old-fashioned clothing chatted and laughed with each other, some playing cards, as their outlines occasionally wavered and flickered. His wife sat in her bathrobe next to Gertrude, and the two focused on the Ouija board that filled the table between them. The grandfather clock chimed midnight.

No one noticed him. He scanned the other occupants of the table, then looked back and forth from each person to their corresponding oil painting on the wall. "April? Who are all these people? I thought you said you didn't have any family left except for Gertrude and me."

The room went suddenly quiet. The others around the table fixed him with cold eyes.

April's hands flew to her mouth. "I'm sorry, John. I asked to meet with Auntie after you were asleep. I just had to tell her about your plan to have her sign over the estate. I love you, but...it's just not right. You can't take over the house and do that to my family. And the rest of them agree."

Gertrude's stare pierced him. "I've always felt a connection with my grandniece. Seeing her again makes me realize that I was right to invite her to come to us. I'm getting old. She can stay for a long, long time, just the way the rest of the family has, as you can see." She gestured around the table.

"On the other hand, we've consulted the entire family, and I'm afraid they don't feel the same way about you."

Tap, then again. Pause.

John felt cold on the back of his neck, and his heart lurched. He whirled around at the sound coming from the foyer behind him.

Tap, then again. Pause.

A muscular, red-bearded man walked slowly into the room, leaning on the orb of his cane.

Tap, step. Pause.

Tap, step. Pause.

Gertrude smiled. "John, meet my husband, Henry."

The bearded man stopped in front of John, raised his cane, and brought it down in a hard and crushing *tap* across John's head.

Tap, then again. Pause.

TAP.

About the Author

Bram Stoker Award® finalist **CAROL GYZANDER** writes and edits horror and sci-fi from the northern NJ suburbs of NYC, with a special fondness for all things tentacular. Carol has short stories in numerous anthologies and magazines, and a cryptid novella, *Forget Me Not* (April 2022). She co-edited the ghost story anthology *Even in the Grave* (July 2022) with James Chambers, and she's edited four other anthologies. Find her at CarolGyzander.com.

GREEN MOTHER
CINDY O'QUINN & PATRICIA GOMES

What lies within a woman's heart?
      Pain, love, contempt and fear.
Bleed it out over the years,
      whether by purging, writing on paper, carving in stone.
Bring it forth, that which dwells inside;
      life will return when you bleed it dry.

Bury it deep, that which dwells inside;
      life will return when you push it aside.
... etchings of the old words carved just beneath silken skin.
      Hidden from the world—draped with anointed flesh to cover
my sins. Keep me there with the Green Mother,
      year times three,
no other amount, no other number.
      Always three for the number of times he tried to kill me.
*Deliver my hands from darkness, and let my soul bathe in the light of the
Green Mother's tears.*
      A pool, like glowing ichor, heals a broken mind from within.

*Punish my mind no more, then let my soul breathe in the waters of
Green Mother's tears.*

   *A pool, like glowing ichor, heals a broken mind from within.
Let her love spill into my center, and fill me again and again.
   Washed clean the thoughts of making all come to an end.*

About the Authors

Poet Laureate of New Bedford, Massachusetts from 2014 to 2021,
author and playwright **PATRICIA GOMES** is published in
numerous literary journals and anthologies. Gomes is the author of four
poetry chapbooks. She is a Pushcart Prize nominee (2008, 2018 and
2021) as well as a Rhysling Science Fiction award nominee. https://
www.facebook.com/patg305.

CINDY O'QUINN is a four-time Bram Stoker nominated writer.
She is a Rhysling and Dwarf Star nominated poet. Cindy lives on an
old homestead in the woods of northern Maine.
Instagram cindy.oquinn,
Twitter @COQuinnWriter, and
Facebook @CindyOquinnWriter.

AFTER THE FUNERAL
JENNIFER NESTOJKO

THEY MADE me plan the funeral, because they said I knew her best. That's a fool's way of thinking if you ask me, but it is true that I knew her better than most. I spent many a night towards the end, feeding her and keeping her blankets warm, and I have the scars to prove it. She lingered a good while, but that didn't surprise me none. She was meaner than Death herself, and that you can tie to. I didn't want anything to do with her funeral, but a woman has to pay her respects, and if there was one thing I've learned about the like of her, it is to respect them. It's no use disrespecting that diamondback hissing up a storm at you with his tail going every which way; I've seen some young idiots get bit that way and end up in a world of hurt and out of this world altogether.

I learned early on to watch for danger and to respect the forces of nature, along with the other forces too. That there survival instinct is powerful in me, and that's exactly why I didn't want much to do with the funeral. No one else would do it, though, and I didn't want to wake up in the night fretful with what might be coming my way.

Now, it's clear as can be that there was no way we were having this funeral down at the pretty little white Baptist church, nor were we dragging the priest from Holy Martyrs out to her cabin in the pines.

The snake handlers might have done it for a kick, but their snakes are gentle little infants, even the mean ones, compared to her. They would have come away handled themselves and not liking it. No, no—a church funeral wasn't what was needed.

I looked at old Hank Pruitt, looked him dead in the eye, and said there would be no liquor at the funeral either. Pruitt runs a big still in the back of those piney woods, and he didn't like that one bit.

"I never heard that old witch being a temperance agitator myself," he told me. "Seems like a little drop would make remembering her easier."

"Yes, sir, it would," I agreed, mild as milk, but he knew I was granite under that meek manner. He'd tested me before. "I'm not sure remembering her a bit more kindly would be to anyone's benefit."

"Man," he said, but without real force behind it, "what could it hurt? A man's got to make a living."

"You should know more than most how much it could hurt to drink around Herself." I replied. After all, his brother no longer needed to make a living; he was lying all peaceful out there in the graveyard off the southbound curve in the highway.

That was the end of that suggestion. There were some of the women wanting to gather flowers from gardens and from the barrens stretching between the trees; it was spring and there were plenty of flowers to gather. Others wanted to order hothouse flowers, but they were in a whole separate camp. I had it out with them on what was allowed; they either had to grow it themselves or find wildflowers. Most of them liked to borrow from the mayor's yard, as his wife had a green thumb, and her roses were the talk of three counties. There was no way we were having that mess. There's just no need to hand over three counties worth of land and souls just like that. Mrs. Cyrus Young looked fit to be tied, but she knew better than to complain. She knew where her firstborn came from and she also knew why he was a bit troubled, so to speak.

What harm could a funeral bring? That was the question being mulled over by folks, and you could see in their faces that they didn't like the answer. No one let on to knowing when that old woman took up residence in that little cabin, and those who could claim true ignorance wanted nothing to do with that little bit of truth. It made for good conversation when walking down the main drag on a Saturday morning or when taking a break during a long workday, but sometimes mysteries need to remain something to talk over, not something to be solved.

Most of those folks who were there were fertilizer anyhow, and had been for quite some time. Some of our best wildflowers, the ones the tourists came by to take pictures of, were on account of those old pillars of the community. There were a few from my time as well, the reason I could get close to her.

If you happened to come across her during a full moon, maybe see her dancing by the waterfall where the tourists sometimes like to picnic at on a summer day, you might get more mystery than you could bargain with, but you didn't talk about it after. If there was an after. I keep my mouth shut.

I about wore out the floorboards in my bedroom in that small cottage of mine, pacing while I tried to figure out just how the thing should go. People would bring a covered dish—that was fine and appropriate, and she liked to see people get a bit fattened up. She liked seeing the gatherings that happened in the fields or in the yards of the townsfolk; she appreciated a good party. As long as she weren't the one providing the food some of us would be safe. I was pretty sure of that, but not so sure that I didn't wear more wood off of those floors.

It was the speeches that worried me. Sure, people liked a good eulogy now and then, but people also liked to paint it on thick with the good memories and exaggerated traits. A little gilding is fine with a regular funeral—people know what's what and they don't mind speaking good of the dead unless the dead was really an old so-and-so. They would be all ready to bring out their flowery phrases, all ready to dab a handkerchief gently with a touch of feeling, but that mess was for regular people's memorials. It wouldn't work with here. Every little lie, every sweet fib, would bring a reckoning.

So would the truth.

I tried to rack my brains for those who were plainspoken yet cautious in their memories and the recounting of such memories. I wanted people with plain sense, but not only is that hard to come by in this town, such folks as had sense didn't have much to do with Herself. They didn't ask for favors from her, they didn't seek her out, they didn't keep charms over their doors and windows for safety because they'd never needed to do so.

Those who had such charms had enough to keep old Widow Tucker in business for a long time, and they prayed nightly that her workings were true. I didn't notice anyone being in a rush to take them down, neither, nor dig them up from where they were buried in the yard and by the fence posts. It didn't do to be reckless; folks would wait a while to see what was what before doing any digging. That was well and good, because I had no plans to put that coffin in the earth. I had no need for digging beyond what a garden with a few potatoes and some lettuce and sweet onions called for.

I had everything planned and ready by the time of the funeral: chairs set out under the trees, a few trestle tables set out with plain homespun tablecloths to hold the offerings of home-cooked meals. Potato salad and sweet tea and a baked ham were already set up, as Mildred Cunningham had arrived early, grim-faced and determined to be the first. She was not chosen to be one of the eulogists; I had my reasons. She knew where to put her fixings down; there was no need to talk. There hadn't been since the night she had abandoned me to face down a judge and jury who had no sympathy for a young girl caught alone on a back road in the middle of the night. The one whose funeral we were having was the one who became my mother then, in a way. I know some with longer memories hold quiet the truth that she had faced the same thing, more than fifty years past, with the same result from the law. She'd outlived those involved; she had become vengeance when justice was no longer an option.

Mama always did make the best fried chicken, though, and I hoped to taste it again, even if she were no longer my mama in anything but blood.

Justine Thomas came soon with her bevy of daughters, each with an armful of wildflowers. Justine had her own reasons to pay her respects; she and her girls made up the tables beautifully and then melted back into the shadows. They knew better than to stay. I wanted to go with them, but I had to be here and bear witness.

When what I could not bear, back when I was young and terrified, had been taken from me by her, I became her apprentice. It was my own choosing back then, which is how I ended up here on this funeral ground where those who were truly mourning would not step foot, not to stay. The rest were cautious, or scared. They weren't mourning.

Eli Wilson was as dapper as ever; he never missed an opportunity to get dressed up. It was probably one reason he had become a politician. His hair had gone grey years ago, and he thought he was the only one who knew that fact, seeing as how he made the trip sixty miles south to get his thinning locks dyed a glossy mahogany. He was one of my eulogists. He knew how to put words together in a delicate way. I knew which way he had voted on a number of laws, though. He may have been married and claimed to be inspired and ruled by the women in his life, but those laws spun a whole different tale.

A quarter of the town came. I reckon they figured that if they came to the funeral that was insurance against her haunt coming to them. There was a right mix of white and black folk, willing to drink from the same fountain of caution, though there were distinct groupings on either side of the aisle. There were more men than women.

Once Eli gave his eulogy, carefully speaking to both groups, carefully leaving out any mention of the afterlife or any specifics that would have been tempting fate, or at least the woman in her wooden coffin, Annie Smith stood up.

Annie wore a lavender dress which looked so good on her, with her deep brown skin, I wished I could wear such a color. Such a thought in that moment was sheer foolishness, but I'd always been fond of Annie. Sometimes too fond, but she had done me the favor of coming forward to speak something real after Eli had worn down his words and illusions.

Annie wasn't flowery, despite the color of her dress. She got to the point: "You all came here today," she said clearly, "because you are too afraid to sleep in your own beds if she thinks you are disrespecting her memory. You didn't dare speak her name while she was alive, and you don't dare stay away now."

Her eyes met mine, holding just the hint of a smile. I couldn't help but watch her closely, though I had part of my attention on the coffin. I wasn't sure if it had moved, but there was a sense of something I couldn't quite catch.

"Here's your truth for this farce of a funeral," she continued. "You would have run her out of these woods like she was run out of town so many years ago, but you don't dare. Your wives and daughters come to her for help, and you are powerless to stop them."

I noticed some of the womenfolk puffed up at that; most of them had never come for such services, but some of their daughters had. A flash of anger, not shame, crossed Mildred's face. I kept my own anger locked inside. My shame had long since been burned away.

The menfolk looked stoic or frowned. Some of them actually had no idea about the daughters of the town needing her services. And mine.

Bless their hearts.

Annie continued: "There will always be someone like her, out on the edges, with strength bought with blood and anger, until you face your own sins and shortcomings. If you fear her, good. You brought it upon yourselves."

Now, such a speech at a funeral out in town would have caused some gasps, and even perhaps an old-fashioned bout of vapors, but here no one moved, no one breathed. I knew cake had been brought, just as it would have been offered at the Baptist church, but the air was thick with tension, thick enough I could have cut it and served it.

Annie stepped back and kept walking, out into the trees, the same direction Justine had gone. I had never been so glad to see her walk away.

I'd been wrong, though; someone had breathed. He took a deep breath and jumped up. His speech had not been planned, even though she had specified asking him. I may have been her confidante, to an extent, but I wasn't stupid.

Stu was dressed somberly, but had a bright red carnation in his lapel. I wasn't sure what he was going to say; it gave me the jitters, not knowing. He was a fair-looking man, even though he had aged considerably over the years. He didn't hesitate, though. He came up in front of the coffin and didn't even lead in to what he wanted to say.

"My pa used to speak of her, for many years," he began, looking straight ahead. "He was going to marry her. It broke his heart to find out she was unfaithful."

You could have heard a pin drop, even on that pine-covered dirt. A wave of uneasiness rose from the crowd. Here, in the light of day, before witnesses, what was only whispered in secret.

"The truth was," Stu went on, "she was a whore. She whored around with more than one man, all at once, and then tried to cry out that she was the one hurt. I'm glad Pa was rid of her, and I wish this town had found the guts to take her out before she became an evil blemish on an upstanding, Christian community." This went beyond the whispers, beyond the rumors. No eyes were on Stu; every eye was fixed on the air, determined not to look at him or at each other. They especially avoided the wooden coffin.

The coffin twitched. I wasn't staring into some middle distance as if I could somehow avoid being complicit in such knowledge. I held the truth.

The coffin twitched again, and even those who were trying not to notice saw the movement. There were gasps, though no vapors yet.

I sighed to myself. Boy, we were in for it, for the reckoning I had been trying to hold back. Right now, though, I wasn't sure I knew why I had even bothered.

Stu either hadn't noticed or didn't care. "We should have rid this place of her long ago," he said, his voice eerily calm. "We should have burned down her house and salted the very earth where she had walked."

I rolled my eyes, not bothering to hide it. That would be much of the town, and we didn't have that much salt. If he wanted dramatics, he would get some soon enough.

Stu saw me, though. He took two large strides to where I was standing and grabbed my arm. "It isn't too late, though," he said, raising his voice slightly. "We have this one."

I didn't like men grabbing me and had spent a fair number of years making sure no one dared, but right now I was not afraid. I knew I was safe enough, despite my scars, despite wresting with a rattlesnake, so to speak. I'd always been safer than I had been in town since I had come to this grove, this clearing in the pines. I knew right now I wanted that reckoning, I wanted what was going to play out to happen.

For a moment no one moved, no one was sure what it was that would happen. Then Mildred stood up. There was a part of me that wanted to cry out to my Mama, but she was long gone.

"I have no daughter," Mildred said. It wasn't the first time. "Do as you will." She sat back down. Stu's grip on me tightened, and his smile came slow but clear across his face. A smile can also be a sneer, but I learned that back in the courtroom. Stu had been the opposing counsel. I still was not afraid.

People began to rise; they'd been given something to do, something to combat their fear, something to regain their power. The witch was dead and they were ready to make sure no witch rose in her place. Their hands were itching for blood.

The coffin exploded, and she came rising up from it on a pillar of flame, like a phoenix in old stories. She always had been a bookish one, telling me once that she had been shy and reticent as a young woman. They had found her reading in this grove, that day of pain.

The fires did not ignite those old pines; she was fond of them. They did ignite a few of the townsfolk. For a while, there were screams, though they were swallowed by the roar of the flames. I wondered what Justine and her daughters, what Annie and the rest of our group of women down by the river, heard. I wondered if it sounded like music. The screams didn't last long, though. Soon it was quiet.

I wandered over to the tables heaped with good home cooking and took a piece of fried chicken. It was the last time I would taste Mildred's cooking, after all. My patron was behind me, in a new form, burst from her chrysalis, in a manner of speaking. I had wondered if she were really dead. Now I knew. She would be hungry, but not hungry for what was on the tables.

My own chewing didn't quite cover the sounds of Herself sating her new-hatched appetite. At least I wouldn't have to clean that mess up.

As everyone knows, after the funeral, comes the feast.

About the Author

JENNIFER NESTOJKO is a teacher and a writer who lives with chaos in the form of a household full of boys and other animals. She teaches English and Ethnic Studies to high school students and Composition to college students, and has, perhaps, had thoughts of making off to the piney woods and becoming a terrifying and mysterious hermit, if only to get some quiet time. The current political and social situations (there are so many) don't help in resisting that urge.

UNTAINTED
CHRISTINA NORDLANDER

AFTER SOME TURNING-POINT, you are condemned to look back and see that it started earlier than you thought. I guess my account has two starting points. The first was when I had taken maternity leave. I sat at home, awaiting my new destiny. My body still looked normal, just a bit broader in the abdomen. I could do everything I'd done until now—the exercise—but beneath the papery layer of my skin I could feel all the reactions that had started. The taste of rusty steel wool, like on the days when I was menstruating. I was a lab.

The doorbell rang. Rudi sat upstairs at his computer, working on his book, and maybe hadn't heard. I ran out in the hallway—I didn't pant yet, I didn't waddle—and outside were two girls, not much younger than I, with a white-painted basket of baby goods from YourPal.

The other beginning was after the science fiction lighting in the maternity ward like a departure lounge for a journey somewhere else, after the midwives placed Dymfna's little weight in my arms. Rudi said I'd picked that name just to fuck with him. Sorry. Just to be a pain. Still, he continued to call her Dymfna, even though he had the option to use her first name, Babette. Was I cruel? The name had grown in me with her.

"Welp, I'm a mother," I said on the way home. "That wasn't so bad."

I started using the breast pump. I'd been on leave for more than two months. I'd be lying if I said that my job in the shop was so darn awesome that I missed it—yes, I did miss it. More than that, I wanted to remember that I was an individual.

(It sounds so strange now.)

Rudi didn't mind serving out his paternity leave. He painted light blue plywood clouds in the nursery and leaned over the big enclosure where she became a bit more of her own person every day, with her transparent brown hair that had grown before she breathed. I left them there, hearing him cooing for her attention with his friendly dad voice as I walked out into the laundry room and lifted down the box with the pump.

I placed the pump on the kitchen table, keeping an eye on it as if circling some unknown animal. Misty tubes, all plastic a symbolic white. The kitchen had large clear windows on the bike path. I went back into the laundry room, pulled myself up on the worktop and unbuttoned my shirt. Sixty millilitres was my goal, to start with. I fastened the cup on the smooth inflated skin and switched it on.

It bothered me. I was used to feeding Dymfna by now, even though I'd had all the revulsion and reactions of: *I can't do this I'm going to fail.* This was something else. It was the nausea of seeing my own milk as a discrete object, something to be put in the top shelf of the fridge behind the frying oil. I'd done some research, I knew I wasn't sucking the milk out, but it felt like the pumping weakened me. I pictured a needle sliding into my nipple, something so thin and delicate I wouldn't see it through the cup. Perhaps it had hurt when she'd started feeding, and I'd already forgotten.

Discomfort aside, it came easier than the first few times I'd breastfed directly. I had to switch off the motor when I saw the pale yellow milk reach the right mark. One of those quick thoughts: what would have happened if I hadn't switched it off?

I was back at work. The first few days I was so tired, I wondered why I'd chosen this. (A nauseating proverb from my mum's generation: "milk in the breasts, porridge in the head.") I wasn't the twenty-year-old Linda anymore. Those of my colleagues who'd gone through a pregnancy treated me with respect. They knew your body isn't just your own any longer: stronger, in some ways. The childless women, and the men, behaved differently around me. They'd never been the kind to harass; it was because they saw me as a different type of being. I was something that could be bred. That sounds foul.

The fatigue didn't ease off. It was always me having to get up when Dymfna woke us: Rudi couldn't always help her. Those were times in the nights when I would have screamed like her, if it would have shut her up. There were mornings when I tottered with dizziness and wondered whether I should call in sick. I got more rest at work, because there I only needed to do one thing.

⬚

One of the first evenings, I told Rudi:

"I did some more research about pumping."

My voice hesitated, but Rudi looked up and I had to continue:

"I should really have started pumping a few days before going back to work. It...takes a few days before the body adapts to the pump, so that you can produce enough."

"Hm?" Rudi said. "But there were no issues, she got enough milk, didn't she?"

I shook my head, an aggressive movement: only against the words.

"That's exactly it, I shouldn't have been able to produce so much."

I glanced down, despite myself. My breasts were two pink weights beneath my white nightdress. They turned the discussion into something pornographic.

"I didn't even feel any discomfort..." I had to break off.

I crept beneath the quilt and felt it slide across my skin, through the nightdress.

"Perhaps it's simply a better model," Rudi said. "The Manson chicks sold it as something new, after all. Not some standard model you can buy at the pharmacy."

"Manson chicks? That's a bit on the mean side, isn't it?" I still laughed.

Rudi shook his head. "You agreed that they looked like they came from some cult. Did you read *Helter Skelter?* The author talked about how he interrogated two of Manson's gals, and they were pretty and nice enough, but they looked like the same girl who'd changed clothes and wigs. That's what those two reminded me of. They weren't *unpleasant.*"

"I don't know that the Manson Family had access to such good breast pump technology…"

I had pumped again, after getting changed.

Rudi grinned at me.

"Or perhaps you're the better model, Linda."

I laughed at it and called him a flatterer, but you always feel better for getting flattered. Isn't that true? Even for something like this.

▭

Dymfna didn't like my nipples anymore.

Rudi said that she drank well enough from the bottles. It wasn't as if she'd stopped feeding from me entirely, but it was hard to get her to take the nipple in her mouth. Once, she started crying hysterically when I tried to turn her face towards it, and that was when I realised how it would feel, having to hear that cry from a teenager or a woman.

For a few days, I kept my spirits up with the thought that maybe the bottle was good, an intermediate step. That was what Rudi would say. My child was growing up; her grip around my finger grew stronger by the day. She was getting enough nutrition. I shouldn't have reacted that way because she was repelled by my body, as if she were repelled by my soul.

Dymfna's sleep deepened to regularity, and I was able to snatch naps in the evenings, but nothing much changed. Returning to the cross-country circuit wasn't an option. The fatigue became like pain. It pressed on my lungs. At work, it was all I could do to focus on not staggering.

I took a lot more than sixty millilitres. Dymfna didn't suckle any more, but I still needed milking. I poured out the excess in the sink and ran the tap so Rudi wouldn't see—but Dymfna needed more, too, she grew. The discomfort had moved inside my nipples. It was like being tickled by something that you didn't know whether it had a sharp point. When I drained the milk, it eased off, and I felt like what was in there had been pulled out.

I should have gone to the healthcare centre. I put it off for the usual reasons: it was going to pass, I had brought it on myself. Breastfeeding wasn't a disease. It was only in a modern industrialised country that women could afford to see pregnancy and childbirth as some kind of sacrifice that made us into martyrs.

The events forced a decision. I collapsed in the warehouse while I was on floor duty. Weeks of compressed sleep hit my brain.

I went to the clinic on a day when the sun blazed from every window and even the lawns were difficult to look at. Was I so unused to the world outside? A large butterfly is what I felt like, maybe a nocturnal one. I don't mean that as a poetic image. I was something frail, exposed to whatever might lurk in the cloudless and glaring sky.

The doctor told me YourPal had recalled their breast pumps due to provable adverse effects, nothing permanent. Customers who could demonstrate that they had been harmed were welcome to call at their office for compensation. She already had their web page up and asked whether I wanted her to call them to book an appointment.

Two days later I went in. I brought Dymfna along. I told Rudi they might feel more shamed if the aggrieved party was a new mum. (Everyone who came there was a new mum.) Truth was, I didn't like leaving her out of sight unless necessary. If I'd been able to bring myself to, this would have ended differently.

The office lay in a townhouse at the outskirts of the city, not one of the fancier ones. A cramped hallway with a staircase in dark oak, densely-patterned wallpaper turning the light murky. A spot of faint light was a reproduction of a painting: two sleeping women floating over a bleak snow landscape. The only warm light lay on their breasts and closed faces, and little threads of sun in the snow.

There was a playroom with a pen, empty when we came. A girl with a black pageboy haircut sat by it, a book in her lap. Maybe she was studying: she looked young enough to still be in college, if that.

"The waiting-room is across from the top of the stairs," she said. "You shouldn't have to wait more than a few minutes."

"Your picture is nice," I said, glancing towards the hallway. "Is there some story behind it, some legend?"

"It's called *The Punishment of Luxury,*" said the girl. "The women are those who cared more about their own comfort than bringing children into the world. They float forever above the sterile land...not seeing anything, in a trance, warmed only from inside by their dreams."

I think she could see my revulsion.

"A depiction of Hell, in other words?"

I'd lowered my voice a little, as if there were any possibility that Dymfna could understand. She didn't care about what the stupid giants were doing; she crawled across a butterfly-yellow square of the playpen in pursuit of a rattle. The only art in the playroom was frames with pressed flowers on the oxblood wallpaper.

The girl smiled. "Many people don't think so, do they?" she said.

I had to stop myself before I got into a political discussion while waiting to speak to the public relations person—but wasn't that a part of the politics, too?

"You thinking of having kids yourself?" I said.

She looked up at me. "I'm on my second."

The waiting-room was decorated in the same antiquated colours, with a mullioned window whose glass looked matte. But now I'm describing things we're both familiar with.

I didn't have to wait long, but I counted every second. The pain inside my breasts had started again. It wasn't a violent pain—it just made me faint and nauseous. I hadn't thought to bring the pump. I could have gone downstairs to Dymfna, but I had to weigh the labour of the stairs against the potential relief. Sometimes I stretched or pushed myself up between the armrests; that was the only exercise I could do here. The discomfort ought to have driven me to pound on the door and demand that they hurry. I couldn't quite link the two.

The door opened and a woman came out: middle-aged, soft-bodied, a gaze that didn't let go of mine. More than once, I thought of her as a doctor and the first-floor landing as a waiting room.

"Come in," she said, and I followed.

But this was no consultation. Inside sat three others, only one of them male, in a circle of over-stuffed chairs. Around so many bodies, the office felt small. There was a window on the road below. All leather was shiny, all fabrics dull and downy.

"Sit down, that's a dear," the woman said.

I assumed she would sit at the desk, but when I went towards the free chair, she brushed its back. As if this were some game of musical chairs in daycare. The seat that was left was a pouffe in violet plush on the floor. I sat down on it. My line of sight wasn't much lower than the others'.

I'd expected the woman to begin, but she sat with her eyes fixed on my face. Her gaze was dreamy, not unpleasant. I had to start:

"I'm here because I used the breast pump. I realise this is nothing you intended, but I've suffered from...the physical sequelae...since I started using it."

My voice became coarse, as if I had to transform myself into someone else when speaking in official contexts—a mum. My breasts weren't hurting at the moment, but I was aware of them. I constantly wanted to press my arms against my torso or pull up on my bra under my flannel shirt.

The woman was still looking at me, and for a moment I wondered if I would have to go into detail. Instead, she leaned forward, resting one elbow on her knee-length woollen skirt.

"My apologies, Linda," she said. "Would you prefer if we spoke in private?"

I said yes: it was always better. The others left the room in single file.

I got up and sat in a chair that was warm from a body. She didn't stop me.

"Well then," she said. "What do you hope to gain from this?"

"I want help with the physical symptoms. That is why you recalled the equipment, isn't it? I spoke to a doctor, but she said you'd handle it."

I said all that as if I were still back in the rational world, but at some point, it had slipped a bit askew, and the things I talked about wouldn't matter anymore.

"Interesting that you don't mention compensation," the woman said.

I was about to say, proudly, "We're doing all right for money," but she was still speaking:

"One thing I'll tell you, Linda: it is not going to get better. But if you continue to pump, you will keep it under control."

I nodded, seeing a bit of pale sky outside the window. I don't know what I thought. I never doubted what she said, and I didn't feel the delay of shock where the words wouldn't come through. What I heard was nothing devastating, no heroic pain to overcome, just slow toil.

"Well," I said. "This is a bit bigger than a model needing recall. Do the police know about this?"

"Remain seated," the woman said.

She waited to speak until I sat back down, as relaxed as I could.

"It doesn't trouble you as long as you use the pump, does it? By all means tell us if it does. We want to improve the process, streamline it as far as possible. None of our producers should suffer."

When I shook my head, she went on:

"You and I, we are surrounded by women who try to leave procreation behind...to consign their femininity to history. Sure, many will have a child or two, then put them in daycare while they return to work."

"What about the men, then?" I interrupted her, but I cannot bring myself to be ashamed of it. The woman gave a brief clicking smile. For the first time, it felt like she was addressing me.

"The men are not innocent. But it is not up to me to judge them."

"What are you trying to get at?"

"That is why we designed the pump, Linda," she said. "To, if you'll pardon the expression, collect the resources of those of you who choose not to breastfeed."

She shook her head, like an apology. A strand of silver hair fell over her forehead.

"But you are different now, aren't you?" she went on. "Natural feeding is our primary aim, but the milk you bottle, too, is something sanctified. I don't use the word in a religious sense, but we have no better words. Our children are more important than us, and the bond we create with them...through the milk...is a continuation of the genetic one. Do you understand?"

All the while I looked her in the eyes and tried to find something that separated her from other people, the ones who didn't say those things.

"I poured it out," I said. "It's not stored anywhere."

"Not physically, no," the woman said. "But your using the pump was also a sacrament. A bond to your daughter, and to us."

Now all I could think about was getting out, to the hospital, letting them see what was wrong in my breasts and cut it out. I think I would have been able to run down to the front hallway and the street, even in my state. When she mentioned Dymfna, I blinked and woke up.

The woman had gone to the desk and taken out white papers, a form.

"I realise that you have been listening to this and only heard threats," she said. "If you'll work with us, we will give you a monthly compensation, the amount that you earn now. It is work, after all. That is money for your daughter and your husband."

Dymfna was in the playroom, so I signed everything that needed signing.

When I was done, the woman put a white-plastic pump and bottle on the desktop.

"Now you can do it, if you want," she said.

They let me go to the car with Dymfna in my arms. Of course she couldn't know that she had been in danger. She was an infant.

I haven't kept track of the weeks since they signed me on. At one point I walked past the hospital with Dymfna, but ended up standing outside the A&E entrance. If I knew that there were some surgery that would set me right, I would do it. Perhaps I will still try.

If not, I can provide for the two of them. The pump keeps the disease at bay.

Rudi doesn't know about it yet. I guess I will have to tell him soon.

About the Author

CHRISTINA NORDLANDER was born in 1982 and lives outside Birmingham with her husband Graham and two cats. She has published more than 20 short stories and other pieces, primarily on the speculative fiction spectrum. She also dabbles in visual arts, game development, and wargame miniature painting, and has a PhD in Classics and Ancient History from the University of Manchester.

"Although the sun shines, there are always shadows." Kimra side-stepped yet another face-glued-to-their-cellphone person doing their zombie walk down the corridor inside Pointe Vista Mall in San Diego.

The late Saturday afternoon witnessed a surge in younger folks and a decline in authentic adults. The big mall anchor store announced its new sale in large, screaming yellow and red signage that shot out of the mall's floor in metallic stands and plastered posters across most of the available surfaces not already covered.

"Do you ever get tired of being gloomy? You're so damn depressing." Vega frowned, making her elegantly drawn, colored, and gelled brows wrinkle. Well, not the eyebrows so much as the skin around them. Her best friend since elementary school, Vega sailed through the crowd like a golden swan, graceful and swift.

"Nope. I'm happy when I'm sad," Kimra replied, fingering her afro puffs. She smirked at Vega.

"Damn, that's weird." Vega sucked her teeth and tossed her waist-long rainbow braids over her shoulders. Everything about her glowed, from her gold bangles on her wrists, her gold earring hoops that brushed her shoulders, and on to her layered gold necklaces around her neck.

"That's okay. I'm goin' get you whipped into shape." Vega pursed her lips with the promise. "You live in San Diego, home to all the beautiful people."

"I like my shape just the way it is." Kimra pinched her love-handles and shook them at Vega.

She smirked, shaking her head. "But you got such a pretty face."

Kimra'd been hearing that her whole life. It played like a well-worn laugh track. She'd been a chubby baby, a thick teenager, and now a "curvy" woman. "Real woman have curves," the television bellowed, but then in a whisper, "...but not too much."

"I have an amazing personality." Kimra shoved her hands into her joggers' pockets. When her hands started to ache, she realized they'd been clenched into tight fists.

"Shush. I got you." Vega swept her hands toward the store ahead of them.

They arrived at the mouth of the large, carnivorous department store. Here, the ugly and unsophisticated entered, their identities devoured by the make-up counters, personal shoppers, and salons.

What remained was cookie cutter culture. Kimra paused at the mouth of the department store. A sliver of worry wiggled down her spine. Vega kept walking a few feet before she realized that Kimra wasn't with her.

"Kimmie? Girl, come on!"

Her voice sounded muffled, but Kimra could make it out. The lights flickered behind Vega. The store seemed to be cackling at her hesitation, daring her to enter.

"I dunno, Vega. I love my face like it is." Kimra hated the sharp whine wrapped around her words. They bore holes in her resolve. The pleading made her sick to her stomach.

"Nuh huh. You'd be happy if you did." Vega snorted. "I know you, Kimmie. You just thirstin' for knowledge."

"I don't want strange knowing like what's in there." Kimra nodded in the department store's direction. "The secrets of beauty, making yourself skinny and creating man-made glamour."

"Everyone wants glamour. I'm not judging you, but we did talk about this already. You said you'd try." Vega's tone was light, but her nostrils flared, signaling her annoyance.

"Yeah," Kimra whispered. She'd confronted Vega with the facts, but that hardly mattered. Vega was always the life of the party. This visit to the mall was no different.

"Oh, I know. Let's split the difference. A new lipstick would do wonders to brighten you up." Vega sparkled despite the shadows lingering and looming in and out of the department store's gaping entrance.

Kimra wondered if the shadows would return to human forms once they exited the mall. Shopping bags seemed too heavy for ghostly arms and rotting hands.

"Just lipstick?" Kimra quirked an eyebrow at Vega. They'd backed off the full facial makeover. So she *was* making headway.

"It's like a fancy lip gloss or your favorite lip balm," Vega reassured her. A warm glow, an aura, softly pulsated around Vega. "It's fun. Come on, scaredy cat."

Another chill raced up her spine, reversing course. Kimra straightened, threw back her shoulder, and faced the store. She could do this. Lipstick was just glorified lip balm. That she could do, a tiny sacrifice to the gods of beauty.

"Let's get some color in your face." Vega guided her toward the entrance.

I'm black. I already have color, courtesy of Mother Melanin, Kimra thought, but didn't say. She hurried along, propelled by Vega's pace and guiding hand. They entered into the stunning fluorescent illumination. Kimra winced, but peered through slits as Vega led her to the equally bright beauty counter.

"Hello. Welcome to Marv's," the slender, hollow-cheeked woman draped in a blood red dress and platform heels said. "How can I help?"

Vega met the store clerk's wolfish grin. "Hey, Linda. We're looking at lipsticks."

Linda rubbed her pale, slender hands together. The grin

remained. Kimra wondered if it was detachable, like the store nametag. She rebuked herself. *You can't always trust first impressions.*

"We have sale on facials. You like one?" Linda asked.

Too many teeth. Kimra shuffled behind Vega and swiftly turned her face away. She couldn't look at the beauty clerk. For starters, Linda's sheet of perfect brunette hair captured the light, trapping it like a spider with a web. Secondly, Linda's flawlessly crafted face was beautiful and terrifying. Too many teeth crowded into a too small mouth. Too perfect. She looked capable of something cruel.

"No! Thank you!" Kimra said, before Vega answered for her.

Linda's mouth widened, if that was possible. Kimra shuddered, cursing herself for taking a peek. The heavy cloak of perfume made her stomach hurt, even more. Something coppery and acidic flavored the air, looming beneath the manufactured aromas.

Kimra closed her eyes and opened them after summoning the remnants of her courage and the protection of her ancestors. *Ready.*

"Just. Lipstick," Kimra said, on the edge of bolting.

Vega laughed. "She's new to this."

"I see. Fresh meat," Linda purred, rolling the R in fresh like her tongue wanted to make love to it. The way she said it made Kimra's skin break out in gooseflesh.

The golden-capped lipsticks were lined in a row, round for sampling, corralled for plucking. Linda's long fingers glided across the luminous rainbow colors. The retail ones hid under the counter in individual boxes, mass produced for consumption.

Linda eyed Kimra's mouth. "Such beautiful lips, full and plump. No enhancements."

Kimra blanched, if her dark skin could do such a thing. The hairs on the back of her neck stood at rigid attention. Those words scared the daylights out of her. She turned, but Vega caught her by the elbow and pulled her forward. Linda's mouth watered. The clerk patted the sides of her mouth with a napkin, and her grin returned.

"Try these." Linda splayed the lipsticks across the glass counter.

"Your skin is so luscious. Do you know? Clear. Vibrant." She licked her lips a moment before the teeth came back into view.

Vega elbowed her. "See? Told you."

Kimra met Vega's smile and tried to relax. "Okay. Let's do the purple one, first."

Vega grunted and shot Kimra an encouraging nod.

Kimra picked it up and leaned in to the large circular mirror. With a quick push of her thumb, she uncapped the sampler.

"Oh, yes! The Deadly Nightshade," Linda cooed, pleasure making her eyebrows rise higher above her artfully decorated and glistening dark eyes.

Kimra froze, the cap in one hand, the sampler in the other. "Isn't that poisonous?"

Vega interjected. "Only in large dosages. I'm kidding! They're just names. There ain't no real nightshade in there."

But Kimra watched Linda, who remained silent, wearing the too-many-teeth grin, her gaze trained on Kimra's every move.

"Lovely shade. Put. On," Linda encouraged after several tense minutes.

Was it her, or was Linda struggling with the language?

"I'm going to try this one," Kimra said and recapped the purple one. Maybe it was her imagination, but Linda's smile had sharp edges that drooped in disappointment when she declined the purple lipstick.

Kimra opened the red matte color. With her heart pounding, she ran the sampler across her lips, turning them from their natural, healthy roseate to a deep crimson.

"Venom looks brilliant on you," Linda exclaimed; a small vein snaking down her forehead stood out in excitement.

"Ooo, Venom," Vega chided. She spun her around to face her. "Beautiful."

"Show me," Linda hissed.

Did this woman know any other words?

Linda's outstretched hand twitched in anticipation but paused just shy of touching Kimra. Kimra didn't think she wanted Linda touching her. In fact, she was certain, but she turned to face Linda anyway. The rail-thin clerk greedily clasped her hands together once Kimra came into her full focus.

Kimra spied her own reflection, out the corner of her eye, in the mirror. It was her. Then again, at the same time, it wasn't. What she saw made her blood ran cold. Her eyes, her chin, her nose all looked the same, original Kimra. But her lips had peeled back, revealing a mouth crammed with teeth overlapping each other. The front top teeth elongated and dripped with saliva against the backdrop of crimson. Bleak. Gruesome.

Kimra reached up to touch her lip. Panic flooded her chest. She struggled to breathe. "What the hell?"

"Don't!" Linda slapped her hand, no longer the bubbly make-up counter clerk.

"Ow!" Kimra scowled and rubbed the back of her hand.

"Leave your beauty. Don't remove it." Linda's eyes widened as she further declared, "This color had flair."

Vega cocked her head to the side. "Kimmie, dial it back!"

"That is what I said!" Linda laughed, hollow and empty like her eyes, like a casket after a thousand years of buried decay.

Kimra caught chills again, backed away from the counter, and looked around for Vega. "V, do you see this right here?"

But suddenly Vega wasn't there.

Her best friend had melted into the throng of shoppers, leaving her alone. Had Vega left to go fill up her gas tank? She always ran her gas down to the fumes. As she whirled slowly around, scanning the seas of faces swimming by, Kimra's stomach balled into nausea. Had she really even been here? *Vega?* Hadn't she come here alone?

Kimra didn't know any more.

"Ah, do not be afraid. You look gorgeous!" Linda gestured her to come back to the counter. She blinked; unrealistic eyelashes brushed her upper cheeks. "There's no solace in beauty, only pain."

The words called up such terror, it enveloped Kimra in its tight embrace. Every fiber roared with alarm, but Kimra drifted forward as if

Linda held her mouth by a tether. Was she facing something sinister? Surely not at a makeup counter. Kimra spied her face again and noted the hideous smile etched into her face. The fear gripped her.

"No! Get this off me! I'm not interested in pain!" Kimra rushed the last few steps to the counter, snatched up the tissues from the box, and wiped her lips until they were raw.

"Try another? Facial?" Linda asked, gesturing to the ever-expanding circle of cosmetics appearing on the counter.

Kimra shook her head, too scared to vocalize an answer. She realized that Linda's struggle to speak came from the overabundance of teeth in her mouth. Scared, Kimra tried not to allow it to root her there. She started backing away. Her heart pounded against her chest like it worked at a disco.

"Wait! Sale! Special!" Linda's long, pale arms shot out like vines, but with nails like claws, swatting the air in attempts to snare her.

Kimra thought again about the spider, spinning more web to stop the fidgeting prey from moving, escaping.

"No! No!" Kimra backpedaled faster. Too afraid to put her back to the store clerk, Kimra kept moving, bypassing shadows and face-planted-in-screen zombies. Her throat was too dry for her to say more, so her hands waved Linda off until she plowed into something solid.

"Watch it, there!" Vega's husky voice shouted in irritation. "You could lose a body around these parts."

"Where have you been?" Kimra screamed. Fury rolled forward, making her face hot. She grabbed Vega's shoulders and shook her gently.

"Um, clearly we're still fine tuning our boundaries, Kimmie." Vega shrugged her off. "What happened to your lips? They're bleeding."

"That lipstick! It's horrid!" Kimra touched her sore lips and cringed. "Where were you?"

Vega shrugged. "Damn. I spent a lot of emotional equity on this trip to Linda."

Perhaps finding the anger burning in Kimra's face, Vega dropped her gaze and mocking tone.

"Okay, sorry! Something grabbed my attention and drew me off your path. I got carried away looking at jewelry. Calm down. I left you in good hands." Vega spoke with all the care of one who just lost a sock.

"Linda?" Kimra shook her head.

Vega shrugged again. "Yeah. She's no pressure sales and a free spirit."

"Demonic spirit, is what you mean," Kimra said.

As they exited the department store, Kimra released a breath she didn't even know she was holding. Still a touch of foreboding made her pause. Vega waved her on. They took the side door exit to the parking lot. Finally, the numbness started to fade from her lips.

Vega gave her a side-eye glance and shrugged although her plans to get Kimra to wear makeup hit a snag. "Still free."

"About that, Vega, we got a little more to discuss," Kimra said, a bit unsure if she should convey what she'd seen. They fell silent as they walked through the parking path to Vega's car.

Kimra buckled her seatbelt and waited for Vega to start the car. Vega lowered the driver's side visor and flicked up the mirror. Outside, a soft rain fell. In the glistening surface of the water-drenched pavement, the vehicles shimmered. In the twilight, the mirror's light flashed on. Vega pulled out her gold-capped lipstick from her purse.

"Vega, is that..."

"Yeah. This one is Blood Moon." Vega puckered and applied the lipstick with a practiced hand.

Kimra froze. *Now what?*

Her heart started to inch into her throat, even as her blood slowed in her veins. Next to her, Vega had this weird smile on her face. But Kimra only saw the profile view.

"V? Linda is a monster."

"Hmmm?" Vega slapped the visor back into place. *Whack!*

"A monster..." Kimra whispered, throat going dry.

"I'm not that kind of person. Yes, I became that person. This is not me," Vega said, before turning to Kimra, her rainbow braids spilling across her shoulders with a smile.

Filled with teeth.

"Ain't I pretty?" Vega leaned closer to Kimra, eyes glazed over, wide with wonder. "Ain't I?"

Kimra screamed and tried to melt into the passenger side door. Her hands couldn't seem to get a grip on the latch.

With eyes as large as saucers and nostrils flared, Vega leaned over the gear shift, saliva dripping down the corners of her too-broad smile. "This. Is. Love-ly. Yeah?"

Kimra shut her eyes tight. "No beauty is worth this much pain!"

A soft humming took up residence in her ears, and she tried to ball herself into a tight knot. Maybe, just maybe, if she prayed enough, she'd wake up in her bed.

Minutes elongated, stretching out like the long canines in Linda's mouth. Shuddering against the still hot car, Kimra emitted a "please, Lordt," against the thick air.

"Kimmie?" Vega's voice sounded normal, not laced with gravel as it had a few minutes earlier. "You okay?"

Kimra peeked through her hands, and then lowered them to find Vega scowling at her.

"Girl, it ain't that hot. Give the air a minute."

Kimra sat up straight in her seat and looked around. Everything seemed normal, even Vega. She shook her head to clear the lingering cobwebs and chill of the encounter.

Had she imagined it? Been dreaming?

"I'm okay," and then with more confidence, "I'm okay!"

Vega smirked at her as she shifted the car into reverse and began backing out of the parking lot.

That's when Kimra spied the sprinkle of saliva dotting the area around the gear shift. Vega didn't appear to notice it, and she put the car in drive, they headed off into Charlotte's clogged and congested streets.

Kimra swallowed the hard lump of fear down her dry throat.

As Vega drove, she said, "You know, we should check out the cosmetic counter over at the mall in Rock Hill..."

"No! No, I'm good," Kimra screamed.

Vega flinched. "Wow! Well, okay. You know, you have such a pretty face..."

About the Author

NICOLE GIVENS KURTZ is an author, editor, and educator. She's the recipient of the Ladies of Horror Grant (2021), the Horror Writers Association's Diversity Grant (2020) and the Atomacon Palmetto Scribe Award-Best Short Story 2021. She hails from the south where gothic and strange are part of the culture. You can support her work via Patreon.

FAILED LOVE LESSONS
LINDA D. ADDISON

THIS IS NOT MY BREATH, it is yours, the false start,
    mis-aligned emotions sliding past the cut in
    your chest. That is not my opening revealing
    all secrets, it is yours, it used to be our hearts
        beating together.

This is not my hand, it is yours that caressed my
    face, breath quickening as the cut at your
    wrist released it, lies written in sleepy
    moments seeping out, crimson script,
        patterns of mis-used affection.

These are not my eyes, they are yours, can you
    finally see me, the real me, now that I have
    freed them from your confusing need to control.
    I suspect the tears of blood on your cheeks
        contain some truth.

It is not my skin, it is yours peeled away to allow the
    history of pain to write itself in the veins
    underneath, a map from the past to unseen future.
    There, there now, admitting wrong is no sin,
        hiding it is...

These are not my muffled cries, they are yours,
    denying, pleading for redemption I can not give,
    only seek out the truth of your abuse, interpreted
    through the echoes of devotional song, here in
        distant woods where you first seduced me.

This is my recovery, my need to understand how
    false love came to be, so I will know better
    next time, so I can learn...

[reprint from *The Place of Broken Things* (Crystal Lake Publishing,
2019), HWA Bram Stoker Award®]

About the Author

LINDA D. ADDISON grew up in Philadelphia and began weaving
stories at an early age. Ms. Addison is the first African-American recipient of the world-renowned HWA Bram Stoker Award® and has
received five awards for collections: *The Place of Broken Things*,
written with Alessandro Manzetti; *Four Elements*, written with
Charlee Jacob, Marge Simon, and Rain Graves; *How To Recognize A
Demon Has Become Your Friend*, short stories and poetry; *Being Full of
Light, Insubstantial*; *Consumed, Reduced to Beautiful Grey Ashes*.

In 2018, she received the HWA Lifetime Achievement Award. In 2020, Addison was designated SFPA Grand Master of Fantastic Poetry. She co-edited *Sycorax's Daughters* anthology of horror fiction & poetry by African-American women with Kinitra Brooks, PhD, and Susana Morris, PhD, which was an HWA Bram Stoker finalist in the Anthology category. She currently lives in Arizona and has published over 400 poems, stories, and articles. Look for her story in the *Black Panther: Tales of Wakanda* anthology (Titan/Marvel).

A MONSTER'S CHILD
BRIDGETT NELSON

"I really wanted a boy, but I got my Ems instead. Isn't that right, Emma?" - Emma's father, Ted

"Mom! Do we have to play with Emma? She's a girl. She won't get this game." - Emma's parents' much longed-for twin boys, Jax and Jay

"Sorry, Emma. I would have invited you to my slumber party, but you're not really, you know, into the girly stuff. I didn't think you'd have fun." - Emma's so-called friend, Gina

"I guess I have to pick Emma since she's the only one left." - Emma's classmate, Daniel, during gym class

"Listen, Emma, I've met somebody, and she's more...adventurous. It's over." - Emma's (ex) boyfriend, Levi

"This sucks." - Emma, sitting home alone during her senior prom

"You weren't chosen to be our sister this year, Emma, but you can always try again next year!" - Emma's (future?) sorority sister, Lexi

"Emma, what were you thinking? Is it your time of the month? I can't publish this story as it's written! Get your emotions under control, quit being biased, and rewrite this shit...NOW!" - Emma's boss, Fred

"Emma, babe, can you bring me another beer? And maybe make some of those chicken wings I like so much. Oh, and sweetie? When you're done, a foot rub would be great." - Emma's husband, Maverick

"Hey, bitch!" - Emma's rapist, name unknown

"Yes, Emma. I understand the sensitive nature of your pregnancy and that you have no interest in having this baby, but there is nothing I can do—no referrals I can make. My hands are tied. It's the law." - Emma's obstetrician, Dr. Maloney

"No, I'm not taking you to some goddamned blue state to get that baby sucked outta ya. It's your damn fault it happened. I saw what you wore to work that day, Emma. You're lucky I haven't divorced your skanky ass." - Emma's husband, Maverick

▭

It was a struggle getting my newly curvaceous body up the stairs. This pregnancy had been rough on my petite frame. My hips and back ached constantly, I was now the proud owner of some truly grand cankles, and I thought I might melt into a blubbering ball of self-loathing if I peed myself one more time.

Dr. Maloney had warned me years ago that, if I ever got pregnant, my narrow hips and pelvis would likely necessitate a Cesarean section. Shortly after I'd married Maverick, we'd discussed having a family. Remaining childless suited us both. I hoped he'd have a vasectomy but, unsurprisingly, he refused. "That bullshit baby stuff is the woman's responsibility, Emma. Ain't no way anyone is snipping my family jewels."

I consulted Dr. Maloney about surgical sterilization, but even with insurance, our deductible was too high. I'd reluctantly gone on birth control pills instead. Mav bitched and moaned about the resulting weight gain, and the iron in them made me sick to my stomach, but since my 'compassionate' husband also refused to wear condoms, I had no choice. The pills worked for three years.

Until they didn't.

Two months after I was assaulted, an at-home pregnancy test confirmed my worst fear.

Since I'd been with two men in a short period of time—neither by choice—and despite Mav being an imbecilic caveman, I still hoped the baby was his. Turns out, DNA testing was really expensive and wasn't covered by our insurance.

I had no clue whose baby I was carrying. It was a mind-fuck.

I don't even know what my attacker looked like, although I'd briefly heard his voice just before he knocked me unconscious. It felt so very wrong not knowing the ethnicity of the baby that carried half my genes. I do remember coming to once and seeing the outline of a tall, slender man...and the glowing, neon orange tip of the cigarette he smoked. That image haunted me.

Mav got angrier and more controlling with each day that passed. He gave me no options. I considered traveling solo to a state where abortion was still legal but simply didn't have the means. I was forced to carry a baby conceived in fear and violence. I hated my body for betraying me. But, I'd endure this like I'd endured everything else— with a steel spine and miserable smile.

Out of breath and decidedly uncomfortable, I pushed open the door to *our* apartment and stepped inside *my* prison. Mav was unreasonable. With the exception of work, I was no longer allowed to go anywhere by myself. He claimed he "couldn't trust" me not to "use my feminine wiles on unsuspecting men." The only shocking thing about that statement was that he actually used the word 'wiles' correctly. He'd installed a tracker on my phone, and we shared multiple video calls each day for verification of my whereabouts.

Mav's "social drinking" became full-blown alcoholism. With the drunkenness came abuse. Last night, he'd kicked me in my lower back with such force, I'd fallen to the ground, right on my belly. Maybe that was his intention—abortion by abuse.

I sighed, hating my meekness, but unsure how to be any other way. Walking into the bedroom, I stopped before the mirror mounted to the wall above the dresser. I pivoted so I could see my back. A dark purple, size twelve bruise dominated my lower spine. I was wearing that son-of-a-bitch's footprint! No wonder I was so uncomfortable. The waves of pain just kept coming.

Objectively, I knew I was supposed to be all mother-y and fall in love with this baby, despite the circumstances surrounding its conception. I had not—could not. Every time I felt it move, my body cringed in revulsion, knowing part of the man who had violated me might be sitting inside my womb. It was the equivalent of finding out I had parasitic worms in my gut. My only choice was to simply sit and wait for the medicine to do its work, despite my desire to rip open my abdomen and pull them out—a mass of slimy, writhing leeches, living in my body without my consent.

A trickle of warm fluid ran down my thighs.

"Dammit, again? For fuck's sake, I didn't even feel the urge to pee!"

I hurried to the bathroom and immediately realized this time was different. It didn't smell like urine, and there was something in my underwear—something that looked a great deal like a quarter-sized, yellowish, blood-streaked wad of snot.

I began to panic until I recalled reading something about a 'mucous plug' in one of my pregnancy books.

"Well, that's gross."

As I cleaned myself up, I wondered if my water had broken. *I'll find out soon enough!* I headed to the closet to get some fresh clothes and glanced outside, hoping to see the setting sun.

Instead, I froze, my gaze laser-focused.

Three stories down, in a shadowy corner of the parking lot, my husband was locked in an embrace with our downstairs neighbor, Fiona.

Our *sixteen-year-old* downstairs neighbor, Fiona.

I'd put up with years of endless abuse, years of waiting on Mav hand and foot, and was possibly even carrying a *rapist's* baby because he demanded it...only to find out he was fucking a child. I'd married a goddamn pedophile.

I paced furiously around the room, trying to find an outlet for my fury.

For so long, I'd taken the heaps of shit everyone felt the need to pile on me...and smiled.

For so long, I'd never been enough. Not for anyone. Not even my parents.

For so long, I'd felt like a big, fat *zero*.

Never again! I was done being the world's punching bag. Feeling a scream rising in my throat, I placed a pillow to my mouth and let it out —an animalistic roar that reverberated throughout my body. The baby kicked.

An idea began forming. In the closet, sitting in a metal box on the top shelf, were Mav's hand and ankle cuffs. My anger grew as I thought about all the perverse ways he'd used them on me. I pulled the box down and was struck by back pain so intense, it brought me to my knees. More warm fluid ran down my legs. Oh, yeah. I was *definitely* in labor. No matter; I'd focus on that later. Right now, my only job was to teach my husband a valuable lesson.

Taking both sets of handcuffs from their fur-lined box, I exited the closet and looked back outside. Mav was no longer in the parking lot, which meant he was on his way upstairs. Grabbing a baseball bat from the utility closet, I gripped it tightly in my hands and waited by the front door for Mav to make his appearance.

A contraction hit, leaving me bent over and gasping for breath. Something thicker, more viscous, ran down my legs. I didn't bother looking. Mav was apparently sharing a very drawn-out goodbye with his girlfriend, but I was grateful for the extra seconds. I only hoped he'd show up before the next one.

Footsteps sounded on the landing outside the apartment door. I knew it was Mav—those heavy, steel-toed boots that strolled so slowly, so casually, so *arrogantly* to our home's entrance. Hearing the sound of the key in the lock, I raised the bat above my head. Adrenaline coursed through my body. I would only have one chance.

Mav walked through the door, gaped comically when he saw my murderous stare, but had no time to react further as I brought the bat crashing down onto his skull. His eyes rolled back into his head, and his hefty body went limp. My husband crashed to the floor in a boneless heap. *Bastard.*

I wasted no time dragging his body in front of the couch. Thankfully, the couch wasn't far from the front door—adrenaline, desperation, and pure grit were the only reasons I was able to move his much larger body. The pain was damn near unbearable as another contraction struck, but I soldiered on. Once his hands and ankles were cuffed, I used some thick twine from the utility closet and took my time securing the man I'd once vowed to love forever to the couch legs.

When he regained consciousness, I'd be waiting.

His eyes flickered open, disoriented and full of pain. They circled the room, eventually landing on me. Clearly pissed off, his body immediately reacted, hands and feet straining to reach me. When Mav realized he was restrained and helpless, his anger spiraled. "Goddammit, you stupid cunt, untie me right now!" I smirked as the yelling caused him to cringe in pain and attempt to grab his throbbing head.

Understanding who had the upper hand, he switched tactics. "Come on, Ems. Why are you doing this? You know how much I love you."

I fucking hated when he called me "Ems." Reminded me of that dickhead I called "Dad."

"You love me, huh? Well, that's good." I peered into his hate-filled eyes. "More than Fiona?"

I watched what little color he had drain from his face. The strong jaw I'd been so attracted to in college clenched. He played dumb.

"What the hell are you talking about, Emma? I don't know any women named Fiona!"

"Maybe not. But you do know a very young girl named Fiona— quite well from what I saw, you rotten sack of shit!"

Undeniably caught, and taken aback by a side of me he'd never seen, he heaved his weight away from the couch, trying to break free. "Are you calling me some sort of deviant kiddy fiddler, bitch?"

I smiled pleasantly. "I wouldn't do that if I were you, sweetie," I said, pulling the cleaver I'd hidden from beneath the couch cushion.

Mav immediately stopped moving and started bribing. "Ems, come on. Put the cleaver away. I'll take the tracker off your phone. You can drive wherever you want, whenever you want! Just please let me go, babe."

"I am *not* your 'babe.' I am nothing to you anymore except the woman who is going to teach you all about body autonomy—and what happens when it goes bye-bye."

He didn't dare struggle, even as I wrestled his pants down around his knees. Though his feet were cuffed, there was just enough give to let me force his legs apart and access the part of his anatomy I desired.

"So, *darling*," I said. "Let's start with a few simple questions, shall we?" I waited for him to respond. He begrudgingly nodded his head, his eyes never leaving my weapon. "Excellent! So, Mav...do you remember all the nights you wouldn't take no for an answer? All the nights I was forced to let you stick your disgusting cock inside me, always for your twisted pleasure and never for mine?" I stared into his petrified face. "Thought so. Here's my response to that."

I clutched one of his shrunken balls, stretching his scrotum as far as I could from his groin, and brought down the cleaver. Mav screamed, the ropey veins in his neck and forehead prominent.

"This just won't do. Can't have the neighbors hearing you, now can we?" I stuffed the severed testicle into his mouth—a perfectly suitable substitute for a dirty sock. Duct tape prevented him from spitting it out.

"Let's move on with our lesson, Maverick. You're a big guy—probably outweigh me by at least a hundred pounds. Do you remember all the times you slapped my defenseless body? Hit it? Kicked it, even? All the times you knocked me to the ground or slammed me against the wall? Here's my response to that."

Testicle number two came off with another quick whack of the cleaver. Mav noisily groaned and whimpered.

"You really don't learn, do you?" Peeling back the tape, I tried to force the second testicle between his teeth. His jaw was clamped, mouth unyielding...so I pinched his too-large nose. When he finally gasped for breath, I crammed it inside.

"Gosh, having things forced into you when you don't want them there kinda sucks, huh?" I said, as I reattached the duct tape.

His face had turned an alarming shade of purple. The truth was, I wasn't sure if he was just *really* angry, or choking on his balls. Frankly, I didn't care either way.

"Finally, my *cherished* husband, do you remember that time I was innocently walking through the parking lot, the parking lot owned by my *employer*, and was attacked from behind without ever seeing the man who assaulted me?"

Mav nodded and tried speaking. I ignored him.

"And, my *most precious* partner, do you remember how you blamed me and my choice of clothing? How you left me no choice but to have this baby—a baby I never wanted, who will always remind me of the most traumatic moment of my life? And let's be real here, Mav...that's saying something, having lived with you." I rolled my eyes and continued. "Do you remember how you willingly put my life at risk, knowing it would be difficult for me to carry and deliver this baby? Did you give a damn?"

I spoke in a playfully falsetto voice, impersonating a child. "I have the answer to that, Ms. Emma! No! Maverick Macari did *not* give a damn!"

At that moment, Mav must have realized he wasn't getting out of this alive—his long-suffering wife had lost it. He twisted and turned his head, as garbled noises came from his throat. His eyes pleaded with me. He wanted to say something. I removed the tape, ready to slap it back in a hurry if he tried to scream.

Mav managed to spit the testicles out of his mouth and offered a wheezy reply. "I did care, Emma. I was trying to help you, by teaching you a little less—"

"A little lesson?" I cut him off. "Yes, about that...lessons are so important. Here is yours."

His limp penis sagged against his thigh. I tugged it upward and held it flat, using his lower abdomen as my cutting board. The first chop sheared through the underside of the shaft and hacked partway into his guts.

The lack of tape over his mouth wasn't an issue; he passed out. I poured most of a water bottle over his head, bringing him back to consciousness. When his vision cleared, I showed him the flaccid tube of flesh in my hand. He shuddered...whether from pain, grief, or revulsion, I wasn't sure.

"Kinda pathetic, Mav," I said. "I could stick this in your mouth, but we already did that with your so-called balls." I paused thoughtfully. "Up your ass? That seems so cliché...and, besides, you'd probably like it."

Red froth bubbled from Mav's mouth.

I paced the room, still gripping my husband's detached penis. "Hey, maybe your special fishies would like a little treat! Black Ghost Knife fish, right? The ones you just *had* to have because they were predatory and so 'cool,' despite the expense. And surprise, surprise! Guess who got to clean the goddamned tank!"

Making sure he was watching, I tossed his dick into the aquarium. The ebony fish immediately swarmed the fresh meat, shredding it into bloody clouds. Mav gave a primal moan, just before his eyes turned dull and lifeless.

All I could feel—aside from the contractions, which were coming hard and fast—was relief.

▭

"911, what's your emergency?"

I let out a sob. It wasn't hard...by the time I'd cleaned up and set the stage, the contractions were agonizing. My plan was dangerous, but it was a risk I was willing to take.

"My husband! I just got home and found him on the floor...someone killed him! He's dead! There's—oh my God!—so much blood!"

"Please stay calm, ma'am. What's your name?"

"Emma, Emma Macari."

"Are you safe right now, Emma?"

"I think so. I don't know. I think I'm in labor...please, send help!"

"I've dispatched a unit, and they're on their way. Did you say you think you're in labor?"

I screamed as another contraction ripped through my exhausted body. This baby was tearing me in two. "Oh God, it fucking hurts!"

"How far apart are your contractions?"

"I don't know! Just hurry!" I said, panting heavily. "Oh my God, I smell smoke!...I think something is on fire...whoever did this must have started it...Christ, it's burning fast...please hurry!...don't wanna die...oh no, here comes another one!" I howled with pain.

"Ma'am, Emma, stay with me, okay? They'll be there in less than two minutes, and I just dispatched the fire team. You're going to be fine. Hang tight."

As expected, I needed a Cesarean section, though the onset of labor and severe smoke inhalation made it more of an emergency than the scheduled procedure Dr. Maloney had planned.

Thanks to the blue, sterile drape in front of my face, I couldn't see what they pulled out of my body, but I heard the surprisingly strong, lusty cries.

"Congratulations, Mrs. Macari, it's a girl!"

A girl. A daughter. Maybe Mav's—whose burnt, unrecognizable body was downstairs in the morgue of this very hospital. Maybe that of the unknown, faceless rapist.

A monster's child, either way.

"No!" I said, as the nurse lifted the squirming bundle to show me. "Please, take her away. I'm putting her up for adoption."

"But, your husband..." began the nurse, before another member of the surgical team leaned over and hissed urgently into her ear. Her expression, above her blue mask, went from confused to shocked, then filled with pity…and a hint of accusation. "Don't you at least want to see her? Hold her?"

"No!" I repeated, my voice firm. "It's my choice, damn it! Finally, for the first time in nine months—for the first time in *years*, it's my choice! *My* choice, and I'm making it. Take her away."

A nurse did so, and the crying receded. I shut my eyes, breathing as deeply as I could with the damage to my lungs, as the surgeon sewed me back up. I lay there, feeling nothing, caring about nothing.

What was it I'd just been thinking? Maybe Mav's, maybe the rapist's. A monster's child, either way.

And maybe they'd also made a monster out of me.

About the Author

Once an operating room registered nurse, **BRIDGETT NELSON** so enjoyed playing with human organs, she decided to turn her macabre interest into a horror writing career.

Bridgett has contributed to multiple anthologies, including *Counting Bodies Like Sheep*, edited by K Trap Jones. Her debut collection, *A Bouquet of Viscera*, is now available in ALL formats.

Bridgett is the HWA: WV Chapter co-chair. Visit her website at: www.bridgettnelson.com.

A CRUCIBLE FEAST
RACHEL A. BRUNE

Lodya McCorrin used her fingernail to pick at the slight gap between her cuspid and her back teeth. A piece of pork from lunch had escaped the hasty brushing, and her tongue had spent the last hour fiddling with it while Gerrod was in the stylist's chair. You'd never guess from Gerrod's virile, masculine stage presence the amount of time it took for hair and makeup to sculpt and primp and craft him that way.

She stepped back, unobtrusively holding her breath, as the stylist covered Gerrod's eyes with one hand and blew an atmosphere-destroying amount of hairspray over her creation. Lodya took the opportunity to seize the offending scrap and toss it on the concrete floor of the backstage area they'd commandeered for a dressing room.

Gerrod—preferred form of address *Congressman* Porter—hated seeing anyone pick at themselves. Her first day on the job, one hapless junior aide had made the mistake of wiping a minuscule spot of mustard off his otherwise impeccable tie. There hadn't been any actual bloodshed, but the shreds of the aide's dignity and self-respect had littered the floor of the congressman's office like a trail leading the young man straight out the door.

He also hated when Lodya left his side for any reason. "I'm hiring you to be my wolfdog," he'd said at her final interview, right before her personal security firm had secured the plump, ripe contract. "I expect you to show your teeth." Therefore, as the stylist dropped her hand from his eyes, Lodya straightened and clasped her hands behind her back, sighing at her dental hygienist's inevitable lecture about flossing.

"There you go, sir." The stylist smiled at the congressman's reflection in the locker room mirror.

Porter stared deeply into the mirror, looking into his own eyes. From Lodya's perspective, they were blank gray canvases, although she'd seen them glow blue under the right lighting. Every blond hair was neatly arranged in a pseudo-military fade, an homage to four years of post-ROTC service in the infantry. His massive shoulders strained against the expensive dark blue wool, the patriotic elements completed with his solid gold flag lapel pin and red tie with the tiny white stars. A little bit of theater, a little bit of flair to complement the red-white-and-blue of the signs, bunting, and clothing that would shout their allegiance to him throughout the arena, even way back in the cheap seats.

Lodya shifted and refrained from picking away a piece of lint on her own navy blue lapel. No one would notice the white speck. But a uniform is a uniform, even the finest and most custom-tailored, made from the most expensive of wool blends, and the speck offended her. She did adjust the jacket, which had once again snagged on the holster she wore over her shoulders.

In the mirror, Porter frowned at the gesture, then went back to surveying his look. Finally, he snapped his fingers, that single gesture that let everyone around him know it was "Go" time.

Already forgotten, the stylist shrank back as Lodya's second-in-command, Mike Monteiro—a tall, Black man in yet another navy blue suit—took the lead, followed by Congressman Porter's assistants and then the congressman himself. Lodya shadowed his steps as they left the locker room.

"Falcon is moving," she muttered into her earpiece.

"Falcon" was the code term for Gerrod Porter that they used when he could hear them. He tried to maintain a neutral expression, but whenever they muttered that phrase—*Falcon is moving*—he straightened even taller, smiling, his straight, blunt teeth flashing in his not-too-deeply-tanned skin. It was the same expression he wore when he did a meet-and-greet at the local Army base or watched one of his talk show interview appearances, where his blunt style eviscerated his less-vicious, weak opponent.

The men and women stationed at key points in the facility muttered their statuses back through the earpiece. The wire almost disappeared in Lodya's thick, black hair, neatly pulled back into a braid and twisted into a bun at the nape of her neck. She was almost exactly one-half-inch shorter than Porter, and even though she was in top physical condition, next to him, she appeared almost waif-like. He enjoyed the contrast—liked to refer to her and her employees as the Falcon's Wingmen. Lodya paid no attention to what Porter called her and her colleagues. He wasn't the first promising young candidate they'd shepherded; they were there to do a job, and every single agent she commanded was a consummate professional.

The hallway was wide, the stark concrete echoing at the slightest sound. The crowd's excitement filtered through the walls, a dull roar that leeched through harsh stone. Porter turned to make sure his wolfhound was following at the prescribed distance. As the fluorescent lights caught his eyes, Lodya thought she glimpsed a spark of something that only came alive when he was walking toward these crowds—these massive, undulating, cheering, *alive* crowds that taunted and pleased and worshipped the congressman from North Carolina on what seemed his almost inevitable path to the White House. Even if he hadn't formally announced his intentions—yet.

Porter made a sound in his throat, and as he turned away, Lodya understood the sound and the darkening swell that tingled like sharp sparks in his eyes. The crowd's energy and the promise of the arena awoke a reaction in the congressman, a reaction that she sensed—scented—was not sexual, but a hunger nonetheless, and the maw of its appetite was not Porter's groin or stomach but the deep burning in his hooded, gray eyes.

At the front of the entourage, Mike ducked to the left, a strange, erratic movement that caught Lodya's eye. She reached out to place a hand on Porter's shoulder, even before the code word filtered back through the earpiece.

Eagle Wolf Eagle Wolf Eagle Wolf!

Eagles and wolves—two of a falcon's natural predators, closely followed by humans. Humans like the woman with the sign who had lain in wait around the corner.

Lodya pushed the congressman behind her, ignoring his aides milling in confusion. She keyed her mic, keeping her eyes on the scuffle ahead. "Report."

Mike grunted, and Lodya dropped her free hand to her torso, hovering at her weapon.

"What the hell is going on?" Porter hissed in her ear. "Why the hell haven't you pulled your weapon?"

Lodya ignored him. The scuffle ended before it even began, with the protester's sign flung facedown on the floor next to the protester herself. She was middle-aged, slight, with gray hair that peeked out from beneath her nun's wimple.

"Let her up, Mike." Lodya didn't bother with the earpiece.

"I want that bitch arrested," Porter snarled. "I want her—"

"Sir, Agent Monteiro will ensure that she is properly removed." Lodya nodded to the rest of the entourage, then keyed the mic again. "Door 2, we are almost at your position. Fall in on Falcon 2."

With that, she took the lead down the rest of the short distance to the stage door. As they passed the nun, still sprawled out on the floor, Lodya spared a glance. Mike had her well in hand, the only trace of her resistance the bright red blood that streamed from her nose. Lodya took a quick glimpse behind her to make sure Porter was following within arm's reach. As they passed the woman, she could swear that the light in his gray eyes glinted a dark, brooding red.

But then, the moment was over, and they headed to the stage, Lodya's weapon un-drawn. Porter still frowned even as they waited behind the curtain while a trio of adolescent bluegrass singers sang the

National Anthem in three-part harmony. Lodya didn't have to see them; she already knew that their outfits would be reminiscent of ruffly pioneer dresses, jazzed up with red, white, and blue sequins.

She also knew that Porter wasn't frowning because of the music. Rather, he clearly enjoyed it when his security team got the opportunity to demonstrate their skills on those who would violate the sanctity of his rallies. The violence expended on his behalf would be taken up by his disciples as proof of his virility, his male energy, and the leadership that he brought to the corridors of power—that he *would* bring.

The only thing that could have made the scene outside the stage door more perfect, more obliging for the cell phone pictures his staff had snapped as they filed by, would be if Lodya had drawn her weapon on his behalf. As the song wound to an octave-crushing close, she patted the holster resting snugly under her left arm, secure in what she carried there. Softly, the rest of the security stations reported in, their movements rehearsed and adaptable, as fluid as any pack of well-trained sheepdogs herding their charges to safety.

The applause for the trio blended into the introduction from the local mayor, a frosted blonde who had wooed Congressman Porter to her city for this penultimate rally, one at which it was rumored that he would finally—*finally*—announce his candidacy to the men and women who longed to see someone with strength and purpose in the Oval Office. Someone who would understand them, who would understand what it meant to fight your whole life to get ahead, only to see it wasted on those who spat on the values on which this country had been founded. Someone who understood military service, who preached that masculine strength wasn't toxic, but a pillar of society that saved it from corruption and decline.

"...and now, ladies and gentleman—y'all *are* ladies and gentleman, right? Anyone who identifies as an imaginary creature should leave right about now, am I right?"

Porter kept frowning as he darted glaring looks at Lodya and then back at the mayor. Lodya understood. The glares weren't because he didn't agree with the joke; it was that the mayor had taken exactly forty-five seconds longer than she was supposed to with her time in the spot-light, and that stage was waiting for him. Not her.

"...your congressman—and who knows in the future?—Gerrrrrrod Porter!"

The flash of rage—at the insinuation, the potential spoiler, and the possibility that any part of his announcement might be diluted by this dumb woman's need for attention—twisted Porter's face in a grimace of disgust, and then evaporated as the curtain rose.

The smile on his face was nothing less than genuine as the powerful photo flashes from the press, gathered in their little corral to the side of the stage, went crazy. They were accompanied by the tiny sparks of thousands of little stars—cell phone cameras snapping blurry, grainy photos, trying to get this once-in-a-lifetime picture of the future leader of the free world. Lodya thought they looked like a swarm of fire-flies, but instead of an undercurrent of wonder or innocence, they gave off a frantic air, a desperate hunger that contrasted with Porter's confi-dent, vigorous lust.

Porter kept his hand raised, his attention focused on the crowd, the gesture only mildly reminiscent of another wave of acknowledgment that history had long since condemned and forgotten. From the crowd, whistles, adoration, returns of the gesture.

Lodya took up her position at the side of the stage, safely out of the way of any photographs or attention, but close enough to respond to any dangers. Porter had insisted she be present, the face of his security entourage. He had even hinted that once he made the announcement, he would keep her firm on as a private augmentation to the federal security. Lodya privately thought it was bold of him to assume he would get that far, but she did not doubt his ability to claw his way through the ever-more-packed field of potential candidates, all crowing their accomplishments and bravado.

She knew, more than most, the singular focus and purpose with which Congressman Porter conducted every single interaction, fundraiser, networking opportunity, and zealot-filled arena. That hunger lurked behind his eyes, shone free as he grinned and dropped his arm.

A few final spatterings of applause, and the last couple of cell phone flashes died away. Porter launched into his familiar spiel. He gave a nod to the military veterans in the crowd, the first responders, the "essential workers," the mothers and fathers. He referenced his own upbringing, his time in the Army, his dismay at seeing the country he loved and served become fodder for those whose political agendas would desecrate—yes, *desecrate*—the sacrifices of those who had built the country from scratch and those who had died in its service. He spoke to the crowd, and they received his words not as a net cast over the widest possible stretch of the ocean, but as a spear aimed right at them, and he told them it was okay.

That it was okay to be straight. That it was okay for them to be a man or a woman. That it was okay to work with your hands. That it was okay to be angry at those who demanded safety and shelter and food and fulfillment without first working hard for those things. That it was, of course, perfectly possible to be proud to be white, especially in a country that celebrated pride for those of every other color.

Here, Lodya caught Mike's eye. Her colleague stood in the shadows. She raised an eyebrow, asking a silent question, and he nodded in response. The bystander was out of the way, and they were clear to proceed. She wasn't worried about anyone asking further questions regarding the incident—likely Mike had just pushed the nun out the door and locked it tight behind her.

On stage, Porter was hitting his stride—the congressman drew the undivided attention of everyone in the arena, including the press box, where the men and women covering the event fought against the wave of energy that drew them under Porter's charismatic tide.

Lodya breathed in, feeling the energy sink like gentle lightning into every pore of her body, the sharp, familiar shocks joined by the same transformation that lit Monteiro's eyes across the room.

That energy wrapped itself like a nervous cat around the stage, preening and dancing with the vitality crackling from the congressman.

As Lodya and Mike kept their alert watchfulness from the wings, Porter's eyes deepened, going dark blue under the lighting. The heat from the adrenaline and the spotlights sent sweat trickling down Lodya's side. A similar glistening shone at Mike's temples.

Even Congressman Porter, normally powdered and pale, began to flush. He paused at the center front of the stage and pulled a handkerchief from his pocket to dab at his brow. He turned towards Lodya, but she stared back, unwilling to take the hint and find someone to turn up the A/C. She was security. He had aides for that. Besides, the heat felt comfortable. Delicious, almost.

Someone might have started a grill; the heat and smell were filtering inside. Out in the parking lot, Lodya knew, they had food trucks parked, but most of them had started to pack up.

Porter tucked his handkerchief away and raised both hands, this time to quiet the cheers and the groans from the crowd—the men and women who stood, unmoving, entranced. Waiting.

His skin above his collar grew redder, darker, glistening under the lights and the heat.

"My fellow Americans," he began, his deep, smooth voice burring in the utter silence with just the faintest hint of a drawl.

Lodya held her breath with the crowd.

"I come before you today, a humble man who has thought long and hard about the sacrifices—the burden—that the mantle of leadership demands." He swallowed hard, face alarmingly red.

Lodya stepped forward, staring intently. Was that the beginning of a blister on the back of his neck?

Porter coughed, and the smell of roast pork and charcoal smoke wafted across the stage. Lodya's mouth watered. Mike swallowed and surreptitiously wiped his mouth with the back of his hand.

"I come before you," Porter continued. "I come before you to—"

Another round of coughing interrupted what he was going to say. Lodya took another step forward. She reached out.

Porter struggled to get just one word out; he grabbed his throat and heaved, trying to breathe around whatever reaction he was having. In his eyes, Lodya detected, rather than panic, an overwhelming rage that his announcement had been derailed by whatever this mysterious ailment was.

Porter blinked back against the sweat that dripped in his eyes, against the red burns now raising welts on his exposed skin.

"Sir, let's get your jacket and shirt off." Lodya pretended to ignore the spread of the blisters on his skin as she eased the wool suit jacket off. As tenderly as possible, she peeled back the cotton shirt. It stuck to the skin of his arms, and she tried to gingerly pry it off before giving up and ripping it off in one quick gesture.

Porter screamed and fell to his knees. His exposed skin blistered and bubbled, sticking to the white tank top, filling the air with the scent of the most delicious grilled pork Lodya had ever imagined. Porter ran out of air as his throat finally closed all the way—the scream cut off. He frantically scrabbled at his neck, trying to pull at a tight collar that was no longer there. The red and blisters spread until he couldn't move, couldn't see—eyes shut—hair falling out in stiff, oily bristles.

The silence in the arena crackled as if with the lightning that heralded the approach of a storm. The bright flashes of professional bulbs from the press corral had vanished; now, the reporters and the photographers and the bloggers and the literary sycophants stared at the stage with a hunger that leapt across the distance. A hunger echoed in each eager face that stared up at the stage from around the arena. The anticipation stretched and expanded with vicious claws and rapacious teeth.

Porter trembled violently, his entire body shaking in minute trills. As Lodya bent to touch him again, he flinched, but his joints had locked, and he could not escape as she gently stripped him of his white tank top, Italian suede dress shoes, black cotton socks, and gray wool suit pants. She maneuvered his large frame as softly as she could to divest him of his last article of clothing, his red, white, and blue boxer briefs.

A murmuring began in the crowd. Wordless. Barely perceptible. It was the sound of thousands of throats groaning in pleasure at the man who had promised them everything, who had vowed to serve proudly, had sacrificed and stood before them, swearing on the Bible of his faith to assuage their hunger.

From her left shoulder holster, Lodya drew the bottle that had replaced her weapon for this occasion. It was large, heavy. As she uncorked it, the smell of apricot and cayenne wafted across her nose, mingling with the smell of the pork that roasted at her feet. They had waited long enough. Finally, Porter had succumbed to the vicious maw of his own outrageous appetites, and now his thwarted desire would season his fruitful demise. Smoothly, gently, quickly, Lodya spread the sauce on Porter's blistering, disfigured, burnt skin, making sure to leave not one patch of crackling hide unbathed.

The murmuring grew louder, the urges of the crowd reaching a peak from which it would be nigh impossible to divert them from the feast that lay, sizzling and tender before them. Lodya felt the appetite of the crowd press in, pushing and eager. They would not remember one frame of the scene that currently unfolded before them; once Lodya and her voracious colleagues left, the crowd would awaken, as if from a dream, their electronics shorted and useless, their bellies and minds still hungry, still craving. And yet, even as they filed dully to their cars and drove away, they would remember the dream feeling of being fed, of feeding, and the need to return to the trough. But now— they waited. No, they *awaited*.

Lodya caught Mike's eye and nodded. He spoke a single word into the earpiece, then smiled. The sharp, white fangs glinted in the spotlight, his saliva thick with anticipation.

Porter had called them his Wingmen. He had seen them as his to command, his protection detail—his guard dogs. But the men and women Lodya led were not birds of prey, nor canine herders, but a different breed altogether.

Lodya and her colleagues—her pack—threw their heads back, howling in the broken silence of the arena, shedding their skins with the visage of humanity. They stalked, sleek and agile and *hungry*.

Time to feast.

About the Author

As a military journalist, **RACHEL A. BRUNE** spent five years telling the Army story. Now, the soldiers in her stories keep company with werewolves, Fae, and a mad scientist or two. Her debut short story collection, *Side Roads*, won the 2022 Imadjinn Award for its category. She is the founder and Editor-in-Chief of Crone Girls Press.

T HE P RESENCE HAS PASSED *from us. It's safe again.*

Tommy knew it was a lie from that alone. Nothing could be safe *again* that had never been safe in the first place.

So why am I here? He pondered that question as he waited for the driver to retrieve his duffel. The North State bus stank of diesel, and he'd been surprised by how much it cost to buy a ticket all the way up to the gas station on the edge of town, but now he was here, and the bus ride was over. At least there was that. The giant blue "F" on the orange sign for First Off The Block Fill'er-Up had been repainted at some point, but the rest of the station looked like a shipwreck. A sign by the road read "North State Stops Here" and Tommy hmphed. *It sure does. And civilization stops with it.*

The driver handed Tommy his duffel, and Tommy held out a couple of singles. The driver's eyebrows went up. "Much obliged, sir. Don't see a lotta tips on this route."

"I bet not." Tommy hefted the duffel over his shoulder and strode across the gravel surrounding the island where the gas pumps stood. No card readers or digital displays, these were the kind you started by turning the handle on the side.

This wasn't Tommy's first time at the very last stop on the North

State line terminating on the outskirts of Wedge Holler. It was his second. The first time, Tommy had stolen a hundred sixty bucks from Great-Grandad's cash box, the one he used for "off the books" transactions—moonshine and occasional "friends" he let visit with the teenaged members of the Wilkerson clan—then hiked by light of the full moon down the side of Boylston Ridge to the creek, followed its zig-zag path to the road, and turned left.

That had been six years ago.

Now he walked back under full sun.

The mailbox still leaned. Tommy remembered the first time he noticed it standing slightly off-balance. *Probably some kids hit it out hot rodding,* his mother had said. *Always somebody out hot roddin' around, up to no good.*

No one had been up to much good at the other end of the driveway, either: not Great-Grandad Wilkerson, nor his son and daughter (*Presence protect them,* and Tommy hated how quickly that reflexive phrase slipped through his tired mind), nor their children and grandchildren in turn, known collectively as The Line. They weren't all bad up on the ridge, but the good ones didn't last, and two or three simply vanished. When someone escaped, Great-Grandad would preach on them the next Saturday night—the *real* Sabbath, he would always remind them—all about the wicked world that had lured them away. *If you want the Presence within you,* he would tell them, *you will not run away. You will stay loyal, stay here, and keep their commands.*

The kids all had stories of how the runaways made it. Mostly their myths of the former occupants of empty seats at dinner—removed from the tables and stacked in the corner after one meal passed in silence—came from their own imaginings of the world past the close fields, the pasture, the barbed wire fences running between them, and then the tall fence beyond the bushes as covered in thorns as they were in black-berries.

Tommy had volunteered for blackberry duty, a punishment as often as an assignment, three weeks in a row. Wrapped head to toe in denim in the hot sun of early June, he'd pushed his way past the briars to work a plank loose one nail at a time. The price of freedom had been lying to his mother, stealing from Great-Grandad's cash box, and all the blood he'd shed getting pricked and sliced crawling through those goddamned blackberry bushes a hundred times.

He'd have paid it again a hundred times more.

Great-Grandad kept the cash box behind his special books—*The Word*, *The Presence*, *The After*, bound in burgundy and gold—on the top shelf of the bookcase in the Round Room. Tommy had been tempted to take those, too, just to spite The Line, maybe fuck with Great-Grandad's communion with the Presence, but the last echoes of what Tommy guessed had been eight hundred Sabbath sermons had stayed his hand. He knew by then that Great-Grandad was not sacred, and The Line was not "special," at least not in the elevated sense Great-Grandad meant when he said it.

The Presence was another story.

Tommy had decided he wouldn't take anything with him The Presence might use to track him down.

Forty-five minutes passed from the time Tommy stepped off the Fill'er-Up lot to when he spotted Great-Grandad's mailbox in the distance, but no cars.

Looks like no one's getting out of Wedge Holler today.

Tommy stood at the first gate, the one twenty yards up the driveway from the road. A part of him panicked for a second—*doorbell camera, security system, CCTV*—but of course none of that existed here: no wi-fi signal for a camera, no mile of co-ax for a closed-circuit TV. Only a doorbell screwed into a capped-off metal tube beside the gate.

He pressed the doorbell once, waited a beat, pressed it again, waited, and then pressed it three times in rapid succession. He'd watched his mother do it the few times she took him with her on a run. *It means family coming back*, she told him. He'd rung the bell like that in nightmares ever since.

Five minutes later, a sister he didn't recognize pulled up in Great-Grandad's truck.

▭

"You look so different now." Tommy's mother stood halfway between the carport sheltering Great-Grandad's pickup and The Line's two minivans and the front door of the main house. The dormitories still stood off to the right, behind it, and the barn and the Round Room still stood to the left, but everything had a weather-beaten quality to it. Cold winters and summer hail had pounded the paint right off the wood. Tommy did carpentry work now. He knew it wouldn't last like this. They must have been running short of hands. That's how it went up on the ridge: food came first, then plumbing, then preaching, then everything else. In more fruitful times they'd had to scrounge for tasks to keep his sisters' tiny hands busy. Now it seemed clear The Line withered on the vine. One of the pastures stood visibly overgrown and two fields at the back lay fallow. They didn't even bother to mow the lawn anymore. That had been one of Great-Grandad's most forceful commandments: *We must keep ourselves and our surroundings tidy to be of use to the Presence. We must always be well-groomed. We must always be prepared.*

"I know," Tommy said, "but it's me all the same. More myself than I ever was here."

Some of his sisters—young ones, girls not yet born when he left— had begun to emerge from various places. One clambered down the old oak in the front yard of the main house. Two more crept from behind the bushes on the other side of the carport. Around corners and from behind the old wagon Tommy's mother and aunts kept filled with flowers in spring and autumn, and from every other hiding spot, girls from four or five up to twelve or thirteen came into view and formed a loose half-circle perhaps as far from Tommy's mother as she stood from Tommy himself.

Tommy wanted to inspect his sisters, gauge the brightness of their eyes, check for signs of the thinning of The Line, but he kept his eyes locked with his mother's as she stared at his face, his short beard, his broad shoulders and chest. Fifty hours a week climbing ladders and driving nails had made Tommy into a strong young man with biceps as rounded when he flexed as Boylston Ridge itself. He put his hands on his hips, casually confident, not threatening but also not willing to be threatened. "I take it Great-Grandad finally went to be with his children?"

Fourteen young voices echoed, *"Presence protect them."*

Fear bloomed in Tommy's chest like a clenched fist opening to let something go.

"You stand as one set to fight." Tommy's mother's voice sounded flat.

"It would pain me to hurt you, but I will if I must." It didn't even occur to Tommy how easily he slipped into the old-fashioned cadence of high mountain speech.

"But you won't fight *them.*"

Fourteen girls rushed forward to grasp at him with tiny hands.

▭

Tommy's mother had been right: he wouldn't—couldn't—fight fourteen little girls. The Line raised them to be meek *and* ruthless, a vicious combination when unleashed. Great-Grandad Wilkerson had perfected his technique across three generations of offspring: starve them emotionally, feed them just enough physically, and tell them they had to best each other to be loved.

Tommy allowed them to get his arms behind him. One of them produced a thin strip of leather and bound his wrists in a quick hand-cuff knot. He could easily free himself of the misnamed knot, of course. The trick was to demonstrate his submission by not bothering to try.

Tommy never broke eye contact with his mother the entire time.

"Search the bag." Tommy's mother gave the order in a strained tone. *She isn't thrilled about this,* he thought, *but fuck her anyway for going along with it.*

One of the sisters dug around in the duffel where it hung against Tommy's hip and then piped her report. "Nothing but clothes and some carpentry tools, Mama Jean. A hammer, some other stuff I don't reco'nize."

His mother nodded at the girl. "Take 'em to the barn. We need to get over to the Round Room right away."

▭

Tommy and his mother had written infrequently. He never gave her a real address, signing up instead with a service that simply scanned and emailed him anything they received for him. The address he used for his mother, in turn, had been the Fill'er-Up station. She went there once a month to purchase whatever couldn't be made or grown on Boylston Ridge and to ask if they'd gotten anything addressed to her. The family who owned the Fill'er-Up didn't ask questions. Nobody asked questions about The Line if they knew what was good for them.

Two simple sentences had shattered the tiny amount of healing and trust Tommy had started to feel they were building. *The Presence has passed from us. It's safe again.* It wasn't safe. He'd known it when he read those words. She wouldn't have told him it was safe unless it wasn't. She'd have told him the Presence had passed to *her.* She'd have told him they were no longer seeking signs of him in the paths the stars etched upon the sky.

She'd have told him Great-Grandad Wilkerson was dead.

Great-Grandad was not dead, but when they took Tommy into the Round Room he realized the old man would be dead awfully soon and parts of him already were. The stench of a death long in the making hit Tommy's nostrils like a punch and he nearly gagged. The littlest of his sisters covered their mouths and noses with the collars of their shirts, shyly ashamed of their disgust at Great-Grandad's literal decay. The old man's bloodshot eyes were wide but not wild, the pupils tiny, the whites turned yellow-brown. His hair, always such a point of pride even as he taught them never to be prideful of their bodies, had been reduced to a few greasy strands. His skin, covered in weeping sores, sagged like a too-large suit. He sat in the tall chair at the front of the Round Room, from which he had passed judgment and delivered instruction every Saturday night, but now he had to be propped up with two pillows. His feet were bare, and Tommy could not help but notice they had turned black and mottled green. The man was dying from the ground up, and Tommy did not hesitate to think it a tragedy for the rest of the world that death had not come for him in the opposite direction.

Great-Grandad Wilkerson's tongue wormed out and spasmed across the splintered edge of his lower lip. He drew a whistling breath, and Tommy strained to hear him speak. "The Presence told me it would call you back."

"The Presence didn't call *shit*. Your lying daughter did."

Great-Grandad's chest lurched, and only when the corners of the old man's mouth tried to rise did Tommy realize it had been a laugh. "Always the strongest. Always. And we have need of that strength now."

"The fuck you do."

One of the sisters raised her hand as though to strike Tommy for using such language, but Great-Grandad's fingers fluttered, and she lowered it again.

He coughed once, and something yellow-green landed on the filthy shirt swaddling his too-thin torso. "Chapter 17 verse 201 of *The Word* tells us one day a child transformed shall bring into this world the husk The Presence shall embody. The Presence says you are ready. You are *the one*. It is time you repaid us for all the freedom you've been granted, the gifts you've been given. It is time for you to manifest."

Great-Grandad had to pause to rest after speaking, and Tommy wondered who did the preaching. The Round Room had been one of the ways Great-Grandad messed with kids' heads, telling them the Round Room had no "front," no "head," because in The Presence they all were no more than vermin, utterly without value, devoid of reason for pride. *The Presence disdains us equally,* Great-Grandad would say, *and that is the only real equality possible.* But the Round Room was not round. It had corners, and an obvious front, and the tall chair sat at the head of it in a position of visible authority. Calling it the Round Room, Tommy eventually realized, had been one of the ways The Line trained them to ignore the evidence of their senses in favor of what they'd been told.

No other adults had shown up to Tommy's homecoming, so the whole ridge was probably down to just Tommy's mother, Great-Grandad, and the sisters here in the room with them. Some of them had been born to other mothers, or that one wouldn't have called Tommy's mother "Mama Jean," but the other mothers were absent.

That meant they had failed to manifest The Presence and been returned to it.

"This is a great honor," Tommy's mother said, and he realized she must do the preaching. "It's the greatest honor any of us can ever know. And I was not convinced at first. I want you to know that. But years of studying the books with Great-Grandad have shown me the light. The Presence must move to its next phase, and you are the one to manifest it. We're giving you a gift, even if right now you think you don't want it." Tommy's mother moved to stand beside the tall chair. She began to undo the piss-stained trousers bunched around Great-Grandad's legs and waist. "I know you'll hate us for this at first, but in time you'll understand."

Two sisters began turning the hand crank on the wall. Dust puffed out as a seam slowly opened between the two halves of a sliding trap door in the floor of the Round Room. Despite the sun outside, and the windows high on the walls of the Round Room, the light inside the Round Room dimmed and the wavering, uncertain un-light of The Presence began to bathe the ceiling overhead.

Tommy couldn't avoid staring as The Presence was revealed. He'd seen it only twice before, and that had been enough to convince him of its power. The second time it had also convinced him he had to leave. A mother had failed to manifest. *You have failed The Presence and The Line*, Great-Grandad had thundered as the woman tore at the handcuff knot and turned to flee as the trap door opened, *but The Presence has purpose for you yet*. Then two other mothers had pushed the woman over the edge. She didn't even get a chance to scream.

The gaping mouth in the middle of the floor revealed a cave: granite walls streaked with quartz crystals, crushed gravel, and the powdery fragments of old bones. At the center The Presence writhed and wobbled. Its terrible un-light shone like the shadow of a solar eclipse, the edges of everything sharp as razors in its awful glow. It gave off colors that screamed in Tommy's mind and stank of burning tires, dying rainforests, the end of humankind. It squealed like a rusted abattoir singing a child's lullaby, and the agitated edges of its many arms writhed in eager anticipation. The quartz crystal embedded in the walls of its nest reflected and refracted that not-light into fragments of other people's memories, scraps of songs unsung, and the taste of copper.

Quartz from these mountains is powerful, Tommy's mother had said when he was a child. *NASA put it in telescopes to look into space. Sometimes I think The Presence gave them the idea.*

Tommy's mother beckoned, and his sisters dragged him to half-stand, half-kneel before the tall chair. Great-Grandad's pants were around his rotting ankles, and he rasped as he struggled to speak. "You have been transformed, as The Presence foresaw. But you still have a womb in there. It is time for you to accept the fate that comes with it. It is time to bring The Presence to fruition. You and The Presence are uncommon. You are each *profane*. And thus, you are both *sacred*."

"Fuck your *sacred*," Tommy groaned through teeth gritted against the nonstop psychic whine of The Presence Revealed. He slipped the handcuff knot with a flex of his biceps, pushed his sisters aside, and grabbed Great-Grandad's shirt collar in one mighty fist.

"*No*," Great-Grandad wheezed, his voice whistling.

"I'm the one who gets to say no this time." Tommy could hear the psychic ululation of The Presence as it cried out in thrilled disbelief. Its thoughts were a debilitating jumble, like having forty radio stations blasting at once, but Tommy could feel its lusty anticipation for finding out what happened when its own prophet became a sacrifice.

Looks like no one's getting out of Wedge Holler today.

About the Author

MICHAEL G. WILLIAMS writes queer-themed horror, sci fi, and urban fantasy about outsiders finding their people and saving the world, including his sci-fi noir *A Fall in Autumn* (2020 Manly Wade Wellman Award), his vampire series, The Withrow Chronicles, and his San Francisco urban fantasy time travel series which begins with *Through the Doors of Oblivion*. He lives in Durham, NC, with his husband and a variety of animals. More can be found at: michaelgwilliamsbooks.com.

WITCH HUNT
JESSICA NETTLES

Two black mounds of dirt greeted Skid and Kev at the base of their assigned mountain. The hillocks were both about knee-high, and tiny pine trees grew along the tops.

"What do you think they are?" Skid kicked at the edge of one of them with his brown hunting boot.

Kev took a swig from his steel flask. The wide-brimmed hat he'd bought the night before that read "Hunt 40" slid to his shoulders, revealing a shock of pale red hair. "Indian mounds?"

Skid thwacked his friend's temple with his finger. "There ain't no more Indigenous People out here, idiot."

"Yeah. That's why there's them mounds." Kev swung at his friend, lost his footing, and ended up sprawled over one of the hillocks, breaking some of the taller seedlings.

"These can't be mounds. They don't look like they been here that long." Skid picked one of the smaller pine sprigs from the second pile of packed dirt and twirled it between his long fingers. "Besides, if someone was buried, that means they can't be released to the Universe like they should be."

Kev's eyes widened. "Their particles would stay here. No stardust. That's some pure evil right there."

Skid nodded. "Right. No stardust." He kicked a hole in the side of the mound next to him. "I reckon someone tried to start a garden right here but didn't do a very good job."

"You think they live close, like right on this mountain?"

"Bobby said there were two old ones near here. They must be slippin' if they're planting so close to the roads." Skid rubbed some sweat out of his eyes. The morning was getting humid fast. "Easy prey."

"Maybe we'll get back to base before everyone else and get the best beer!" Kev started up the incline, but Skid grabbed his arm

"I'm lead, remember?" He released the younger man and pulled out a machete. The edge of it gleamed from where he'd sharpened it last night by the fire. He stepped between two craggy granite boulders and swung the blade into the brush on the other side.

Kev followed, but not too close. The sun was shining through the canopy of oak and pine. Behind them, leaves rustled and bells tinkled, but not loud enough for the men to hear. If they'd known the old stories and had heard the sounds, they'd have sworn there were fairies in the forest.

▭

Rodalee stopped between a row of okra and white squash and leaned on her hoe. The garden was festooned in broad, prickly green leaves with splashes of golden yellow blossoms and fully open flowers of cream with a center of purple. A group of honeybees moved from the brown-red sunflowers that stood shoulder height and hovered around her like guards as a random breeze ruffled loose greying curls hanging either side of her glasses and gave her a bit of respite from the rising mid-summer heat.

"Y'all go down there and check things out."

The swarm headed into the tree line and vanished in the shadows.

The broad green fronds of the squash and okra plants surrounding her rustled in response to the movement of the leaves in the trees and the kudzu that draped to one side of the yard. A musky, familiar stench floated in the gentle mid-morning breeze. It couldn't have been a year since their last visitors. Time moved faster than it used to.

She pulled off her blue flowered garden gloves, put the hoe over her shoulder, picked up a basket filled with okra fingers, red-green tomatoes, and a few golden-skinned squash, and made her way to the cabin.

She grinned as she stepped up to the porch. *New blood. This should be fun.*

"Hey, Kev, you see this?" Skid adjusted the vapor rifle on his shoulder as he nibbled one of the energy bars the outfitters sold them back in town.

"Oh, that's funny!"

A rough piece of thin plywood was nailed to a two-by-two stud that leaned to one side. The plywood was painted in a faded teal and adorned with flowers. It read: "Leave now."

Kev laughed and tore down the sign. He broke it over his wide knee and threw it to the side.

Skid dropped the energy bar wrapper on the ground. "That really deterred us, huh?"

The two men unsheathed their old-fashioned machetes, and began cutting through the tangle of weeds, vines, and random branches in the hope that using a self-made path would avail them the element of surprise.

Another well-preserved pole stood in the middle of the brush like it had been there since the birth of the mountain. It looked like one of them poles that people used to use for power lines back in the twentieth century and smelled sharp and acidic. On it was another ply-board sign. This time, a dark-skinned woman glared at them with one eyebrow arched. Hair hung in green and blue ringlets around her face. "Danger ahead, gentlemen," it read in hand-painted, blood-red lettering.

Kev dropped his blade and whipped his vapor rifle from his shoulder. "Snakes! Skid! Snakes!"

Before Skid could stop him, the sign disappeared; only a few particles floated and dissipated in the breeze. Half the ancient pole was also missing.

"Dammit, kid! Give me your weapon. You could have caught me in that fire." Skid, who'd just managed to hop out of range, appeared at his fellow hunter's side.

"Those snakes were moving. Didn't you see that?" Kev lowered the gun but held on to it.

"It was a stupid picture. Nothin' moved." Skid grabbed the rifle barrel. "Now let me have your gun."

Kev yanked it away. "No. I ain't gonna miss the chance at one of them bitches now that they screwed with my head." He slid the weapon back on his shoulder and picked up his machete. "Next time, I'll be more careful, okay?"

Kev pushed past Skid and the knee-high pole. He began swinging the machete again.

Skid said, "I'll start working over here. Away from you. Maybe we can cover more ground."

Behind them, unnoticed, the first broken sign hung back on the pole, surrounded and supported by the wide green leaves and sturdy vines of kudzu. The disintegrated sign and the pole reformed just as they were moments before. Thorny blackberry vines and poison ivy grew over the new path the men cut into the side of the mountain as though they'd never been there.

"They're early this year." Odette looked up from her crochet without stopping her work, arching her eyebrow. Her smooth skin was ebony dark and glowed under a sheen of sweat. She sat cross-legged like some sort of goddess under a soft silk skirt of red and gold.

Rodalee nodded as she leaned the hoe by the screen door and dropped her gloves on floor of the porch. "You ready for lunch?"

Her partner sat her project into a handwoven vine basket and said, "I will be after I stretch a bit." Her skirt swished around her ankles as she stood up and reached for the sky, her hands spread like rays of the sun. She skipped down the stairs, dancing to music only she heard at first. It reminded Rodalee of the days they used to dance in the jazz clubs back in 'Lanta when it was a free city. She swayed thinking of those times as she passed through the screen door and pulled plates from the cabinets above the sink.

The soft lilt of Odette's voice wrapped around Rodalee from outside. The notes moved from window to window as Odette danced and skipped around the house. At first, she hummed a blessing, but as she moved from the side of the house to the canning porch around back, Rodalee could hear the shift in tone. It was a song they sang every year the men came. Every year for themselves. For their friends and family. For each other. It was a song of love, sadness, anger, and rage that only they knew because they'd written it with their own blood and passion. Rodalee set down the plates and walked through the kitchen, then through the wide living room filled with the green couch and chair they'd managed to salvage from the house they'd had to leave behind in East Point so long ago, and then past the closed door that led to their bedroom and then back around to the back of the kitchen and the canning porch. She lifted her voice with her partner, and caught sight of her outside the window to the side of the porch. Odette's sway was now a warrior's step. One stomp, then another. Rodalee matched her stomps and energy as they made their way to the front of the house. This culminated with a howl into the forest for every year since they'd arrived at the cabin. The leaves rustled. The branches bent. Odette swished up the stairs.

Discordant notes blew down from somewhere and hung in the clearing where Kev paused to take a piss. On the opposite side of the meadow, Skid cut through more of the vegetation that seemed to grow back as quick as he chopped through it.

He caught himself humming a song he didn't know as he zipped up. It tickled at the last vestiges of childhood inside of him. Skid had warned him about the siren songs of the forest last night over supper, but it had sounded more like one of those stupid stories the computers told in nursery before you were old enough to move to the study towers downtown. He shook his head and started to cut a path up the mountain toward their prey.

Mid-swing, the world tilted, or maybe his mind did, and he let go of the blade. As it flew away from him, a sort of sweetness flushed through him. His shoulders dropped and he felt the way he did back home in the Relax-a-vats—all floaty and empty.

He closed his eyes, but a thought nagged at him: *I should check on Skid.*

Kev opened his eyes and turned to call Skid. A rolling wave of writhing vines sporting leaves as broad as his head rose in the center of the clearing behind him.

Hey, that's kinda cool. I bet Skid hasn't seen this yet.

"Skid! Look at the cool wave of vines! I don't remember any of the training vids talking about the kudzu doing this kinda shit. Hey, Skid!"

The sky turned to the gray of new asphalt and lightning crackled around him. The vine wave arched ever higher above the trees and parts of it caught fire, burning blue and yellow.

"Okay. This ain't so cool."

A maw opened, branches twisted together inside like teeth. A screech that shook the trees and ground knocked Kev to the ground. He screamed with it as it began to drop toward him faster than he could scramble.

In the distance, he heard, "Kev? Kev?"

He had no time to answer. The wall of raging vegetation fell on him and flowed over and around him until he no longer heard a thing.

Skid stopped when the air flashed with a sheet of lightning and the hair on his arms stood up. A torrent of rain came up so fast that there wasn't time to look for Kev. He could only hope the big dummy would find shelter under something that wasn't a tree. He didn't want to face another trial in the city. There was no way he could lie his way out this time. He'd bragged too loud back at Base about heading to Witch's Rise to 'venge Marco and Henzy. The fact was that it was nothing about 'venging anyone and everything about proving that they'd not been prepared. Those mounds hung in his mind now.

The downpour stopped as fast as it had begun, and Skid walked back the way he thought he'd come. Finding his path was impossible between dodging now fallen limbs that dotted the forest floor and the fact that the underbrush showed no signs of being cut at all.

He tapped the badge on his shoulder and called, "Kev? Kev?"

All that returned was buzzing, crackling white noise.

He turned the face of his tracker watch and it beeped. Now he had something. Skid turned in one spot until a blue line appeared on the small round screen, connecting from the center to one side of the circle.

"Don't worry, you jerk. I'm coming." Skid moved in the direction the line pointed.

Several minutes later, the tracker beeped again, and the line disappeared. He stood at the edge of a kudzu-filled clearing. The massive leaves rippled on the surface of vines like one of the lakes inside the perimeters where he boated most weekends.

"Kev?"

A figure rose at the edge nearest Skid. At first, it was all leaves, but then vines twisted around, forming what looked like a trunk of a tree. As the vine-tree rose, arms began to form and twine together to a squared-off point.

Skid turned to run but tripped and fell to his side. The same vines flowed over him, holding him to the ground. A familiar whirr rose behind him. He turned in time to see the vine-man grow a head. Two bright-blue eyes opened in the head and stared straight past Skid.

"Kev? Kev! It's me! Don't shoot, man."

The gun's sight turned red, and the thing pointed the weapon straight at Skid.

"I got her, Skid," the vine-man said. "I got her!"

Skid struggled and screamed, and then there was a light and then nothing.

Rodalee sliced one of the Bigboy tomatoes she just washed up. "I was thinkin' that tomato sandwiches and iced tea would be nice. We could eat on the porch. It's gettin' hot in here."

"We got any of them bottle Cokes left?" Odette looked in through the screen door. Her curls, which were streaked in whites and greys, hung tight. They always got dense when the humidity rose.

Rodalee got out the bread Odette spent yesterday baking. Its yeasty scent was a comfort. "Let's save them for later."

Her partner grinned and disappeared from the doorway. Rodalee plated the sandwiches and put them and two glasses of tea she made before dawn on a tray. By the time she got outside, Odette had the folding table they used to dine on the porch set up. Two ladder-back chairs with cushions were placed across from the other. Odette held to the idea that even if you had to rough it, you should do so in style. Rodalee had to admit that this made her love the woman more. They sat down across from each other and clinked their glasses together the way they did each meal.

A scream interrupted their midday reverie.

"Looks like they could at least give us time to finish our meal." Odette put down her glass of tea and scanned the edges of the yard.

Rodalee took another bite of sharp tomato and fresh homemade bread. "And we're gonna. Ain't no need to do nothin' yet."

Her partner frowned but picked up her own sandwich. "Are you ever going to learn to speak like a lady, Roda-love?"

"I hear tell that there ain't much use in bein' a lady in these parts." She couldn't help but grin and got tickled when her partner struggled to hold that frown as she daintily nibbled a corner of her sandwich.

The sharp crack of a rifle made them both jump.

"They're killing each other now, I guess." Odette reached for her tea.

"Maybe our screamer was too mangled for his lead to want to deal with. I'd say your hexes are getting better, my dear."

"Your traps are getting more creative, my love." Her partner took a lady-like sip from her tall, sweating glass.

"Either way, we're ahead." Rodalee took her beloved's hand. "Another tomato sandwich? I think that fertilizer from last year really makes a difference, don't you?"

About the Author

JESSICA NETTLES grew up in the South where the spiritual and material cross paths daily. This is her realm. Her first novel is *Children of Menlo Park*. She is also featured in the gothic horror anthology, *Off the Beaten Path 4*, as well as *Georgia Gothic*.

To find more about her and her work, check out jessicanettlesauthor.com.

You also can find her on:

Twitter (@steampunkengl)

and Instagram (steampunkenglish).

RUMPELSTILTSKIN
JEFF WOOD

It's NOT my wife's fault she couldn't give birth to a human baby, the way God intended. I held no grudge. I loved her as God loved her.

And because I loved her, I helped her.

God is love.

No, I did not create human life. Only God can create human life, by using a woman's Precious Vessel™ as His divine instrument. I would never presume I could tread on God's omnipotent powers.

I cannot create life. Life is a miracle. Gold, on the other hand, is relatively easy.

Not gold coins, of course. No precious ingots. That's unscientific thinking. But the human body collects gold and stores it in the blood and heart. Raw gold can be birthed, with the proper words, the proper names, the proper care, the sanctions of the church and the court. Like the children's tale of old, in my words lies my force. In my name lies my strength.

I built the room for her. Six walls, a wooden cross hung high on each wall. No windows. I didn't want her distracted by the outside world. Her bed sat at the center of the room, hospital-issue stainless steel, easy to sterilize and cleanse.

I wanted to provide my wife with a comfortable surface on which to lie while giving birth, but I knew the cloth could not stand up to the heat. Cloth would burn, as would mattresses, as would soft blankets. I pondered the problem for weeks until I found a solution.

Wet straw would do the trick. Straw is not the same as hay; it doesn't contain the leafy, nutritionally valuable parts that make it a cost-effective feed for cattle. Straw is the woody, leftover byproduct of the threshing of hay, and the interior of the stalks contains several hollow, air-filled chambers that make it an excellent insulator.

That's science.

I knew that while standard sheets and mattresses would burn, a bedding of wet straw would not. I'm no monster. Any heat with enough force to singe and burn cotton bedding would harm the flesh of my wife.

I medicated my wife so as not to feel the pain before I did anything else. Made in God's image. I, too, am merciful. My first wife never understood that.

I stuffed my wife's mouth with straw. She did not complain. If she did, I didn't hear her. I stuffed her ears and nose next. I didn't want her to hear her terrible cries of pain, or smell her own burning flesh.

I laid her out on the surgical bed in my gentle nest of wet straw. The smell of the straw took me back to the years of my upbringing, the comforting scents of animals on my father's farm. I pictured him in the barn, felt his fingers working in conjunction with my own, the gentleness with which he cared for the work animals, the welcoming way he attached the ropes and reins, the yokes and blinders and saddles. He understood the fealty of nature to man, and of man to God.

My love for my wife grew incandescent seeing her naked skin raw and sterilized, her hair buzzed fully off, her legs spread wide, her eyes open in childlike wonder of the power of the Lord.

I stuffed her Precious Vessel™ with wet straw. I'm not a cruel man. I worship my wife. The material I used to pad her was the finest of straw, all the chaff removed, thorns and burrs and insects and weeds discarded. I winnowed away all but the softest reeds. For her.

Again, she did not cry out. She was a woman of God. God's love protected her from the pain, just as I had.

The straps I used to bind her to the bed existed, like God's love, to protect her from herself. Each tightened buckle was a prayer to her womanhood, each yank on the strap a testament to her holiness.

I intoned the sacred words whispered to me by the priests, and consecrated by the courts.

"We, the people," I began.

I watched the words take root inside her body as I spoke them. Each one burned into her like a brand.

Wealth oozed out of her Precious Vessel™ and spilled onto the table and floor below. Yes, the hot metal tore at her alabaster skin. The sight saddened me. As the rivulets of gold made their way down her thighs and legs in rivers of scorched skin, blood boiled at the sides of her wounds, black smoke filled the air with the stench of death. The room reeked, a charnel house. My wife's body crumpled like that of a doll.

Oh, but the floor below her shone.

Gold.

I had spun straw into gold.

My wife. My straw. My gold. My property.

My wife's body rose, in conjunction with my thought, a scarecrow of flame. Smoke poured from every orifice I'd stuffed with straw, her mouth, her nose, her ears, her Precious Vessel™.

She levitated higher. One foot, two feet, three feet. Burnt straw fell into a scattering of char and ashes on the floor. Her mouth, free of straw, was free to speak.

She opened her eyes then. They shone as brightly as the sun. The molten gold lying at her feet sparked with life, rising in the air with her, a river of shining gold, rotating around her. She'd taken something of mine, something of value, something I owned, and given it life. She'd given life to the gold, a blasphemous act: only God can create life. She'd chosen sin.

She looked at me. She pointed at me. She said my true name.

In my name lies my strength.

How did she know?

The golden river that circled her roiled and spit molten metal toward me like a rain of bullets. My framed doctorates and published works on the shelves behind me soared into flame. A spray of hot gold slashed diagonally across my chest. Sick with pain, I bent down to observe my injury, and felt another blow of hot pain on my scalp. I dropped to my knees.

How did she learn my true name?

Metal flew in every direction, thrown from the spinning ring of righteous flame encircling her. Broken and burnt crucifixes clattered to the floor like dead birds. Drops of fire affixed themselves to the walls and the floor and the ceiling until the entire room had been painted with radiance.

As the walls of the room fell away and my home burned to the ground, I saw outside into the farms and fields beyond. Other figures hung in midair, other women rising above their own burning landscapes. Churning maelstroms surrounded them all. Mine had been made of gold; these women forged haloes of blood and bile and bone, molten rivers of guns and knives and chains. Piled mountains of dismembered limbs, dead babies stacked like poker chips. A swirl of black crows infected the air, feasting.

"How did you learn my true name?" I asked her.

"I've always known your true name," she told me. "But I didn't know I had the power to speak it until now."

And with that she spoke my name one last time, in harmony with the angels, joining the voices of women as far as my clouded eyes could see, their voices finally freed.

She said, "Now I understand. I've always had that power."

Divine light consumed me as my eyes burnt to black. The old world, my world, withered into cold ash. I do not know what new world rose up to take its place.

It's not my world anymore.

It never was.

About the Author

JEFF WOOD lives in Colorado with his wife and multiple cats. He spends a little too much time watching baseball, and way too much time looking at the night sky. Jeff has had over forty short stories published in print magazines and online publications such as the *Dark Moon Digest*, *NoSleep Podcast*, *Boston Phoenix*, *New York Press*, *Wild Musette*, *Fiction at Work*, *Six Sentences*, *The Greyrock Review*, and *Bellowing Ark.*

TWELVE BABIES
HOLLY LYN WALRATH

THE FIRST HAD RED HAIR, a kind of pink peach fuzz that you could almost taste, smell the sweet skin beneath. She couldn't bear to leave her, little kicking limbs and all, anywhere but in the hospital baby box. It opened up like the box at the bank in the drive-through window; places where precious things are dispersed must be foolproof. Has this kept us safe? She wondered, even though it was a lie. You could always walk into the bank and place a gun on the counter. Convinced it was an accident, an aberrance, a mistake she'd never make again—she felt bad for what she had done, but she let it leave her mind like smoke into the air.

▭

The second was a boy, and this made goodbye tolerable. Boys can be cruel, she considered as she held it to her chest, still wet and making noises so small they could only come from the pursed lips of a baby. It felt easy to leave it on the front porch of suburbia, Middle America, land of sweethearts. She rang the doorbell, walked away. The feeling of shame slipped off her back like sweet hot oil. Her fingers pressed against the implant in her arm, the reassuring cold under her skin. A fluke, surely. There was always that 1% chance. One in a hundred. She just got too lucky. She bought a lottery ticket and some cigarettes.

The third came on the road, and heavy and hard. When she'd first missed her red, it took her a month because she wasn't used to counting days. She checked in with a little doc-in-a-box clinic. They asked her the name of the implant company, when she'd got it, did she know it was recalled? The doctors said pills were pointless, that her body spontaneously reproduced. Because of the metal sliver in her arm. Did she want it taken out? It wouldn't stop the babies from coming. She'd have to do that on her own. It was supposed to be the newest, the best, the brightest. Now it made her just as broken as she felt. She tried to focus on their words, to understand the science mumbo-jumbo, but she didn't have the energy. The act of birth felt tranquil now, a cool pool of mind that she could slip herself into. Fall away, fall apart, beneath sweat and pain, releasing herself. The baby appeared featureless as she placed it in the stranger's backseat.

Fourth and Fifth—dead in the womb. Nothing to hide, nothing to forgive.

Six—had it really come this far? Something wrong with this one, its face a little question mark in between the dirty rags. She would never make it to Seattle at this rate. She burned condoms at a homeless man's trash can fire and then fucked his brains out. What use were they anyway? (She wasn't sure if it was the men or the condoms she was referring to anymore.)

Seven—a tiny town in Idaho called Pocatello. There was the heat of the rails, the kiss of summer sparking out into the night. Somewhere in Seattle, a man could save her. A doctor, a Frankenstein of sorts, the architect of the little metal tube. The irony of this destroyed her just before sleep, as her eyes began to see the revolving faces, little white and pink faces like an array of pretty ceramic plates. She could just stop. Stay here. Keep out of beds. Sleep under the stars. But she no longer knew how to say no.

Eight in the forest. Trees are very tall and green. Men like to stand you up against them, maybe they like to pretend you are the ghost of the tree, slipped out.

Nine, ten, Richland. City streets are slick with rain and sex. Men, looming out of doorways and bars and hospitals, like aimless storks come to rest. They wanted to study her. They wanted to take her apart, this reverse psychology of the pill. She broke apart, stole cash from an offering plate, and bussed north.

Eleven. It was supposed to protect her. A little piece of metal, slipped beneath the soft flesh of the underarm. Instead, her ovaries devoured it, and her too. They had their own ideas about things.

Twelve. Seattle. Frankenstein cheats on her with the government. They place her in a white cell. They keep the babies, too. She can no longer hide the evidence, they say.

About the Author

HOLLY LYN WALRATH is a writer, editor, and publisher. Her poetry and short fiction has appeared in *Strange Horizons*, *Fireside Fiction*, *Analog*, and *Flash Fiction Online*. She is the author of several books of poetry including *Glimmerglass Girl* (2018), *Numinose Lapidi* (2020), and *The Smallest of Bones* (2021).

EXPRESS DELIVERY
A.M. GIDDINGS

LILITH'S FINGERS found the tiny ball of potential carnage that her sister had slipped into her coat pocket before she'd left. The marble-like object clung to the fingers of her right hand, and she couldn't seem to leave it alone for more than a few seconds. She shook it loose and muttered under her breath. "Soon." She searched her other pockets for the address her sister had given to her and, pulling it out, checked the number against the faux brass doorplate beside her. Of course the one she wanted was at the end of the hall. That was always the way of these things. Hoping to get this over with quickly, she strode down the hall, the back of her long coat brushing against her calves.

When she reached the door she wanted, Lilith tugged a few strands of hair loose from her braid and made sure they fell forward, hiding the faint scars on her temples. Then she checked to make sure that her sunglasses completely covered her eyes. It wouldn't do to give the game away too quickly. Finally ready, she knocked briskly on the door. There was no answer.

She frowned and checked the time. He should be home by now. She tried knocking again. After a minute or so, she heard him coming. He was cursing, and she thought she made out something about dinner burning as he threw the door open with more force than was necessary.

"Cameron Wallace?" she asked politely, ignoring his glare. Her timing was perfect, as usual.

Cameron looked her up and down appraisingly, noticing the curves she was trying to hide. An obnoxious smirk replaced the scowl on his face. "Maybe. Why? Are you selling something?"

The insolent way he looked at her made her want to rip his face off. With some effort, she focused on the task at hand. Feigning discomfort with his manner, she crossed her arms over her chest. "Um, no. I was asked to give you something."

"Even better." His smirk devolved into a leer as he opened the door a little wider.

The fact that he'd only left her enough room to squeeze by was not lost on her. He was going to make her touch him to gain entry. She unfolded her arms and slid her hands into her coat pockets as she hesitated. As before, the tiny ball clung to her fingertips. This time she didn't shake it off.

"Well? Are you coming in?" he asked, getting impatient.

Pretending to make a decision, she removed her hands from her pockets and slipped inside. As she crossed the threshold, her right hand brushed lightly across his abdomen in an apparent bid to keep some distance between them. She felt the slightest catch as the sphere stayed behind and she had to work to hide a smile. Once she was inside, Cameron closed the door and locked it behind him.

"Is that necessary?" she asked. One glance around his living room gave her the location of several potential weapons, including a pair of throwing axes mounted on the wall, a table lamp that looked like it was made of cast aluminum, and a bowie knife sitting, unsheathed, on his entertainment center.

He shrugged. "I'd rather not be disturbed by nosy neighbors. So, what do you have for me?"

Lilith checked her watch, then leaned against the arm of his couch. "I have a message for you from your girlfriend, Trina."

Cameron blinked. "You know Trina? Are you her friend?"

Lilith inclined her head. "I am."

"Well, it's always good to meet a friend of Trina's. Do you know her from work? I haven't seen you at church or any of the family functions." He came over to the couch and sat next to her, invading her space in a deliberately calculated way.

Lilith edged away from him, playing off her anger as nerves. "She's a friend of my sister's. I'm not exactly sure how they met, but I've grown quite fond of Trina. She's got a bright future ahead of her." In her mind's eye, Lilith saw Trina huddled in Lailah's kitchen, her shaking hands wrapped around a mug of tea as she begged them for help.

"I agree," he said, a hint of smugness in his tone as he turned on the charm. "And I hope to be a part of that future. I'm planning to ask her to marry me when I finish law school in a couple weeks. My dad got me a job clerking for Judge Wilson, so I won't have any problem providing for her."

Lilith couldn't help frowning, though she doubted he noticed. He was too busy trying to give her the sanitized version of his plans for Trina. The version he'd likely given her other friends and her parents. She remembered Trina's voice trembling as she told them how he planned to use her parents to pressure her into quitting her job and marrying him. How he'd been sabotaging the condoms she'd made him wear, trying to get her pregnant so that she couldn't refuse him. "I don't think she's ready for marriage just yet," she managed to reply when he looked at her, expecting a response.

"Is anyone really ready for marriage? For children?" he asked rhetorically as he placed a hand on her arm and gave her his best 'earnest' look. "We've been dating for months. It's time to take the next step, and believe me, she'll say yes."

Lilith glanced down at her watch. It wasn't time yet. She needed a few more minutes, so instead of breaking all the bones in his hand, she just brushed it off her arm. "Some people are ready, when it's something they want. When it's a choice."

"She has a choice. The timing may not be exactly what she wants, but what is in life?"

"And if she says no?" Lilith prodded, wondering if he was arrogant enough to admit his crime when challenged.

He looked surprised and hurt. "Why would she say no? What has she told you about us?"

"She told me that you want more than she is willing to give," Lilith said, wondering how many of Trina's other friends he had conned into believing him with that look of feigned injury.

"Are you jealous? Is that why you came over? To break us up so you can get a little something for yourself?" He gestured to his crotch.

Lilith rolled her eyes, figuring he wouldn't be able to see it behind her sunglasses. "I came over to tell you that she doesn't want to see you anymore. That is all."

His mask cracked, and anger flashed across his face. The muscles in his arms and shoulders tensed, and Lilith thought he might actually try to hit her. Then Cameron forced himself to relax. "It doesn't matter what she wants. I'm in good with her parents. They'll convince her if I can't."

Lilith had had enough. She stood up abruptly and shoved him so hard he fell backwards onto the couch. He rolled off and jumped to his feet, his face suffused with rage.

"You bitch!" he snarled, taking a swing at her.

She deflected the strike and knocked him down again. As he tried to struggle to his feet again, she planted a foot on his chest and used her weight to hold him down.

"The alpha male B.S. really doesn't fly with me, Cameron." She put so much venom in the name that it was almost a curse in and of itself. "I have seen centuries of the crap that men have given women, and until recently, I haven't been able to do much about it." She held out her hand, and the newspaper from the coffee table flew into it. Holding it up in front of his face, she pointed to the headline about the comprehensive abortion ban that had just gone into effect. "Unfortunately for you, this latest round of misogyny has finally gotten under my sister's skin. She agreed to give me the army I've always wanted."

Cameron made a show of looking around as he tried to dislodge her foot. "What army, you crazy bitch?"

"There is that word again. I don't think that you understand that it's almost a compliment coming from someone like you." Lilith checked her watch again. "Anyway, back to what I was saying before I was so rudely interrupted. My sister was in a bad mood when Trina showed up on our doorstep looking for help. Normally, she'd just end the potential pregnancy before it started, kind of like emergency contraception, but with magic. This time though, she agreed to offer the young woman a chance for revenge. Can you guess what Trina chose?"

"For you to come here to talk me to death?"

"Cute." Lilith figured enough time had passed, so she let him sit up. "No, she thought that if you wanted a child so badly that you'd sabotage your condoms, then you should have one."

Confusion replaced the rage on his face momentarily. "What? She's keeping it?"

Lilith laughed derisively and snapped her fingers in his face. "You aren't keeping up here, Cameron. No, Trina decided to let you do the heavy lifting of this pregnancy. Of course, since you don't have a uterus, that blastocyst is going to tear through you like tissue paper, but *c'est la vie.*"

"Wow. You're even crazier than I thought...but thanks for admitting you gave Trina an abortion. Now all three of you can go to jail." He got to his feet and started to come for her.

Lilith evaded him easily. "I'd sit down, if I were you. You're going to start to feel it soon. The egg hatched a few minutes ago, and it looks like it has invaded the epithelium of your large intestine. That can't be good."

Sweat beaded on Cameron's forehead as he tried to reach for her again. He took another unsteady step, and then his knees gave out under him.

"I may have also amped things up a bit. My demonic little blasto-cyst is already re-working your system, destroying all those nice, high-resistance, muscular arteries and turning them into flaccid sacks. I hope you have some folic acid on hand."

He shook his head, trying to clear it. He attempted to stand again, but the softened bones in his legs wouldn't hold his weight anymore.

"Hmm, I may have overdone things a bit," she said with a wicked smile. "Normally the bones are only softened a little so the pelvis and ribs can spread to make room for the fetus. I think we got everything, though. You should stay where you are, your skull is probably as soft as pudding right now, and I wouldn't want you to damage your brain before you get to experience the full effects of what you've created."

Cameron moaned and curled into a ball as a wave of cramps hit him. When they passed, he rolled over and threw up onto the newspaper.

"Yes, things are progressing nicely. I wonder if you'll get the enhanced sense of smell. Some do, some don't. It probably depends on your base hormone levels." Lilith prodded the little foot shaped lump that showed up on his abdomen.

"You...you've done this before," he managed to gasp out between cramps. By now his stomach was three times its normal size as his innards liquefied. She estimated that the demon inside was now about the size of a twenty-four-week-old fetus.

"A few times," she admitted. "It used to be a lot harder to convince my sister that it was justified."

He groaned as another wave of cramps hit.

"She's the one who can remove the fertilized egg and create a neat little energy pocket to keep it safe until I can find it a new home. That's all life magic, and life magic requires an angel. Not my area, I'm afraid." Lilith lowered her sunglasses so Cameron could get a good look at her glowing red eyes. "I'm all about the vengeance."

"Why—" he gasped, tears streaming from his eyes, his face contorted in pain.

"Because as I said earlier, dear boy. This is how I grow my army. Also, we had to make sure you couldn't make life difficult for Trina."

"You're evil," he managed to groan between cramps.

"Now, don't be a hypocrite. I just used Trina's fertilized egg as a weapon, like you were planning on doing."

He shuddered and tried to crawl away from her, but he couldn't make his limbs work and his swollen belly kept getting in the way. Lilith stepped around him and went to the kitchen in search of something to snack on while she waited. She watched his slow, desperate progress with mild amusement as she nibbled on the chips she'd found in his cupboard. Cameron had almost made it to his front door when he screamed in heartrending agony and fell over. As she watched, he started rolling on the ground as his abdominal muscles contracted uncontrollably.

Lilith put the bag of chips down and strode over. "You don't mind if I help the baby out, do you? I don't want her to hurt herself." She knelt beside him, her right forefinger shifting to a wickedly sharp talon.

Cameron tried to shove her away, but his internal bleeding and shock left him too weak to do anything more than bat ineffectually at her claw. Lilith slit him open from groin to sternum and then pulled his shirt, skin, muscle, and fat aside. "Let's just see where the little devil has gotten to, yes?"

Her hands twisted inside his peritoneal cavity until she found what she was looking for. When she pulled the baby and placenta free, a large section of his intestine came up with them. She cut it free and dropped it back into the hole she'd made. As she worked, blood oozed out of the gaping wound. It soon soaked through his torn shirt, and began pooling on the floor beneath him.

Lilith gently opened the placenta with her claw and pulled the baby demon out. After cutting the cord and siphoning off all of the fluid and gore, she set the baby down on a cushion she'd pulled from Cameron's couch. Then she wrapped her in one of his blankets to keep her warm. Once she was sure her new daughter wouldn't roll off and hurt herself, Lilith began cleaning up the rest of the mess. She retrieved the bowie knife from the entertainment center and measured the width of the blade with her fingers. Then she pulled the edges of the cut closed and sealed it with a little bit of her saliva. She slid the knife into the section she'd left open and positioned the body so that it looked like an accident to anyone who bothered investigating. As she stood up, most of his bodily fluids, except for the puddle of blood around his body, flowed into her and disappeared. Satisfied with the result, she scooped up her newest demon and left through the bathroom door.

━━

Lailah was waiting for her on the other side with a pot of tea and a knitted onesie for the newest member of their family. She got to her feet when Lilith came in the back door. "Did you get what you needed, sister?"

Lilith held out the baby, its pink, prehensile tail curled instinctively around her arm. "I did, thank you."

Smiling, Lailah came over and peered down at the tiny baby with the blood-red eyes. "She's adorable. And the sperm donor?"

"Dead. Knife attack."

Lailah nodded. "Trina will be glad to hear that. I'll let her know as soon as we get the little one settled."

"Excellent, let's go see if we have room in the nursery, shall we?"

About the Author

A.M. GIDDINGS is a writer, scientist, and independent filmmaker from North Carolina. She has a PhD in Microbiology and wrote scientific articles in virology, cell line design, and gene therapy. She is the author of the futuristic dark fantasy series, Dance of Ages. In addition to her writing, she has worked on short and feature-length horror films with Sick Chick Flicks, and is the co-director of the Sick Chick Flicks Film Festival.

https://www.facebook.com/profile.php?id=100013149190221

A CALL TO ACTION
MARC L. ABBOTT

A BREEZE CARRIED the thick black smoke from the fire across the late afternoon sky. The villagers, who had come to watch the burning of another suspected witch, covered their noses and mouths with their hands and clothes, hoping to keep the smell at bay. A small group of women, friends of the victim, stood together crying.

Constantine Hudson stood with the magistrate, John Mather, and the priest who was loyal to the church's witch hunters. His hands on his hips, chest stuck out like a peacock, he sported a devil-may-care grin. His gaze fixed on the charred remains of Martha Trench.

"That makes sixteen, Constantine," John said. "The local women should know better than to practice their heresy around here."

"Such a shame too. She seemed like such a nice woman," the priest said. "Should have known something was wrong when she stopped coming to church. What was it she said? She had the right to commune with God or any God she saw fit?" He scoffed. "Lunacy, I tell you."

"Well, the good Lord saw fit to give us Constantine," John said, "and we're better for it."

"Which reminds me, I have been meaning to ask, when do you think you'll take a wife? The women seem to fancy you," the priest said.

Constantine glanced at the group of crying women. Several of them stared at him angrily. He looked around at the faces of several young ladies. None of them were swooning at him. They refused to meet his gaze, trembling slightly as they looked to the ground.

"I haven't found the one that could catch me yet, Father. When that day comes, trust me, you will hear me cry out loudly to the heavens." He chuckled. "I think it's time for me to have some drink. Witch burnings always leave me thirsty."

"If you're going to the tavern, be careful. They have quite a beauty behind the bar working there. She started there yesterday." John looked quickly at the priest. "Not that I have given her a lingering glance."

"You're married, not dead, magistrate," Constantine said, laughing. "But I will heed your words. If she is as beautiful as you say, I may have to get better *acquainted* with her. Gentlemen, I will take my leave."

Constantine put on his riding gloves and made his way to his horse, standing a few feet away.

He started to mount it when a black carriage caught his attention. A woman sat inside with a black veil over her face, staring through the window at the burning stake. The carriage never stopped. After a moment, it picked up speed and disappeared on the road leading to the tavern.

Constantine turned back to the stake and glared at Martha's body. He got the feeling someone was watching him. He turned and saw John's daughter, Esther, staring at him, rubbing her belly. She glanced down at it, smiled, and looked back at him. Constantine shook his head and rode away.

He arrived at the White Candle Tavern a few minutes later. The black carriage was parked to the right, just shy of the building. No one, not even the driver, was near it. He wondered who it might be as no one in the village had such a handsome vehicle. He would know when he went in and looked around. Anyone not familiar to him had to be the owner.

Constantine nearly took the door off the hinge when he burst into the tavern, pulling his riding gloves off and holding them up triumphantly.

"The witch is dead!" he bellowed to the customers. "Martha Treach is no more."

There was a small contingent of customers sitting around looking somber. They all turned in his direction and collectively banged their mugs on their tables, signifying that they agreed with his celebration. But no one cheered.

"Thank you." He slammed the door and surveyed the room. Before he could put a fix on the carriage's owner, a soft, almost angelic voice called to him from the bar.

"Evening, sir, welcome to the White Candle Tavern."

He turned and saw a beautiful young woman, no older than twenty-five, with long blond hair. As he strutted to the counter, he took notice of her blue gown with a corset; her breasts pushed up, showing her cleavage. He fixed his gaze on them until he reached the bar and then looked into her blue eyes.

"Hello, and who might you be?"

"Name's Abigail, sir. Abigail Lamont. I just started working here."

"Ah, the new girl. The magistrate said you were beautiful. I would have to say that's an understatement." He put his gloves down. "Well, Abigail, may I have a pint of ale." Constantine produced a small leather pouch from his belt, opened it and removed a coin, and placed it before her. "And here is a little something extra for you."

"Thank you, sir." Abigail smiled as she turned to a barrel behind her, put a pint mug under the tap, and filled it to the top. She set it before him and then slid the coin away. "Here you go."

Constantine held the mug tight and drank deeply. Then he turned and looked at the faces of the customers watching him.

"Pardon me, sir, but did you say you killed a witch?" Abigail said softly.

Constantine turned quickly to her. Their eyes met, and he felt a warm sensation go through him. "I didn't kill her, no. The good Lord saw fit to do that. I just find them and bring their evil to light."

"Are you a witch hunter?"

"That I am. Constantine Hudson is the name."

Abigail's breath quickened as admiration filled her eyes. "*The* Constantine Hudson?"

"In the flesh, my dear."

"I heard you came in here to drink from time to time." Abigail placed her hand atop her chest, swooning and drawing his gaze. "I never thought I would actually meet you."

"Whereabouts are you from?"

"New York, sir."

"New York? What brings you to these parts?"

"My family used to live close to here. We moved away some time ago before I was of age to be out on my own. I always wanted to come back here to live."

"And you come back and find a job already."

"William Thomas, who owns this place, is an old friend of the family."

Constantine sized her up, his eyes admiring the curvature of her figure. "Well, he made the right choice putting you out here instead of the kitchen." He took a sip of his ale. "Welcome back. I had no idea my deeds went so far south as New York."

Abigail nodded. "Fifteen witches, I hear. All captured at your hands."

"Sixteen, if you count Martha."

"You must tell me how you do it." She leaned forward, smiling innocently. She placed her hand on top of his.

He looked down as her fingertips folded over and tucked into his palm. They were a bit chilly. He was about to draw back when his eyes focused on her cleavage again. He felt her grip tighten. Their eyes met again and locked.

"You would like to know how I capture witches?"

"Yes. Witch hunters fascinate me. I haven't met many. And I've never been *this* close to one before."

Constantine started to feel strange. Looking into her eyes, he felt compelled to tell her everything. He took another sip of ale and began to speak when a smokey, hypnotic voice called out from across the room.

"Dear girl, stop that!"

Startled, Constantine pulled his hand back from her grip. He and Abigail both looked in the voice's direction. A woman sat in the far corner, dressed in a black gown with red trim. A black veil, pulled back and shrouded behind her head, revealed her handsome features and a stern look. Next to her, a handsomely dressed footman sat straight as a board.

"Excuse me?" Abigail said.

"You do not want to be fawning over that man," she said. "He is not an honorable one."

"This man is a great witchfinder," Abigail said.

"Great? He is a hypocrite and a murderer."

The customers began to stir nervously.

Constantine placed his mug on the counter and stood straight. "You must be the owner of the carriage outside. I've never seen you around here before."

"And what of it. I have a right to here like everyone else."

"I didn't say you didn't." He placed his hands on his hips. "And you are?"

"My name is Elizabeth Vane. Not that you deserve to know it. But out of courtesy, I give it to you."

"Well, Elizabeth, I—"

"*Madam* Vane to you," she said. "And let me assure you before you open that lying mouth of yours, I am not susceptible to your charms like that young one there is." She glared at him with angry eyes.

Constantine cracked a smile and placed a hand over his heart. "Madam Vane, let me assure you that what I do is no easy task. I am an honorable man. I am a God-fearing man. What I do is in service of Him and the good of the Christian people of this area." He nodded slightly to her.

"Oh please, that might work on that wench there, but you are no honorable man. You're a liar, and I would go so far to call you a murderer, but you manage to save yourself from that moniker because you don't set the fires to the stakes yourself."

"I'm sorry, but did I do something to offend you?"

Abigail placed a gentle hand on his arm. "You owe her no explanations of who you are." She looked at Elizabeth. "What is your problem? He is just a man doing a service for..."

"Don't you dare say it." Elizabeth pointed a warning finger. "Only the weak use that as an excuse." She turned her glare to Constantine. "And yes, you have. You have innocent women killed by falsely accusing them of things you know nothing about."

"All the women I have brought to justice were guilty of consorting with the devil."

"Which is it? They are witches, or they consort with the devil?"

"There is no difference."

"Ignorant man, there is a difference. Witches do not follow your religion, therefore they would not consort with the devil. They wouldn't know who the devil was."

"And how would you know that?" Abigail stepped out from behind the counter and stood in front of Constantine. "You sound like a witch supporter to me."

"What does that even mean, dear girl, witch supporter? That man is having women killed who refuse to fall for what he is selling or think for themselves."

"You don't know that. All the women he has brought to justice have been guilty." She turned to Constantine. "Right?"

"Of course."

Abigail took his hand and stepped closer, staring up at him. "I can tell you are a man strong in your convictions."

Constantine looked down at her and gently stroked the side of her face with the back of his index finger as he smiled. Once again, captivated by her beauty.

"You're very perceptive," he said.

"So how is it that you know a woman is a witch? You never answered my question on that."

"My dear, Abigail. I would gladly tell you. But not here." He placed his hand on her waist. "At least not in the presence of that woman."

"I know where we can go to speak privately," she said coyly.

"Silly girl," Elizabeth said. "You won't get the truth out of him that way."

"Why not?" Abigail broke her glare from him.

"Honorable, my foot. There is more lust and lasciviousness in him than you can measure. He's not the type to bed you, then talk. And if he chooses to tell you anything, it will be as little as possible. Men like him fear women with knowledge. That's why he had Martha killed."

Several customers stood and made their way to the door quickly. Constantine moved Abagail to the side and then slowly approached Elizabeth's table. She didn't flinch. She watched him as a grin formed in the corner of her mouth.

"Who are you,"—he pointed an accusatory finger at her—"to make these false allegations against me? Huh? And what is it about Martha that has you so riled up? Maybe Abigail is right. Are you a witch supporter? Maybe I should take you before the magistrate and test you."

Elizabeth's footman rose and stood between them.

"You will not touch Madam Vane," he said.

"It's alright, I can handle him," Elizabeth said. "First, you're not taking me anywhere. You put your hands on me, and it will be the last thing you do on this Earth. And believe it or not, that's not what I want to happen. Second, Martha was my very good friend, and she told me all about you and what happened between you two; that's why I know what I said is true."

"And what lie did she tell you?"

"It wasn't a lie. I see how you're trying to bed the fair-haired maiden over there, and, unlike her, Martha balked at your advances. Because of that and some other improprieties you have had with the women in this area, you declared her a witch, and she was burned at the stake."

Constantine chuckled. "For the record, she threw herself at me, poor thing. Tried to use her magic to tempt me."

"Oh, is that what you call it, magic? The temptation you feel is of your own making."

"That is the work of the devil through which she works her magic."

"Again, with the devil."

"The Holy Book..."

"Contains no mention of witches nor Satan consorting with them." Elizabeth stood.

The rest of the customers rose and started to move to the door. One woman turned to say something, but the man with her pulled her out of the building and slammed the door.

"So, all the women who just happened to share your bed," Elizabeth said. "Whom you spurned after they professed their feelings to you, those women who suffered at the stake because of your inability to be a responsible man, they were all witches?"

"You've got that all wrong. You're assuming that what I did with those women was out of pleasure."

"What other reason would you have?"

Constantine made a nervous laugh, then stepped back. "Ignorant woman. I did not lay with those women for pleasure. I did so to draw the devil out. I did so to save their souls because they had consorted with Satan to tempt men. I saved many marriages from those women who sought to tempt husbands into adultery."

"You're kidding," Elizabeth said. "Even you don't believe that."

"But then what did Martha do to be labeled a witch?" Abigail called out. "She had no husband to protect. Was it because she spurned your advances? That wasn't it, was it?" She placed her hand over her chest. "Surely you're not that kind of man."

Constantine quickly moved to Abigail and placed his hands on her shoulders. "My dear, I can explain." He guided her back from Elizabeth's close proximity. "She was using witchcraft to keep many women from having children." He gave Elizabeth a quick glance. "She used plants and spells to keep them from giving birth."

"The ones who became pregnant were with your child," Elizabeth said. "They sought the help of Martha for fear of what would happen when you denied the offspring as your own. They would be labeled bastards and the women whores." She pointed at him. "But that's not the real reason. It's because of the magistrate's daughter. You got her pregnant and then ran to Martha for help. Only Martha refused to do anything because the child was too far along. Couple that with her turning you down, and suddenly she was a witch. You couldn't have that getting out now, could you?"

Constantine grew quiet. He felt his face grow hot from his rising anger. The footman, upon seeing this, rushed to the door and locked it, then began to draw the curtains to the window. Constantine seemed to ignore him.

"What proof do you have to that claim?" he asked lowly.

"Martha wrote me and told me some time ago." Elizabeth produced a folded piece of parchment tucked underneath her belt. "In this."

Constantine rushed at her and snatched the parchment. He opened it quickly and read it. When he had finished, he laughed, crumpled it, and shoved it into his trouser pocket.

"I think I'll keep this." He smiled. "Now you have no faux proof to deliver to—" He noticed that Elizabeth didn't seem concerned. "Who exactly had you planned to give that to?"

Elizabeth shook her head. "No one."

"I don't understand."

"I realize that while there is a magistrate here who touts his belief in justice, he is still a man. A zealot who would sooner whisk you away to another part of the country to avoid scandal rather than try and execute you for lying to the courts and church about the women you condemned. He would never dare take the side of a woman over a noted witch hunter. I told Martha this, and she agreed that it would be best if we take matters into our own hands should she be charged and put to death for witchcraft." Elizabeth removed her veil and placed it on the table. Then she removed the bottom of her dress, revealing trousers and riding boots, and tossed it to her footman. "The question is how to exact this revenge."

"Wait a minute." Abigail moved past Constantine and stood before Elizabeth. "You cannot exact revenge against this man." She looked back at him. "Not until I have had him."

"What is wrong with you?" Elizabeth said. "After everything you have heard and what he did to our sister, you still want to bed this man."

"Wait, what sister?" Constantine said.

"Martha, she was our sister," Abigail said. "Well, not our sister by blood. She was part of a little sisterhood we had formed as a way to look out for one another. If any one of us is in need or in trouble, we come to their aid. In matters of death, if it happened at the hands of someone, we punish them."

Constantine laughed. "Let me see if I understand this; you two came here to get revenge against me. You two *women*. A wench and, what are you supposed to be, some kind of assassin?" He moved to a chair and sat down, wiping tears from his eyes. "I'm in so much trouble," he mocked.

"Oh, please let me have him," Abigail said. "My coven would love to take turns with him. And I could make him suffer so much. You stopped me hypnotizing him, so the least you could do is give him to me."

"That was cheating, by the way," Elizabeth said.

"Coven?" Constantine said. "Oh, so you're a witch? Come to curse me?"

Abigail burst into laughter. She laughed so hard the blood started tearing down her face. Constantine, upon seeing this, stopped his laughter.

"Abigail, your tears," Elizabeth said.

She wiped the blood and looked at it. "Oh, that's not good. Spoiled the surprise." She turned to Constantine, her eyes now crimson, and bore her fangs. "I'll have to replenish my supply."

Constantine shot up from his chair and stumbled backward. "What devilry is this?"

"He really loves bringing the devil into things," Elizabeth said. "Witches aren't the only ones who have covens. Vampires also have covens, and Abigail here is a member of one of the larger ones in this territory."

"I can smell his fear," Abigail said. "That's when the blood is the sweetest."

Elizabeth put her hand on Abigail's shoulder. "Take it easy."

"Vampire?" Constantine looked around and spotted a cross hanging over the doorway to the kitchen. He hurried to it, removed it from the nail, and held it out before him, watching as Abigail and Elizabeth looked at it, then at one another.

"Is he serious?" Abigail said. "You know that's not going to work."

"I know that crosses do work against vampires," he said smartly.

"Yes, but only if you are a man of true faith. A man who loves God, not mocks him by perverting the words meant to teach love. Not someone who uses his words to lie and have people murdered."

"Your day of reckoning is here," Elizabeth said. "You had a woman killed who did nothing more than commune with the elements to help all those who were in need. A woman who did nothing more than protect those who could not defend themselves from men like you."

"The good men of this village will do the right thing and see you destroyed if any harm comes to me."

"Constantine, the good men of this village left you here with us," Abigail said. "They already did the right thing."

Constantine glanced around the empty tavern. His eyes grew wide from the realization that he was alone.

"Abigail, I'll let you have him."

"You will?"

"I think an eternity with you and the coven would be a good lesson for him. My curse would be worse. Which, incidentally, Martha was helping me keep under control," Elizabeth said. "Luckily, she left me enough wolfbane potion for a few months until I can find another witch to help."

Abigail bared her fangs and charged Constantine. He dropped the cross as he tried to scurry back. She leaped at him with her arms forward, seized him by his shoulders, and brought him to the floor. She leaned into his neck and bit him hard in his jugular. He cried out in agony as she started to drink. He fought to get her off him, but she clamped down more and sucked hard. He started to flail.

"Abigail! Wait, stop!" Elizabeth cried out. "I have a better idea."

Abigail let go and looked at her with eyes burning red, blood dripping down her chin. "What!"

"Turn him loose."

"Why?"

"If you turn him into a vampire, simply to torture him, he'll still have immortality. If I bite him and he turns, he'll exploit the curse."

"You said you weren't going to curse him."

"I know, but hear me out and listen to what I'm about to say. With him in the state he's in right now, we can get our revenge, and the villagers will too."

"You're not making sense, Elizabeth. The villagers know what we are. We had to tell them."

"But they are on our side, and that works in our favor. So here is what we're going to do." She approached Abigail and whispered in her ear.

Constantine watched as Abigail's eyes returned to normal, and a smile grew on her face. She laughed as she looked down at him. Elizabeth stepped out of view. He heard the sounds of tables being overturned and chairs being smashed. Abigail bent over and began to wipe the blood from his neck and smear it all over hers. She then took more and spread it on his lips. She disappeared for a moment and then returned with a lit candle. She leaned over and put the flame to his neck, cauterizing the wounds she had inflicted. He cried out in pain.

"I'm done," Abigail said. "I'll go get the magistrate and the priest."

"No, my footman will do that," Elizabeth said. "You go outside and wait. When you see them coming, let me know, and we go from there."

Elizabeth walked over, lifted Constantine into a seated position, and put him up against the bar. Then she told the footman to bring the magistrate, priest, and as many villagers as he could.

"Tell them a horrible incident is occurring at the tavern with the witch hunter. They must hurry. When you get back, Abigail will play her part, and you play along."

The footman nodded, and Abigail left the tavern. The sound of the horse neighing could be heard then it galloped away with the sounds of the carriage wheels squeaking behind it. Elizabeth stepped back a considerable distance from Constantine and got down on her knees. She stared at him.

"You think you'll get away with this?" He clutched the bite marks on his neck with one hand and, with a shaky hand, tried to wipe the blood from his face, but all he did was smear it more. "You wenches will pay!"

Elizabeth smiled. "For all the women who have left in the grip of fear, we return the 'favor.'"

Approximately ten minutes had passed when Abigail opened the door and looked in. "They're coming! I see lantern light."

Elizabeth closed her eyes and began breathing heavily. The sound of bone breaking resonated in the room. She cried out in pain as she fell forward on her hands and knees. She pounded it with her fists as she arched her back. Her remaining clothes began to tear away. Thick black hair grew from her skin while her face contorted. A snout pushed out of the middle of her face. It was unusually long, and its upper teeth hung long over the lower jaw. She let out an inhuman cry that morphed into a howl.

Abigail then rushed in, holding her neck. She fell onto a table and then onto the floor, writhing in pain just as John, the priest, and others entered with the footman. Their eyes fell on the final moments of Elizabeth's transformation first. Cries of terror filled the tavern.

"Dear God!" The priest crossed himself.

"What in God's name?" John screamed.

Then Abigail stood and started acting frantic. "Thank God you're here! He's a warlock!" She pointed to Constantine, who was sitting on the floor. "It was horrible. I told him I didn't fancy him, and he went mad. Spewing incantations at me. He then bit me and tasted my blood." She pointed to Elizabeth. "That poor woman tried to help, and he pointed at her and said words I did not understand."

"I heard them!" the footman yelled out. "I saw him point and speak in tongues!"

"That is a lie!" Constantine roared. "I did nothing to her." He pointed at Elizabeth, and she howled and started to run away from him. She snapped back and then ran to the far end of the tavern as though she were trying to escape. "You foul woman!"

"You see. He points, and she cowers," Abigail said.

"This can't be." John looked at Constantine. "What..."

"Sir, that woman is a vampire. She bit me and tried to turn me into one of her. She is an agent of the devil!"

"Good magistrate, look at me." Their eyes locked. "I tell the truth. That man bit me and then forced me to bite him. Then he burned the wounds. I have heard of this with warlocks. They burn the wounds as part of their rituals."

"But he is a witch hunter," the priest said. "Why would he...I mean, why would he...?"

"How do you think he's so good at finding witches? He is one," Abigail said.

"This is outrageous." Constantine tried to stand but was too weak to properly get on his feet and fell over. "She is lying, I tell you. She and that thing over there are monsters."

Elizabeth walked on all fours slowly toward the middle of the room. Her eyes locked on him. She growled and barked, startling everyone. When Constantine raised his hand, she backed away and started convulsing. Everyone watched in shock as Elizabeth painfully transformed back into her human self. Her footman hurried to cover her naked body.

"What...what happened?" She looked over at Constantine and cowered. "What did you do to me? And who is Esther?"

"What about her?" John said. "She is my daughter."

"Oh dear, the poor girl. I heard him in my head. He said he was going to have carnal ways with me and Abigail as he did with Esther."

Abigail turned to the crowd. "Esther? Where is Esther?"

Esther was guided through the crowd. Terror on her face. Her hands on her stomach. She and Abigail looked at one another as Abigail placed her hand on her belly.

"Are you with child?" she asked. Esther looked at her father, then at Constantine.

"Do not worry. You have done nothing wrong. Are you with his child?"

Esther looked at Abigail, and tears formed in her eyes. "He said he loved me."

"Esther, no," John said.

"Father, forgive me." She ran into his arms. "He said things to me. Told me he would marry me, and then he..."

"It isn't her fault, magistrate. It is the work of a warlock. To deceive to get what he wants," Elizabeth said. "I have seen this before. You saw what he did to me with your own eyes. He has cursed me to be a were-wolf for—" Elizabeth stopped short and started to transform again.

Everyone fled from the tavern and into the evening air.

Elizabeth approached Constantine and seized his pant leg with her mouth. She dragged him like a rag doll out of the tavern to an awaiting crowd that was now turning into a vicious mob. She then fell onto the ground and turned back into her usual self.

"Magistrate, it's not too late for Esther. You can save her if you destroy the warlock," Elizabeth said. The people cheered. "If he has tasted Abigail's blood, turned me into a werewolf before your eyes, and forni-cated with the magistrate's daughter, which one of you will be next?"

Several men picked up Constantine by his arms. One punched him in the stomach. Someone with a rope began to tie his hands behind his back.

"No, wait, you're all being deceived. I am a God-fearing man. Esther is lying. They're all lying."

"Prove it," John said.

"What?"

"Prove to me they are lying. That my own *daughter* is a liar."

Everyone went silent. Their eyes locked on Constantine. Abigail gasped, then whispered to the footman; he nodded and went back into the tavern. After a moment, he returned with something behind his back.

"I can prove we're not," Abigail said. "There is a simple test we can do." She and the footman approached him. "If he isn't a warlock, then the sight of something holy shouldn't affect him."

Before anyone could speak, the footman handed Abigail the cross from the tavern. She thrust it in Constantine's face. Fearing he was about to be stuck, he screamed, flinched, and as the cross burned Abigail's hand, she dropped it immediately and backed away in agony.

"Look what he did! Cowered before God. Spurned the cross with his breath and burned me with it!"

"*Warlock!*" someone screamed.

"No!" Constantine said.

"Take him to be tried!"

Constantine screamed in terror as the villagers seized him and began to carry him off into the night.

Abigail helped Elizabeth to her feet, and they stood together watching Constantine be carried off.

"I thought crosses don't work on you."

"Only in the hands of a righteous man." She looked at the footman, who nodded at her. "I have to admit that was a better idea than turning him." She turned to Elizabeth. "I didn't know you could change like that."

"I'll be in pain for the next few days. That's the problem with serving justice against the wicked. No matter the good intention, it's gonna hurt like hell."

About the Author

MARC L. ABBOTT is a Brooklyn-based author, actor, and storyteller. His short stories are featured in the Bram Stoker Award® nominated horror anthologies *A New York State of Fright* and *Under Twin Suns: Alternate Histories of the Yellow Sign*, as well as *Even in the Grave, Hell's Heart,* and *Hell's Mall*. He is the co-author of *Hell at Brooklyn Tea* and *Hell at the Way Station,* the two-time African American Literary Award-winning horror anthology. He is a Moth Story Slam and Grand Slam Storyteller winner and one of the hosts of the podcast *Beef, Wine and Shenanigans*.

Find out more about him at www.whoismarcabbot.com.

HOW DOES YOUR GARDEN GROW?
SAMANTHA BRYANT

MEG NEVER LOOKED BACK as she walked, even though she could hear tendrils reaching for her and small, damp jaws opening and closing. Some things were better left unseen. She might be ignorant—Lord knows there were many things she didn't know—but she wasn't stupid.

She remembered the stories and understood the unspoken warnings between the words, the truths about the dangers a woman faces in looking back. Keeping those lessons in mind kept her resolute.

Eurydice would walk free upon the earth if her foolish lover had only kept his eyes on the prize, but he'd been unable to trust that she followed without direct evidence. His doubt separated them forever and trapped her in the ghost realm below the earth, victim to her misplaced faith in the man who sought to be her hero. She'd have done better to plot her own escape than to rely on a fickle man who demanded validation for rescue.

Lot's poor unnamed wife let nostalgia taint her hope for the future and ended up relegated to a cautionary tale used to scare women into obedience. She had looked upon that which men had not wanted her to see and had been silenced forever as a result of her temerity. Her mistake had been in letting them know what she wanted. Secrecy could be a woman's friend.

Looking back was a chump's game, and Meg had finished playing. Her eyes fixed on the horizon; her feet trod the path out of this life. She had only to remain true to her task, and it would soon be over.

Just as the old woman had instructed, Meg walked steadily with unfaltering steps, shoulders back and head held high. "Project confidence. You must feel the sureness in the marrow of your bones." Mama Johntae's glower still burned in Meg's memory, along with her words: "Don't let the slightest seed of doubt take root in your mind, or it will grow until it overwhelms you."

Meg daintily dropped fat, dead flies from her silver bowl onto the earth, sowing them like seeds as she strode toward the house where Jasper slept, a serene smile on her face. Her husband's excesses would probably have kept him unconscious without a soporific, but she'd hedged her bets with a tincture of melatonin, valerian root, and terpenes, ensuring he remained in a stupor. There would only be one opportunity—no second chance to grab her second chance.

Living with Jasper had become like nesting with a rodent or an insect—hidden and scuttling, dark and unkempt, dirty and disgusting. Strange that something that began in romance and adventure ended on a mattress on the floor of a shabby hovel. Her daring liaison with a dark and dangerous man had deteriorated into another boring account of libido defeating wisdom, and she'd become one of those women she'd always despised: trapped by her own fantasies, deluded into limiting her life to the orbit of his by the fear of the very violence that had attracted her in the first place.

Even with her palms bloodied from the corpses of the flies and the sweet-rotten scent of rot accosting her nostrils, Meg gloried to walk in the light, feeling as though she had stepped from a cave where she'd been lost for far too long. She was only ashamed it had taken her this long to act. Some part of her must have held out hope, despite all evidence to the contrary. Some stupid part that denied facts just because she didn't want them to be true.

That was all over now. She was through lying, especially to herself.

The warmth of the afternoon sun on her skin was tepid compared to the heat of anticipation rising in the dark pool of her heart. Sunlight still permitted shadows to hide the dark things, but the light of justice sent beams into every cranny, leaving no place for rot to fester. Purifying as fire.

How fitting to rid herself of this insect disguised as a man with Venus flytraps and pitcher plants. Her green thumb had proven good for more than daisies and rutabaga. Jasper had dismissed her plant work as useless, even as he consumed the fruits of her garden. Even before the drugs ate the kinder parts of the man, he had never understood her connection with the earth and her joy in bringing life from it. He sneered at the nurturing side of her, calling it weakness.

Now that spring had arrived, and her plants had grown strong and hungry, they'd see who was useless, what fed and what was eaten. The harvest had ripened, and her moment had arrived. Anticipation glowed on her face with a feverish sheen.

The path of flies she'd sown drew the scrabbling plants behind her like Hansel and Gretel's breadcrumb-thieving birds. Enormous pitcher plants and Venus flytraps dragged themselves across the dry earth with a rasping scrape, seeking the salty-sour meat of the fly corpses soaked in Jasper's blood. She'd trained them to crave the taste of him and kept them slightly underfed. Now they were ravenous.

For night after tedious night, she had extracted vials of his blood after he'd passed out. Crouching by the mattress on the floor, ready to bolt should he stir, she slid a needle beneath his skin and drained more. He didn't notice one more hole in his flesh among the needle tracks that already marred his once-beautiful skin or wonder if his weakness stemmed from anything besides the drugs. He remained sure of his hold over her, convinced she had been permanently cowed.

While he slept, held in oblivion by his addictions, she swept the corpses of flies from all the windowsills. She'd needed hundreds. Luckily, squalor attracted them in droves, and spread sugar called even more. Her macabre collection grew until her silver bowl swam with dark fuzzy carcasses, wings stained red and bellies bloated.

If Jasper noticed her odd new obsession at all, he must have mistaken her preparations for an attempt to clean up the pigsty their home had degraded into. As if any home with him in it could ever truly be clean—he dirtied all he touched. When she made her new home, it would always smell of antiseptic and lemon oil. She'd make sure of it.

Meg didn't look back even when the plants scuffling behind her grew noisier. Leaves rustling against the earth became more like voices calling her name with each step. "Mmmmmmeg, Mmmmmmmmmmeg, Mmmmmmmmmmmmmeg."

"Dark magic wants to go bad, to turn on its user," Mama Johntae had warned. She'd been right. Even knowing, even prepared, the magic twisted the sounds in her brain, making her imagine the plants called her name. She had to fight to keep her head facing forward.

The old woman had tried to talk her out of this, even while she taught her what she needed. She'd told tale after tale of the failures of women who sought to bend dark powers to their will but hadn't had the backbone to follow through completely and had paid the price. Her unblinking gaze expressed apathetic doubt that Meg had what it would take.

Meg would not be deterred, had practiced the incantations until her teacher had to admit her proficiency. The old woman's last words still echoed in Meg's memory, "Follow all the rules, or you'll fall victim to your own devices. It'll be your funeral instead of his."

A murmuring rose, like a crowd burgeoning into an angry mob. The smacking sounds seemed more human now, like the noise of an old man's lips as he eats ribs with only half a set of teeth. Distracted, Meg had slowed, and the sun was beginning to dip lower in the sky. Nearly time.

Vines scraped at her heels, tugging at the hem of her skirt, urging her to turn around or to stop walking and let the hungry vegetation feed. The temptation to lay down and let the plants overtake her made her wobble on her feet. It would be easy to stop. To give in.

But Meg wasn't one for easy. Not anymore.

Without looking down, she dropped another handful of flies

behind her, grimacing at the wet smack against her calf when one of them bounced off her flesh on its way to the ground.

The tension on the cloth of her skirt released, her plant army distracted by the offering, and Meg lengthened her stride, keeping ahead of the troop of viney soldiers snaking from the forest valley where she'd nurtured them. She could see the peeling red paint on the door of the shack she'd shared with Jasper now. The building tilted askew, even the architecture knocked off kilter by the mockery of a life lived within its walls.

She laid a hand on the doorknob. Once she'd led the plants to their intended victim, she had to keep walking, straight through the house and out the other door, picking up the bag she'd placed there.

She longed to stay and watch but knew that if she stayed, the plants would devour her, too. Maybe after a week or so, she could return to see what remained. But even that was risky.

Better to wait until after a full cycle of the moon.

Better yet to keep walking and never look back at all.

The way forward was all that mattered now.

About the Author

SAMANTHA BRYANT may look like Laura Ingalls Wilder, but inside it's a lot more like Wednesday Addams. Check out her other horror offerings at http://bit.ly/SamanthaBryant alongside her lighter work, like the Menopausal Superhero series. You can find her on Twitter and Instagram @samanthabwriter, or if all else fails, check the woods. She likes to get lost there at least once a day.

TO THINE SELF BE TRUE
ALP BECK

"W‌HAT DO YOU THINK, Liz? Should we take it?" Greg looked at his wife, hopefully.

"Doesn't the price seem a little too low? Too good to be true, maybe?" Liz toyed with the hair on her troll doll key chain, a sign of her anxiety. "You know what my dad says, *If it's too good...*"

"Yeah, I know. For God's sake, please stop quoting your father every chance you get. You married me, you know, not him. *Why did she constantly have to bring up her freaking father every chance she got?* You heard the agent, it's because the house comes with a tenant. That's a good thing, as far as I'm concerned: built-in income."

Greg didn't know how much rent the tenant was paying—that was part of the contract. The real estate agent was very specific; he was not to ask. Whatever it was, it was worth it. The house was an incredible steal, especially in this neighborhood.

"C'mon, honey. We'll never get a deal like this again. Have you *seen* this house? Do you know where we are?" he said. Liz saw the hunger in his eyes, his desperate need to impress, so she relented.

"Okay."

"Yes!" Greg grabbed Liz and squeezed her, a little too tight, then turned to the agent. "Lady, you've got yourself a sale!"

Greg stood at the center of the kitchen, staring up at the ceiling, then looked at the rent check in his hand, a measly 102 dollars. It was from the Hekate Society: a company that didn't exist—according to Google. Two years into homeownership and they still hadn't found a way to get the old woman out. It didn't bother Liz, she reminded him she didn't disturb anyone, and their mortgage payment was low enough they didn't need the extra cash, but what she really meant was that her *daddy's* help was always there, on the back burner, waiting to be summoned.

Greg had other ideas. He wanted the hag gone. He was sure he could make a fortune in rent from that apartment, even though he'd never seen it. It had to be at least as large as his own on the first floor and that was plenty big; with at least three bedrooms, a living room, and an eat-in kitchen.

Besides, the whole upstairs situation was freaky.

Once a week, some big guy delivered stuff, groceries, he guessed, to her apartment. He'd use his own key to let himself in. His *own* key. Unbelievable! *They* didn't even have a key, and they were the owners of the goddamned house! A few minutes later, he'd let himself out. Greg would watch the guy out his window as he climbed back into his van and took off. Once a week, without fail, regular as her goddamned check.

To this day, he'd never laid eyes on the woman. Quiet as a church mouse. He'd heard her moving around upstairs a couple of times, but, for the most part, she was invisible. And what kind of a name was Chelleach? There it was on the check, plain as day: *RENT—FOR CHEL-LEACH MORRIGAN.* He hadn't figured out how yet, but he was going to get the bitch out of there, one way or another, no matter what Liz or that damn contract said.

Liz looked at the garbage piled by the front door. It was Greg's job to take it out twice a week and put it by the curb. But lately, he wasn't interested in doing much of anything. He left early and came home late. She'd been patient. She hadn't mentioned how lonely she felt. Every night he'd get home later and later. He'd grab a beer out of the fridge, pop the tab, turn on the TV, and park his butt in the shit brown La-Z-Boy. She didn't mention the liquor on his breath or the stink of old cigarettes wafting off him, even though he'd supposedly quit two years earlier.

She grabbed the five bags of trash and clumsily made her way out the door. As soon as she did, the door shut behind her. Panicked, she realized it was set to auto-lock, and she didn't have another set of keys. Greg had taken the spare set with him months ago when he'd lost his, and never replaced it.

"*Ciallaionn se a gortaitear thu.*"

She looked up, startled. Her tenant stood at the top of the stairs. Liz gaped. This was the first time she'd laid eyes on the woman. She was small with penetrating cobalt-blue eyes that looked out of a face so etched with lines it might have been made of bark.

Long, white hair cascaded down to her waist, so luminous it appeared to light the darkness that surrounded her.

"*Ciallaionn se a gortaitear thu.*"

"Excuse me?" Liz said.

Chelleach continued to stare back, as if willing Liz to read her mind.

Liz shook her head, not comprehending. "I don't understand—"

The old woman harrumphed with evident frustration. She tossed a small metallic object at her feet. Liz bent down and picked it up, amazed to see it was a key. She glanced up, ready to thank her, but the landing was empty. She'd never heard her leave. Sighing, she turned, inserted the key in the door, and turned it. It fit perfectly. She let herself in and tossed the garbage bags where they had been earlier. Let Greg deal with them. Instead, she ran to her laptop and opened Google translate, selecting '*Detect Language Automatically.*' Then she typed the phrase phonetically, as best as she could remember, and hit, *Enter*. Google spit out the translation.

'*He means to hurt thou.*'

It was Gaelic.

<hr>

Liz startled awake. She heard a commotion outside her front door. Then the clumsy fumbling of a key in the lock. She sneaked a glance at her bedside clock: 1:30 a.m., and he was just getting home; the third time this week.

Greg stumbled in, rancid smelling from his evening. She got up off the couch, still not fully awake.

"Don't you *dare* say anything," Greg snarled as he tossed his jacket on the back of a chair.

<hr>

He'd been fired from his job at the bank earlier this week and had not yet told Liz. The bastards. Frustration boiled in his system as he relived having to sit quietly in front of the chinless HR stooge as he recited from a list of imaginary grievances:

Behavior that has been perceived as abusive and hostile; General belligerent and disruptive attitude; Refusing to do the work assigned to him; Frequent missing of deadlines; Chronic lateness; Making unwanted advances to his female coworkers; Creating toxic, confrontational atmosphere for those around him.

The drone reminded him that it was his third offense, so there was no need to rehash the specifics. He was out for violating the company's Code of Conduct. Ha! More like the company's Code of Chumps. *Friggin' snowflakes.* Screw 'em, he'd show them all, the pricks.

<hr>

Liz took a deep breath before speaking.

"Greg..."

"What? What are you going to say?" Spittle flew as he shouted. "The same old bullshit?" His eyes were mean. "I knew you would be up, waiting for me," he said mockingly. "Just looking for something to tell *daddy,* right? To show him how I screwed up. Just looking for an excuse to get on my freaking back. If you've got nothing good to say, just shut the hell up and leave me alone!" The anger came off him in waves, and it was obvious that he just didn't care. "I have a right to blow off some steam!"

"Greg..." Liz tried again. Greg advanced on her fast until he was just an inch from her face.

"I. Said. Shut. The. Fuck. UP!" He raised his fist threateningly. Liz backed up, alarmed, forgetting the basement steps were right behind her.

Too late, she realized her mistake. She lost her balance and fell back.

▭

Greg watched with mingled surprise and horror as his wife tumbled backward, her arms flailing uselessly as she tried to find purchase. Everything happened in slow motion: Her hands reached out for him, but in his current state, all he managed was a clumsy brush of his fingers across hers—then she was out of his grasp in a millisecond. Her body tried to right itself, almost made it, then failed as she plunged downward. Her mouth released a muted "Oh" as she realized what was happening; then came the horrible *crack* of her head as it hit one of the concrete steps; her body catapulted, feet over head, not stopping until it landed on the basement floor.

He shouted her name, taking the stairs two at a time until he was next to her. He knelt beside her. Her head was bleeding, and one of her legs was bent at an odd 90-degree angle. She was unconscious.

He grabbed for his phone to call 911, then realized it was still in his jacket pocket upstairs. He ran up, and that's when he saw it—the melted candles, the porterhouse steak in the congealed butter, sliced the way he liked it, the fresh mashed potatoes beside it—his favorite meal—and in his plate sat a little, yellow onesie with the words, *'Nine Months 'till I Meet You, Daddy!'*

In the distance, an inhuman keening sounded, muffled by the roar in his head, like that of an angry river. He thought he saw movement in the corner of the room, a streak of bright white; then it was gone.

The wail was his own.

▭

After the loss of their baby, things settled down. Greg tried to be attentive and kind as Liz recuperated at home. He found a new job at a bottling plant. While Liz didn't hold him responsible for the fall, he knew better. The memory of that night was etched deep into his psyche, keeping his guilt at the forefront of everything he did. He took comfort in the fact that they could try again. *No permanent damage,* the doctors had said. He stopped drinking. Got himself into Alcoholics Anonymous. Made the meetings and took stock of his life. He was determined to make good on his resolve. He would never let things get so out of control.

Liz's father had insisted on paying for a full-time nurse to help with Liz's recovery. Greg resisted the urge to toss the woman out. He was sure his father-in-law enjoyed throwing his wealth in Greg's face. Greg bottled up his resentment. He wasn't that guy anymore. He looked down at the AA, 2-year sober chip, never too far from him.

Yeah. He was a new man, and he'd surprise them all.

▭

"So, you're sure about this?" Greg asked Dan.

Dan was a recent hire at the plant. They became buddies the day Dan had covered for Greg's lateness by punching in Greg's timecard.

He'd done this without being asked or even knowing him that well. For Greg, a man who didn't trust anyone, it was the first time someone had done something without an ulterior motive.

Soon, they were taking lunch together. Greg discovered that they were very similar. They were both hungry and ready for more. Dan, like Greg, wanted to leave a mark in this world. They discussed ways to make more money, hatched wild schemes and outrageous scams designed to bring them wealth. Their favorite activity was imagining what they would spend their fortune on, and then the focus of the exercise would invariably turn to flaunting their success to those who had belittled them.

"Yeah. I'm telling you; this will make us both rich." Dan said.

"Tell me again how this works?"

"We go in, fifty/fifty, on a vending route. I have a cousin who is selling his—90k, and it's ours. We make money from day one. It's a very profitable route, at least four to 5k a week. He's retiring to Boca. In a couple of years, we'll have enough to buy other routes."

"Ninety thousand? You sure he won't take any less? That's a lot of cash."

"Yeah. He already sliced 10,000 dollars right off the top 'cause of our relationship. The route is a guaranteed moneymaker. You only have to come up with 45k since I got the other half."

Greg had gone over this in his mind, numerous times. This was all they had in savings, a wedding gift from his father-in-law. But if he did this, it would be for Liz and their baby, for their future.

"All right. I'm in." Dan jumped up and high-fived him.

"Yeah! Millionaire's club, here we come!" Then he looked at Greg. "Don't forget. He wants cash. That's part of the reason he gave us a discount, plus he wants to keep the IRS's greedy fingers out of his pockets."

"Yeah, yeah. I got it. I'll have it to you by Tuesday. I need a couple of days to get to the bank."

He got up from the table, thinking that Liz would never find out about the missing money. He managed all their finances. The account would be overflowing way before she ever got wind of the withdrawal.

———

Tuesday, Greg brought the cash in a thick manila envelope and stashed it in his locker. After work, they would meet with Dan's cousin and close the deal. He could see his future, and its color was green.

Dan didn't come to work that day, so Greg left him a couple of messages to make sure he was okay. At the end of his shift, he went to his locker. When he opened it, the envelope was gone. He frantically yanked everything from the cabinet, not caring where stuff landed.

"NonononoNONOOOO!" He yelled and howled with frustration and rage as he violently and repeatedly slammed the door against the locker's frame, drawing nervous stares from the coworkers in the room.

Nope. No envelope. As if it had never been there.

He had been duped.

It took three security personnel to calm him down, and then his boss sent him home.

He left and turned into the nearest pub.

———

Liz raised herself from the bed. She carefully made her way to the edge of the mattress. In the last few weeks, Greg had raised the stakes. Punches, kicks, slaps, all were fair game. He didn't even need a reason anymore.

A sharp pain of warning left her gasping as her bruised ribs complained. Her arms were covered with small welts of various hues, some faded, some fresh, ranging from pale tan to angry blue and purple, where Greg had pinched her. He'd grown very fond of his little game. If she didn't get him his beer quickly enough or displeased him in some way, he'd pinch her somewhere hard, then laugh uproariously as if it were a big joke. He'd kiss her gently on her cheek and slap her bottom hard enough to leave another bruise. "It's all love, sweetie, all love." He made sure never to pinch her somewhere the marks could be seen, but just in case, he always demanded she wear long-sleeved blouses when dining with her parents. She didn't tell them. She couldn't bear the thought that her dad had been right. He'd warned her, but Liz had gone ahead and married Greg anyway. He'd seen right through him, or more to the point, he'd probably recognized himself in him, and maybe Liz had too.

She had married her father.

Liz stared at the bank statement incredulously.

She rifled through all the pages again, just to make sure she was reading it correctly.

The total amount in the savings account read: $0.00.

She shook her head in disbelief. She was baffled. She was sure her father's gift should be there, but it wasn't. Dread pooled in her stomach at the realization she'd have to ask Greg about this when he got home.

That evening he was in a worse mood than usual. She asked him how his day had gone, and he just grunted. *Might as well just go for it,* she thought. Then, she took a big breath.

"Honey? We got the new bank statement today. I was looking through it and—"

Greg froze and turned to her. "What the hell were you doing looking at the bank statement?" His voice was icy.

"I was just curious. With the interest rates being what they are, I wanted to see how our savings was doing..." She made sure to place the accent on *our.*

He lit a cigarette, all the while continuing to stare at her. He smoked so much now that his index and middle fingers had permanent tobacco stains between them.

She met his eyes, trying to hold her ground, and saw a calculating, cold stranger there. She barely recognized the man before her.

"Oh? What the hell do *you* know about it?" He said, then paused. The room grew unnaturally silent. Everything around her was still. She felt her heartbeat reverberating in her ears. Then, without warning, he punched her hard in the stomach. She doubled over and vomited. He backed away from the spew in disgust; when she stopped, she collapsed the rest of the way. She lay there, gasping for breath. He glared, disgust evident on his face. She realized what was coming next a second before his heel hit her face. Then she blacked out.

When she came to, he was gone, and it was morning. Thank goodness. She could barely move. Maybe she needed a doctor or even a hospital. Liz tried standing, but a wave of dizziness overcame her. She lay back down. She'd wait a few minutes and then try again.

Greg was out doing God knows what. She didn't care anymore. She was done. He'd worn her down. Her relationship had become a cautionary tale. She was not angry or sad. Worse, she was indifferent. Everything was gray. No highs. No lows. She'd call her parents later. It was time to admit defeat.

In a bit, she managed to stand. She gingerly put on her bathrobe and then slowly made her way to the front door to get the mail. When she opened it, she saw a small basket sitting there. She bent down, picked it up, and brought it to the kitchen table. Inside was an old-fashioned bag of ice like in old cartoons, and a little glass jar filled with a green and phosphorescent unguent. She opened it, and her eyes teared at once at the pungent smell. She looked at the front of the jar and saw only two words written in beautiful cursive on a yellowed label:

For Pain.

Puzzled, she took the jar to the bathroom vanity. She opened her robe and raised her pajama top. Gently, she applied a bit of the concoction to the parts that hurt the most. The pain disappeared at once. Then she smiled for the first time in months.

▭

Liz stood in front of the apartment door and nervously knocked. She didn't think she'd get an answer. She'd tried at other times. C, as Liz referred to her—because who could pronounce that name?—never opened the door. Other than the time she had locked herself out, she had never seen her again. Greg hadn't succeeded in getting her out. He'd blasted acid rock on the stereo system at all hours. He'd snuck mice under her door, knowing full well that they would invade the entire house but that never happened. They had simply disappeared.

He'd shut off the heat and electricity to her apartment, despite Liz begging him not to, but nothing had come of it. Nothing. No response. Liz reminded him daily of the contract they had signed: they were not to evict the tenant or do anything to jeopardize her living quarters. And yet, he persisted. After a while, Liz stopped saying anything. The grays made that possible.

Now, here she was. Trying again. She needed to thank the old woman. Her miracle balm had not only taken away the pain but had also awakened her from her catatonia. Life had color again.

She knocked again. This time the door opened just as her knuckles made contact with the surface.

"Hello?" She pushed on the door gently, widening the gap. "Hello? Is anyone there?" She walked into the darkness, using the wall as a guide.

As soon as she fully disappeared into the apartment, the door slammed shut behind her.

▭

Greg walked into the house slowly. The front door was open. All the shades were up, and the house was totally dark. The glow of the TV was the only light in the kitchen, and Liz was nowhere to be seen.

"Liz? Honey?" Nothing. No Liz. Where the hell was she? She was supposed to have dinner ready for him; she knew that. He turned on the overhead light.

Nothing.

Weird.

"Liz? Stop fooling around, you know I don't like games." He walked into the bedroom. The bed was unmade. Liz always made the bed. The glow of the streetlight cast odd shadows into the room. He turned on the bedside lamp...

...and jumped.

Liz sat in the corner wing chair.

Unmoving.

"Liz, what the hell are you doing?" Something was off. The way her eyes fixed on him was unnerving. A chill ran through him.

She didn't respond. After a minute, she tilted her head slightly so she could look past him.

Behind him.

He turned. A small, wizened woman stood there. She had the whitest hair he'd ever seen; so white, in fact, it appeared to glow. Her glacier-blue gaze froze his body in place. He gasped and began to pant without knowing why. He blinked and tried shaking off the frost building in his bones. The crone smiled a dark toothless smile, fathomless and deep. It widened past her face, impossibly large. Then, she grabbed his wrist with an icy, dry grip and with a quick twist, she snapped it breaking his paralysis. He screamed then for all he was worth, and her smile widened with evident joy. With her other hand, she grabbed the same arm, further up, and shattered it. He watched in disbelief. She alternated her grip as she traveled to his shoulder, her grip unshakable, methodically breaking bone as she moved. She switched to his other arm and began the same process. Greg collapsed to the floor. His bladder let go, and he felt himself fade, but he refused to surrender to the impossibility of this moment. This could *not* be happening. He would not let it. He struggled against her, trying to escape. She grabbed his ankle then and snapped it in two. Mercifully the pain took over, and he passed out.

———

The old woman continued to methodically break the bones; first one leg, then the other. Then the neck, the torso, and the hips. She folded the various parts as she went. Nothing hampered her progress. She saved the head for last, imploding it with a swift heel to the nose until Greg's corpse was nothing more than an indistinguishable mass of bloodied bone, muscle, and tissue.

———

Liz stood up then. Chelleach waited. She made her way to where the old woman stood, leaned in, and carefully wrapped her arms around her, feeling the weight and solidity of the older woman against her. Chelleach relaxed into the embrace. The longer Liz held her, the more insubstantial she became until only Liz remained and no other.

Then Liz made her way up the stairs slowly, feeling her age, as she entered her apartment and closed the door behind her.

———

The young couple roamed around the house. It was the sixth one they had looked at that day, and, incredibly, it was exactly what they were looking for, right in their price range. They could not believe their luck.

Mike turned to the real estate agent, his pretty, young wife doing a poor job of hiding her excitement.

"Okay, this house seems to fit all our criteria," said Mike. "So, what don't I know?" He was naturally suspicious, and his gut told him the price was too good to be true. These real estate people were always taking advantage of dupes. They were no better than used car dealers.

"Ah, yes. There is one condition to buying this house." The agent smiled a predatory smile. "It comes with a tenant."

About the Author

ALP BECK lives in New York City. She writes in all genres but prefers horror. Her essays have been featured in *The NY Times* and *NY Blade*. As an ardent fan of the short story, she believes in mastering the short story before tackling novels.

Currently, she is working on her horror novel, *Fresh*, and a series of short stories, including *The Underride*, with her co-writer, Laurie Jones.

You can find more information here: www.alpbeck.com.

THE FALL OF THE HO-MAN'S EMPIRE
PAIGE L. CHRISTIE

She says, "Anytime," as she watches him walk away into the desert. His back is hard and straight as a steel beam, and if he looks back at her, his eyes will be as cold as that beam in winter. As cold as his hands on her flesh. As cold as the response in her stomach to his touch.

He doesn't turn. She doesn't really expect it. She doesn't want him to. She doesn't want anything from him, that's sure—though he gives her that—that anything, that crimson entirety of all she doesn't want—and that is why she waits for a reply.

She turns and goes back into the house. The space around her seems to grow larger as she closes the door behind her and shuts herself into a world too full of windows. The house stretches before her as she walks through rooms cold and blue with darkness.

There is no furniture.

.   .   .

She stops in the large room beyond the stairs, gazing out through the barred French doors that lead out into the wild-grown back yard. A bolt slides home in her mind. Between her thighs.

Darkness descends inside the house while the sunlight dances with the pull of the moon on the dew on the green and red jungle plants outside. The light beckons her through the steel-cabled windows. The house laughs at her, like a knife stabbing upward over and over again, battering the entrance to her sanity. The green land beyond the empty house cries out for her.

A shape drags at the corners of her vision and she turns her head to gaze at the puddle on the floor. Red, like rose milk, it laps furiously at the splashes of sunlight that bruise the ridged stone floor. The golden patches seem out of place in the cramping blueness.

Slow steps carry her toward a closet on the far wall. She opens the door, pulls an apron from a hook, and slides the garment over her head. She reaches for the mop. She should clean up the evidence so the next one won't have to ignore it. Her fingers curl around the mop handle. She should leave the evidence for the next one to try to ignore.

A click sounds down the hallway, and an arid breeze flicks up her legs as the front door opens to allow it entrance.

"No time," she says and closes the closet door.

Apron draped loosely around her, she walks from the room, haunted with every glance by barred images of freedom. She stops in the doorway and stares toward the entryway.

He moves down the hallway to where she waits.

"Anytime," she breathes, and he does not hear the rage and frustration in her voice.

He is paid to come here. To rest his taxed nerves. She is paid—to receive his desire—for a peace—for control. Her time is his. She is paid.

She pays.

She says, "Anytime," as she watches him walk away into the desert. She does not wait to see if he will look back. The sand burns her feet as she turns and walks toward the house. She doesn't feel the heat. Inside, a second puddle of red is running into the first. They are blending, blurring, becoming one, trying vainly to rinse away the widening patches of rhythmic sunlight.

She thinks puddles have been running together inside her for a long time. That their wavered edges have been a long time in meeting, in forming, in resolving into a bright mirror. Resolving into resolution. Revolution.

She smiles. She will dip her fingers into the red pool that has been forming. She will smear a wet message on the lock of the French doors, let it rust away, open a way into the wild, green yard.

Let them try to ignore the growing chaos. Let them try to ignore the opening growing in her cage, while searching for the opening in her.

"No time," she says, on fire.

About the Author

PAIGE L. CHRISTIE is originally from Maine and now lives in the North Carolina mountains. She is best known for the Legacies of Arnan fantasy series, and her work can be found in several anthologies, including *Galactic Stew*, and *Witches Warriors & Wise Women*. When she isn't writing, Paige runs a non-profit soup kitchen and food pantry, walks her dog too early in the morning, and practices belly dance. Website: paigelchristie.com

CHURCH OF WOMEN
KATHLEEN SCHEINER

R**UTH HAD BEEN GOING** for almost three days straight. At first, she fled at a full tilt, sure the men were after her. But she figured out after about a day that nobody was coming for her, and that hurt more than anything. She wanted to die, and the quicker, the better.

Now Ruth headed north toward a place that she heard about as a young girl while playing at the knees of the older women. "They're a coven of witches who feast on the sweet meat of babies," Gretchen said, a great-grandmother three times over who had outlived most of her daughters. "When the men go hunt, they talk about these feral witches who go about in blue robes and offer treats. That's how they lure you, and then—" Gretchen had slapped her hands together, making Ruth flinch. She'd never forgotten those stories, and if the men wouldn't kill her, she was sure the witches would.

There had been no new births in ten years, but every night the village girls and women had to participate in breeding rituals, where the men picked who they wanted to mate with. Ruth was fifteen when she married, a fair age, and she gave birth to two beautiful daughters, Portia and Athena. But she could no longer bear what was happening to them. Only ten and twelve. It was unspeakable.

Ruth emerged from a scrubby forest of dead trees, no longer having the strength to walk, and saw a stone wall with an iron gate set inside it. A huge building with towers loomed up behind the wall, and Ruth sat at the base of a dead tree, watching and listening for hours while deciding what she would do. At one point, she heard hundreds of voices—the register sounded female—singing, and she was struck by the peculiar beauty of that noise. Windows were cut into the tower, and sometimes Ruth would see shapes go by that looked vaguely female. She could also hear children playing, and that made her want to cry, but there was no water left in her body.

Eventually, a woman unlocked the gate and came outside, placing a cloth-covered basket in the dust with a pail alongside it. The woman was dressed in long sky-blue robes and wore a golden crown heavy with jewels on her head. She was plump, and Ruth could smell rich meaty odors coming from whatever was in the basket. The woman stepped back inside the gate, then closed and locked it before disappearing.

Ruth waited as long as she could while saliva pooled in her mouth. But then she couldn't help herself any longer. With the last of her strength, she scrambled toward the basket, the temptation too much. Once there, she ripped the cloth off the top of it and saw crispy brown meat. She seized it in her hands and gnawed it to the bone, then discarded the gray nub. Ruth slurped water from the bucket and then went back to the basket, taking out a dense loaf of bread. She smelled it, remembering the past when wheat and yeast had been available. The earth no longer gave crops in her village, and the people baked under a sun that grew hotter and hotter, leaching the dirt until it was dust where no seeds could take root. Ruth tore a hunk off the bread and stuffed the piece in her mouth, then picked up an ugly purplish-red fruit with a bumpy rind. She turned the fruit around and around in her hands, trying to figure out how to eat it.

The gate squeaked, and Ruth looked up to see the woman in blue opening the caged door. She did it carefully as if she feared that Ruth might run away.

"Hello, good afternoon," she said in a gentle, jovial voice. "I saw you out there when I was doing my morning meditations and thought you might be hungry and thirsty. It looks as if you've come a long way."

Ruth nodded and ducked her head down, ashamed of her appearance. Her green dress was tattered and worn, and now it was also dirty from her long travels. She wiped her greasy hands on her skirt.

"Thank you," she whispered and then had a nauseating thought. "That wasn't a baby, was it?"

The woman threw her head back and laughed loudly, a guffawing noise like an animal might make. Finally, she wiped tears from her eyes. "No, we don't eat babies. How ridiculous."

Ruth looked up at her, seeing fair blond curls of hair underneath her crown and kind blue eyes. "I'm ready to die," she said. "Do with me what you will."

The woman squatted down so she faced Ruth. "Where do you get these ideas? I'm the High Priestess here. We call this the Church of Women and we celebrate life, not death." She reached out and touched the fruit in Ruth's hand. "Do you know how to open this? I can help you."

Ruth released the object, and the High Priestess dug into its hard rind with her fingernail, then peeled back the thick skin, showing something like ruby-red jewels caught in the fruit's pith. She popped a seed out and placed it in Ruth's hand. "Here, try it. I think you'll like it."

Ruth put the seed into her mouth and sucked on it, first tasting a sweetness and then a tart undertone as she chewed it.

"It's called a pomegranate. Have you ever had one?"

Ruth shook her head no.

The High Priestess said, "It's the fruit that symbolizes women, so it's sacred to us. Only we are allowed to eat it, not the studs or geldings."

"The studs or geldings?" Ruth repeated nonsensically.

"The men we employ here. We take only the finest specimens and barter with the outside world, giving them tea, meat, and bread for their services."

Ruth thought of the men in her village who went off to hunt and came back with bloodied weapons but no meat or bread. They returned from their trips with barrels of tea that they ladled out to all the villagers. They called it sarsaparilla, and it did help to ease hunger pains. Ruth had wondered who they killed for that tea—bloody spears meant a battle—and she noticed that the hunters sometimes returned down a man. The hunting party never spoke of what happened to him, and Ruth assumed the missing man had died while fighting. She had been happy when Jordy disappeared, the man who took Athena's virginity, sure he was dead. But now she realized he might be alive and why the hunters thrived compared to the rest of the village.

A bitter look came over Ruth's face, and she asked, "How many are there?"

Anger choked her as she thought of all she had to do because men told her those were the rules: mate whenever they felt like it, carry their children when that had still been a thing, make food when there was any, and clean—so much damn cleaning. On top of that, she had sacrificed her daughters. Supposedly for the greater good. That's what they told her.

"We keep five studs and have eleven geldings for the women to use as they see fit." The High Priestess dropped a wink, and Ruth understood what she meant.

"Do you have to do it?" she asked.

The High Priestess seemed so tall and commanding. Ruth couldn't imagine her cowering in front of a man.

"I have used the studs before, but it's not something I desire anymore. They're here to provide their services if a woman has needs of the flesh but doesn't want to bear a child. Or she can use one of the studs if she does desire a child."

Ruth's interest was piqued. *These women are in charge of what they do? They don't have to answer to anybody.* "And you don't eat the children?"

The High Priestess gave her a sad smile and raised her right hand. "I promise, we do not eat the children. They're integrated into the church, and they have the choice to leave when they come of age at sixteen if that's what they wish. But in the two hundred years our abbey has been here, only three have chosen that path."

The High Priestess stood up from the ground and dusted off her light-blue robes before opening the gate.

"Would you like to come inside and shelter for the night?" she asked over her shoulder. "I can show you around and offer you a room. You're welcome to stay with us if you want, but you'll have to earn your keep. Or I can just make sure you get a good night's sleep and then send you off with supplies tomorrow."

Ruth nodded and rubbed her belly, which was making gurgling noises because it was so happy with the food. She got to her feet and waited for the High Priestess to lead the way. *It might be a trap*, she thought. *What happened to those three?*

The woman opened the gate with a key she took from a ring in her pocket, and then she asked Ruth, "What's your name? Tell me about what your life is like."

"They call me Ruth." She was suspicious of the High Priestess's intentions but tried to pick out words to describe her life. "Once I was a wife, and I thought I was happy. I had two girls, Athena and Portia, and everybody said they were born lucky. Pretty girls that men started competing for when they were only five and seven. My husband said they would fetch a fair price and be taken care of because they were so valuable. But then the famine came, and everything changed."

"You've been hungry," said the High Priestess with a knowing look. "I believe we've traded with your village, and our church is compassionate. We can't bear to see so many starve."

Ruth frowned. "I was talking about no babies. There have been no babies for ten years, and now marriage is outlawed. There's breeding, and my girls—they're the most in demand. I look at them sometimes and wish I had killed them at birth."

Tears sprang up in Ruth's eyes, and an idea began to form in her mind. If she wasn't being deceived, maybe she could save her daughters. To bring them to this Church of Women.

"Oh, dear," the High Priestess said, and something made her face cloud over. "We were only trying to help," she mumbled.

She took Ruth down to an underground room in the big stone castle, where many women in similar blue robes used paddles to stir large vats of brown liquid. Ruth recognized the smell of sarsaparilla and knew this was the tea she had been drinking for several years. She noticed all the women had cheerful expressions and flesh on their bones.

Next, the High Priestess led her down a passageway to a small room where more women and some girls sat at long tables in front of books and paper, many of them writing. Older men in her village knew how to read and write, but nobody else did. It had fallen out of favor after the dissolution of the States. You can't eat books, after all. However, Ruth was curious about what the women found so interesting in those books. They seemed so happy, at peace, and content.

Tugging her out of the sunny room by an arm, the High Priestess said, "This is where we bathe." She opened the door to a bathhouse where steam billowed out. Ruth could see the wispy shapes of women in the clouds, their faces pink from the heat while they clutched bars of soap. "We make our own soap out back in the barn. Five acolytes are assigned to that duty, and we vote on what scents we want to use."

Ruth heard the cries of children behind her, and she ran out of the bathhouse, trying to find the sound. She found herself in a large play-room with floor-to-ceiling windows that let in light. She was stunned to see more than twenty children of various ages, from infants to ten or eleven years old, milling about her. But one thing puzzled her.

She heard the High Priestess's steps behind her.

"How?" she asked. "We haven't had children in ten years. Not one baby. How have you done this? And where are the boys?"

"Oh, we don't keep them," said the High Priestess, and she tucked her hands into the large bell-shaped sleeves of her robe. "They're not necessary for our society."

"B-b-b-but—but how?" Ruth sputtered. "Are those the ones you eat?"

"We do not eat children," the High Priestess said sternly. "And if you're going to stay here, I don't want to hear another thing about it. We simply don't let the boys take root—it's easy enough to do. We source our males from outside the abbey, so nobody gets too attached and the gene pool remains robust. Depending on how our sisterhood votes, the men are sorted as studs or geldings and castrated accordingly."

Ruth marveled at the riches available to these women and girls. Their world was tilted compared to hers. The High Priestess showed her many rooms, vast underground chambers where plants were tended to with clever sliding metal windows that only allowed sunlight in for a few hours a day so the crops wouldn't wither. Chickens passed by in the halls clucking and Ruth watched them go, stupefied. When had she last seen one?

"I'm going to show you the fertility rooms now," said the High Priestess. "This is where our most important work is done, I believe."

She opened a portcullis and tilted her head at Ruth, indicating that she should go forward. A staircase led up to another floor with flambeaux set in the walls, and Ruth climbed the steps, hearing faint bellows and moans from above, like rutting animals.

She entered a cold chamber where she faced five closed doors and spun around, confused. Then she heard something.

There was the sound of whiplash and then a deep male voice saying, "How do you like that, you weeping mama's girl? How does that feel?"

The voice sounded familiar. She ran to the door where the sound seemed to be coming from and flung it open. There stood a fully nude middle-aged woman with black curly hair who had her hands tied above her to a post. Behind her was a black-haired young man, stripped to the waist, with a braided lash in his hand. It was Jordy.

At first, Ruth was terrified and stared down at the floor, not meeting the man's eyes, as she had been taught to do since birth. Ruth heard the lash of the whip once again, and her spell of silence was broken. She rushed at Jordy and pushed him with all of her strength.

"Stop it! Stop it! You're hurting her!" she yelled.

Jordy fell to the floor, kneeling in front of Ruth, but not before she saw the fear in his eyes. He recognized her as well.

"I beg your pardon, ma'am. I only did what Ellie wanted. This was her fantasy."

The High Priestess took Ruth's arm and marched her out of the room. "Come with me," she whispered. "I know it's a lot to take in. Let's go to my rooms where we can talk."

The High Priestess took Ruth to her quarters on the top floor and gestured with her hand at a bloodred love seat in front of a large wooden desk.

Ruth sat down, carefully gathering the loose ends of her dirty dress and holding them in her lap so she could spare the sofa's luxurious fabric. But at the same time, Ruth mimicked the posture of the High Priestess, holding her head up high and squaring her shoulders.

The High Priestess sat down at her desk and picked up a pen and paper. She began writing something, but Ruth couldn't decipher the scribbles.

"Now, I know this will be a difficult adjustment for you if you do decide to stay with us. You have so much education to catch up on, and I'll need you to dedicate at least five hours daily to your studies. As well as that, you'll need to work. All acolytes have to work to keep their place here."

Ruth nodded and found it easy to look into the High Priestess's blue eyes. They were so much kinder than what she was used to.

"If you decide to leave, I'll brew you a tea and give you three days' worth of food so you can make it back to the village you came from." The High Priestess laid her hands flat on her desk.

Ruth looked down at her dirty fingernails and pictured herself in the billowy steam of the bathhouse that the High Priestess had shown her. She would take one of the fat slabs of soap and scrub herself clean before donning the light blue robes of the order.

"I've decided that I'd like to stay if you'll have me," Ruth said, thinking about Jordy. The rules were different here, and she would make him pay. She would rescue Athena and Portia, and they would all make him pay.

"Wonderful." The High Priestess wrote something else onto the pad in front of her. "Do you have an idea of where you would like to work? With your experience with children, I could see you fitting in at the nursery. Would you like to try that work detail first?"

Ruth shook her head adamantly. "No, I have the most experience with m— The geldings and studs, I mean. I'll help take care of them."

The women shared a look, and then the High Priestess stood up and held out her hand. Ruth had seen the men do this in her village but had never actually participated in such an exchange before. She rubbed the palm of her hand on her skirt, then stood up and shook with the High Priestess.

"Welcome, Ruth, to the Church of Women."

About the Author

KATHLEEN SCHEINER is an editor and writer living in Brooklyn, New York. She has written for *Publishers Weekly*, *Scholastic*, *Chime for Change*, *L'Ecran Fantastique*, *Toxic*, and *Penny Blood*. Her novel *The Collectors* was published in 2013, and her short fiction has appeared in *Memoirs of Meanness*, *A New York State of Fright*, *Under Twin Suns*, and several Girls Write Now anthologies. Her reviews, essays, and criticism appear at horrorfeminista.com.

COLOSSAL

TARA LASKOWSKI

AFTER MY HUSBAND discovered my lover and she fled town, everyone declared me damned, fish food for Kraken. I was not asked to defend myself, not that I needed to. The men did not offer a final meal, but I'd had a decadent last dinner regardless—a rich lamb chop stew, cooked by my lover just before we'd been caught. She had wiped the corners of my mouth with her napkin before kissing me. It was that memory I chewed on when they forced me onto a ship.

They told my husband he did not have to make the journey to the squid that the men all feared and worshiped, but he said he needed to see me die for himself. It was his cleansing. His retribution. He was, like all the other wronged men before him, willing to risk it all to see my pain.

He stood beside me, anxious, staring not at my face but at the heavy, damp ropes bound around my wrists, my thighs, my ankles.

"You'd better run quickly, my dear," I whispered, and laughed. "You know what happens to the ones who stay too long."

He unwrapped the ropes and tied them again, tighter this time, licking my blood from his fingers.

We sailed for an eternity, to the edges of nowhere, to the deepest part of the ocean, to the middle of the end. When the ship finally drifted to a stop, bobbing like a child's toy in a swimming pool, all I could smell was salt and rot. An eerie quiet. The men waited, poised with their guns, their eyes darting nervously.

And waited.

And then we heard it. A tremor, like the most devastating of earthquakes. An apocalyptic wail so overwhelming it washed the color from the men's faces.

"She's here," I murmured, and my husband, the coward, backed away from me.

"Let's go. Quickly!" another shouted, his lips trembling. For he knew what could happen if they lingered too long—if the husbands insisted on seeing it all. The greedy ones who thought their wives could satisfy the Kraken enough to spare the ship.

The men untied me, dragged me to the gunwale. They heaved me over the edge, trembling. "Kraken! Our gift."

Down, down, down. I hit the icy water so fast it felt like my back had split open, that I had turned inside out. At first, the water was emerald green, the color of my lover's eyes, but as I sank further, the sea darkened, swallowing the sun. I drifted down, like hot wax, swelling and bulbing, nudging up against unseen things, a soft yielding here, a nip there.

The squid bellowed again. What had sounded chilling above, though, worked its way through me like a lullaby here in the depths. I saw nothing but her—a pulsating gray glow as colossal as a mountain, bulging and twisting in an impossible silence.

I did not try to get away. I found I did not want to. I opened my chest, slung my arms back, parted my legs. The squid contracted. Her tentacles, long, twitching, suddenly tensed like rubber bands. One whirled around me, wrapping. Hundreds of tiny sucking membranes fed on my cuts and burns. She rolled me toward her horrific, trembling mouth.

Then. Darkness.

When I woke, I was dead. When I woke, I was inside Kraken—no, I *was* Kraken. I could see through her large eyes, sense her loneliness and anger, feel her—*our*—drifting tentacles clench and unclench. I was Kraken and all those who came before me. I could see that child's toy above us, its defiant dance on the surface. Could feel my husband's self-righteous gaze. He believed he'd won—that he'd forever separated the two women who'd lain in a field of heather under a full moon.

I twitched.

Feast, I said and didn't say. *Destroy*, I whispered and did not whisper. I trembled as we descended and I remembered all the things that would never be again—the way my lover's backside warmed in a patch of sunlight through her bedroom window, the soft indented curve of her chin, the gentle lilt of her laugh.

It was then we stopped, suspended. We writhed—all the whores and bitches and mothers and harlots and lovers and teachers and scientists and witches and gypsies and sluts that had come before. Our pasts came back—the soft midnight whispers, the dangerous scent of sulfur on the sleeve of a laboratory coat, the children that were and never were.

Rise, we pleaded to Kraken, but she was already bellowing, already pushing up, up, up. The light green waters didn't suit her, but her massive belly undulated with the rage of a thousand women.

We were the size of a city. We were the size of a small country. We were the size of all the nightmares of all the men in all their sweat-stained beds. A collective force of sadness and terror and beauty. Up we came, our tentacles slicing through the water, dwarfing the ship in shadow. The men screamed their man screams as we swept one of our feelers out and across, a terrific arc, snapping the mast like a toothpick. They couldn't hear us, couldn't hear the sweet song we sang as their cabins filled with seaweed and salt, as their bones began to break and their skin began to bleed, as the sharks began to circle. *Oh boys*, we sang and sang.

About the Author

TARA LASKOWSKI is the author of the suspense novels *One Night Gone,* which won the Anthony, Agatha, and Macavity Awards for Best Debut Novel, and *The Mother Next Door.* She has also written two short story collections, *Modern Manners for Your Inner Demons* and *Bystanders,* and has won an Agatha Award and a Thriller Award for her short fiction. Follow her on Instagram and Twitter @TaraLWrites. Web site: www.taralaskowski.com

EVEN BLINDFOLDED, Nadia knew one was watching her. Then the smell hit her, warm and heady and animalistic. "Mother fucking banana!"

Her safeword. The flogging she had been receiving stopped instantly and her wrists were uncuffed from the cross. Nadia ripped off her blindfold and struggled to put on her robe. Dreg looked at her with worry.

She took a deep breath and stepped into his offered embrace. "Sorry, Dreg. There's a Were in here."

He nodded and looked around the room, squinting in the dim light. It was a Friday night, so the dungeon was full. Bodies were scattered around the room, some withering in pain and ecstasy, while others watched.

Nadia turned around and began to slowly walk around through every part of the building, trying to find out where the trespasser went. Coming to the office door, she whipped it open.

A sigh sounded from one of the chairs in the room, and Selene Monte, the club's owner, stood up. Spotting Nadia, she wearily motioned to a chair. "I assume this isn't a social call. I'm going to make myself a strong drink."

Nadia shut the door behind her and sat down. Inside, the thumping music of the dungeon was barely a whisper. Once Selene got her drink, she sat down and crossed her legs and waited.

"There was a Were in the dungeon tonight. A Were...in the club on a non-sanctioned night... Three nights before the full moon to be exact," Nadia ground out.

Selene tapped the glass's crystal rim with her fingernails. "You're absolutely sure about this?"

Nadia growled, "Of course not. I just noped out of an amazing scene and came in here to bother you for fun."

Selene stood up and walked to the security monitors. Her fingers flew over the keys as Nadia came and stood behind her. Selina looked up at her questioningly. "How long ago did you first sense them?"

"I felt them watching me first. I know that happens in a dungeon; this was different. It took me right out of my groove fifteen minutes ago. I followed their scent, but by the time I got here, it was too faint."

Nodding, Selene tapped more keys and stared at the screens. "Any registered Were who comes through the doors would set off the sensor, and they would be stunned; the alert system never went off." Selene looked at Nadia with remorse. "I'm sorry, Nadia. I know after every-thing...it's difficult... I'll alert the Regulation Department and start the evacuation protocol. How long before you can be dressed and take point at the door? Maybe someone will have the Were's scent on them."

Nadia stood up. "I need seven minutes. Don't hold your breath, though. I'm sure any residuals are long gone. Whoever they were, though, was fast and here for a reason. I could feel them; it was focused...personal."

▭

The shower water was so hot it should have made Nadia's skin blister. Instead, she stood under it, hoping it wouldn't cool down anytime soon. It pounded on her back and ran down her legs, leaving scalding trails. The angry, puckered skin on her upper thighs didn't feel the heat at all.

It had taken three hours to excuse every attendee and the staff at the club. Knowing the Were she'd sensed would be facing possible incarceration and definite re-education if the Department got a hold of them made her feel uneasy. She didn't exactly trust the government in general. Groaning as the water started to cool, she went through the motions of washing and got out to dry off and lotion herself. She flinched when she rubbed the cream into her thighs. Every time she touched the scars she saw a flash of fur, felt pain, and heard screaming. Not her voice though; she'd never heard a single sound she made that night, only Evie's.

Nadia shook her head and brushed away tears. Evie had insisted they take a walk the night before a full moon. She hadn't come back from that walk, and her corpse had never been found. The doctors still puzzled over why Nadia hadn't caught the virus that caused people to turn into werewolves from the attack. All she had gained were scars, heightened senses, and a desperate loneliness.

Eating breakfast the next morning was impossible for Nadia, so once she ran out of things to keep her busy, she poured decaf coffee and creamer into a to-go cup and drove to the Club to meet with the Regulation Department. The Department was in charge of the registering, tracking, and education of Weres in the United States.

Pulling up to the Club in the daylight felt off to Nadia. She groaned as she saw three extra vehicles in the parking lot with Selene's convertible. The Department was early and would be expecting her.

Nadia entered Selene's office and nodded in greeting at the two Department officers sitting and typing on laptops. Selene stood up in acknowledgment of her entrance, sat back down careful to not wrinkle her pristine black suit, and continued talking to the Department Supervisor at the head of the table. Nadia took an empty seat and sat patiently to wait for her turn to be interviewed.

A shadow fell over her shoulder, and the hair on the back of her neck stood up. Turning slightly, she saw a tall man staring at her. Selene made an angry sound as he came closer. The man stopped as the Department Supervisor talking to Selene stood up abruptly. He smiled wearily at Nadia and pointed to the door.

Nadia nodded and, clutching her coffee, followed Agent Sharp to the lobby. Once seated, she took a long drink.

Agent Sharp sniffed and frowned. "You know you shouldn't have caffeine this close to the full moon."

Nadia laughed dryly. "You can't tell me what to do anymore. It's decaf anyway."

He shook his head sadly. "Evie's death affected me too."

Setting her cup on the floor between her feet, Nadia tucked her hands under her legs. "You don't get to say her name to me. Let's get this interview done."

Nodding, he began his questions and went by the book. During the questioning, Selene shut the office door. Once it shut, he leaned forward. "I need more than just blanket responses."

Nadia grunted. "I felt someone watching me. It didn't feel like a normal attendee watching a scene, and then I smelled them."

He nodded and wrote in his notepad. When he finished, he looked up at her. "We brought in a Were liaison before anyone else got here, and they caught trace pheromones in the dungeon. The Were had to have stood there for a substantial amount of time to leave traces the morning after. Until this is sorted, the Club is closed." Reaching into his pocket, he pulled out a business card and scribbled on the back. "Here's my new number. If anything happens, call me. I still care."

***

Later that night, Nadia sat in her living room and stared at the pictures on the walls. Evie's face looked back at her. Nadia had taken down all the pictures involving Agent Sharp six months after Evie had been taken. The three of them had been so happy together before that night. Shaking herself from her musings, she stood up, got her keys and phone, and left.

Taking a walk two nights before the full moon wasn't the smartest choice she could make, but she felt like her skin was crawling in their, her, apartment. Too many memories kept popping up. Before she realized it, she was on the same path where she had last been with Evie.

Nadia stopped walking and closed her eyes, struggling to remember what Evie had been saying when they were attacked. Trauma had robbed her of the memory of those moments. She was so distracted she didn't hear the footsteps behind her until strong arms wound around her midriff and threw her to the ground. Her phone went skittering on the hard-packed dirt as her attacker pinned her down. As they struggled, another sound made them both freeze.

From the trees, a howl echoed. Nadia laid still while her assailant rolled off.

"You don't want me, I'm a drunk...eat her." He rose to his hands and knees as a shape leapt out of the darkness and pounced on him.

Nadia sat up and felt for her phone as the man's shrieks turned to gurgle. She stopped moving, her hand on her phone, as the clouds broke from the moon for a moment.

She stared at the creature that had saved her and was feasting on her attacker. She recognized the snarling lips even stained with blood and gore.

Evie feasted ravenously. Every shift of the clouds gave Nadia another glimpse of gore the Were pulled from the man's body. Moving slowly, she brought her phone up and tilted it towards Evie and after fumbling to access the camera with a cracked screen, pushed the shutter button. The flash left dots in her vision. Once they cleared, she realized she was alone with an eviscerated corpse. Sobbing, she dialed 911; she heard Evie's forgotten words ringing in her ears.

▭

It was three in the afternoon the next day before she was able to pull herself out of bed. She kept seeing Evie's blood-smeared face as she ate the man. She hadn't died or been devoured like everyone else assumed, but had survived and now was a feral Were. A knock on her front door made her move painfully from the couch. She wasn't surprised when she saw Agent Sharp with a large cup of coffee and a box of doughnuts on her front step. Leaving the door open, she walked slowly back to the couch and sat down with a pained groan.

He set the doughnuts and coffee on the low table in front of the couch and sat down. "Decaf with Splenda and a staggering amount of vanilla creamer with six chocolate long johns."

Nodding, she reached for the coffee. Seeing how much her hand was shaking, she let it fall limply into her lap instead. "Did the Department send you?"

Agent Sharp reached over and grabbed a doughnut, taking two bites before answering. "I heard about the report from a hospital contact and volunteered to take your statement before they could assign someone else. It seems you've got a stalker and a death wish, not a good combination. Do you have any idea who could be stalking you, Nadia?"

She shook her head. "Does the department know about us?"

He finished his doughnut before answering. "They don't need to know about our past relationship. All they are aware of is that the three of us were friends and that after Evie died, you and I had a falling out. Our romantic relationship is none of their concern." She glared at him. He ran his hand through his hair, shook his head. "The fact that we were in an ethically non-monogamous relationship isn't something the Department would look kindly on."

Nadia nodded and laughed. "Of course. How professional of you." She motioned to her laptop and broken phone. "Hand those to me."

Once he placed them on her lap, she hooked her phone up to the laptop and accessed the phone's photo gallery. She pulled up a photograph and turned the laptop towards him.

Agent Sharp shook his head and stared at the screen. "There's no way. It's been a year. How has she survived without a pack? She's got to be insane by now; lone wolves don't survive for a reason."

Nodding, Nadia smiled. "I know, and yet there she is. She's the one who came to the club. Last night she saved me from that man who attacked me. Tonight's my last chance to get to her before she fully changes. If you ever loved us...you'll help me."

He reached over and grasped her hands in his. "I never stopped loving either of you. But if it is her, she's feral by now. You couldn't fight off a bum last night, what makes you think you can go hand to hand with an insane Were?"

Nadia pulled her hands from his. "She could have killed me last night, but she didn't. She protected me. Part of Evie is still in there. Please don't abandon us again."

Nodding, he pulled out his notepad. "Alright. What do you need from me?"

Two hours before sundown, Nadia paced back and forth in the club's bathroom. She didn't like lying to Selene, but she needed to have a safe place to lure Evie into so no one would get hurt. She had told Selene that she needed to have some time to think after her attack. Looking at herself in the mirror, she chewed on her lower lip. She was wearing the dress Evie had bought her. It was white and went halfway down her thighs. Her scars rose angrily on her skin, and she tried not to feel self-conscious.

Walking out of the bathroom, she went into the office and turned on the security camera feed. After a few keystrokes, she was able to override the system and send the feed to save to the cloud. Smiling sadly, she left a note for Selene with the password to access the footage and walked into the dungeon. She turned down the lights and turned on some soft music and danced by herself.

It didn't take long before she smelled her. Nadia smiled and kept dancing, closing her eyes. "Hi, baby. Come dance with me. I've missed you so much." Dancing in lazy circles, Nadia concentrated on the rhythmic sound of Evie's breathing. The smell got closer, and Nadia stopped dancing. Familiar hands came to her waist and guided her to turn around.

A hoarse whisper sounded in front of her. "Open your eyes."

When she opened them, she smiled. Evie was standing in front of her, her eyes bright with the telltale yellow hue of a Were.

Nadia reached up to cup Evie's cheek gently before leaning forward and capturing her lips. When the kiss was broken, they were both panting and pawing at each other with need.

The sound of footsteps made them stop, and Nadia silently cursed Agent Sharp's timing. Evie growled low in her throat and pulled Nadia behind her protectively.

"Come on, Evie. Don't you remember me?"

Hissing in his direction, Evie squared her shoulders. Nadia slipped in front of her and shook her head. "It's okay, Evie. I've taken care of everything. Trust me?"

Evie looked down and stood tensely. He walked around them in a cautious circle and chuckled nervously. Every time he got a lock on her, Nadia blocked the shot. Finally, he lowered the weapon. "What are you doing, Nadia?"

Nadia smiled and came closer to him. She ran a hand suggestively over her own chest and down her body. "You know, you say you miss Evie. But do you miss me?" His eyes followed the path Nadia's hands traveled on her body. When she started to lift the hem of her dress, Evie growled in warning. Nadia giggled and placed her hands on Agent Sharp's shoulders, putting one behind his neck to bring his lips down to hers. With her other hand, she grabbed the weapon from his slack fingers and fired it into his thigh. He reared back in pain, falling hard on his back, wheezing for air as he knocked the wind out of himself.

Nadia stood over him grimly as Evie stalked towards the now-incapacitated man. Nadia knelt next to his head while he moaned. Tears leaked out of his eyes as he stared at her in shock. "What's going on?"

Making a sympathetic sound, Nadia smiled. "I loved you both so much. It seemed like we were all so happy together. And then, the night Evie was taken...I can finally remember what we talked about that night. She told me what you did, what you made her do. She wanted to go on that walk out in the woods so she could tell me about the rape, and she begged me to run away with her...I would have agreed...then the attack." She grabbed his head and bounced it off the floor. "If you survive, don't try to come looking for us."

Nadia gave Evie an adoring smile and got up. She waited in the van outside for twenty minutes before Evie came in and gave her a blood-smeared kiss. Nadia helped Evie chain herself up in the back of the van. Before they drove away, Nadia tapped at her burner phone and accessed the club's live security feed. Agent Sharp lay on the ground spasming, his legs torn to shreds, bones clearly visible in sections. His face and chest were mauled. The wounds would leave horrific scars if he survived the night. She drove away humming to herself while Evie howled in the back of the van contentedly, becoming more and more quiet as the tranquilizer from Agent Sharp's blood coursed through her veins.

▭

Three days later, the van was found outside the entrance to a national park a couple hundred miles from the club. Nadia's corpse was in the front seat, torn open, blood and viscera coating the van's interior. Her face was left intact; the look of serenity on it clashed with the brutality of how she was killed. Bloody paw prints trailed from the van and into the thick woods surrounding it. In the back of the van, broken chains lay coiled on the floor, tufts of red fur stuck in the links.

About the Author

NICOLE HENNING was raised in a small Wisconsin town. Her parents taught her to love reading, art, horror movies, and strange British television shows at a young age. She is a horror and paranormal romance addict and faithfully uses life as a source of inspiration. Her goal when it comes to writing is to make her readers feel the same spectrum of emotions in the same manner as her favorite authors.

At first your arms caressed us
Enfolding us with grace
You looked into our eyes and said
You know I love your place
Beside us as a partner to forward go as one,
But then you held us tight, so tight
Our breath was taken short
You would not let us walk away
Or turn our head to see
The world outside, away from you
You would not let us free
'I will protect you' you intoned
'Value you, my darling one'
Yet never did you treasure us,
Suborned to fetished need
No freedom ever granted
We did not have before
An incubator for your spawn
Dominance all you craved
Conjoining made us just your slave.

'You lied, you lied you lied' we cried
Yet never did you care
You tried to regulate our every cell
To keep us all at hand
Subvert the fairness of our home,
The promise of our land
Yet you do not know half of us,
The fire in our core
We've reach the limits of your shroud
We now declare a war
No bounds will hold on us
Supreme will be our wrath
You tried to guide our every step
Yet put us on this path
So partner now or clear away
Sisters rise—This is our day!

About the Author

TEEL JAMES GLENN has killed hundreds and been killed more times—on stage and screen, as a stuntman, bodyguard, actor, and haunted house barker.

His poetry and short stories have been printed in over two hundred magazines including *Weird Tales, Mystery Weekly, Pulp Adventures, Space & Time, Mad, Cirsova,* and *Sherlock Holmes Mystery.*

His novel *A Cowboy in Carpathia: A Bob Howard Adventure* won best novel 2021 in the Pulp Factory Award. He is also the winner of the 2012 Pulp Ark Award for Best Author.

His website is: TheUrbanSwashbuckler.com.

THE HIVE
MIKE ROBINSON

When Michelle entered the café, Alison Davis knew instantly there was a problem—that perhaps her worst suspicions, through all the unreturned voicemails, the random cryptic texts (like the recent *hey miss u*, timestamped 2:41 a.m.), the read-but-ignored Facebook messages, had been heart-wrenchingly valid.

Alison had seen that look only twice before in real life, but many times on news reports or in crime documentaries. It resembled what she called the Gilded Glaze, the distant-eyed way someone who'd never *not* known wealth might regard everyone else. She wondered if all such expressions could be traced back to some form of abuse.

Plainly, Michelle Berg looked checked out.

"Alyville!" Michelle said, hastening her pace toward the table. That silly nickname, the first time in years she'd heard it aloud, had been a tennis-volley of Alison's old joke about Michelle's full name being a town: *Michelleberg.*

Alison stood. As they moved toward a hug, she tried to scrutinize her friend's face for any marks or bruises. None she could see.

But the lack of marks didn't matter. There was a drain in Michelle, that visible...reduction, like she'd lost weight (and maybe had), and, of course, those eyes, so glazed and removed.

They sat down. Michelle set her bag on the chair beside her and stared at it a moment.

"Are you okay?" Alison asked.

"I'm okay," Michelle said. "Yeah."

She dove right in. "How're things with Brian?"

She shrugged a little. "I mean, married life is up and down. As usual."

"How up and how down?"

A flash of suspicion on Michelle's face. Usually Alison wouldn't be that forthright, but this was not the time to dance about. Truthfully, though, she'd found it hard to dance around anything since the night at the Hive.

Even just imagining what Michelle's husband Brian, a college wrestler and bank security guard (now moonlighting, probably, as a full-on drunk) might be doing to her friend and long-ago lover, could well have been enough to send her fist into Brian's crooked nose, damn the repercussions.

Lately, Alison felt like she'd dismantled several protective layers around a radioactive Core inside her. It pulsed with the heat of many knotted angers. And if that Core was in her, it had to be in many, many other people.

Maybe everyone.

"It's mostly up," Michelle said. "Mostly up. Trust me. We've just had a little downswing recently."

"Okay. How down?"

Michelle sat back. The old Michelle would've tensed up more, maybe asked something like, *Is this a hangout or a grill session?* Annoying defensiveness, sure, but evidence of a spirit still steely and alive. That steel had melted.

"You know him—"

"I *do*."

Michelle shrank a little.

"Hey there!" A new voice, sharp and chipper. It was the waitress, stocky and cute, whose nametag read TERI. "Can I start you off with anything to drink?"

"Water," Alison said. "Please." She noticed that bright, angry Core seemed to throb brighter when she was dehydrated.

"I'll maybe have a cappuccino," said Michelle. "That cool?"

"Of course it's cool!" The waitress smiled and turned.

Alison leaned forward. "Michelle, tell me what—"

"Oh! Sorry." Teri the waitress turned. "Did you want whipped cream on that?"

Alison's irritation flared. Michelle gave an uncertain smile. "Uh, yeah, sure."

Again, Teri grinned and started to walk away when, as if testing Alison's knack for cynical prophecy, she stopped and turned once more.

"Also! What about cinnam—?"

"For *Chrissakes*," Alison snapped, "get your ducks in a row when you approach a fucking table."

She was suddenly light-headed. Trembling. Teri and Michelle just stared at her with wide eyes. *Don't talk back,* Alison thought. *For your own sake.*

She exhaled. Her heartrate lowered, but not by much. "I'm sorry," she said, though her eyes were closed as she worried the anger might rise again just looking at Teri's pitiable face. "I really am. I'm just... wound tight today."

"Don't worry about," Teri said. Her smile was fleeting, and no longer reached her eyes. "I'll be right back."

When the waitress was gone, Michelle regarded her. "What's going on? Why're you so wound up?"

"Michelle," said Alison. "You know I've never been very confrontational..."

"Yes. At least outside people you're close to." She looked out the window. In a lower register, she added, "I'm the same way."

"Uh huh. I know we had different backgrounds, upbringings, but we were spat out pretty much the same way. We're meek."

Michelle made a disagreeable face, but Alison continued.

"We may inherit the Earth," she said, "but in the meantime we have to weather the gauntlet of fucking assholes, and a society that runs on bullshit and ego."

Michelle snorted.

"I used to get paranoid when someone just disagreed with me *online*," Alison said. "Like, they thought I was stupid, or they no longer liked me. I used to be terrified of teachers and bosses and, hell," she gestured toward the kitchen, "even waiters, sometimes. Bothering people. As if I'd be found out for being an entitled ignoramus."

"I feel like you're about to do some infomercial pitch," Michelle said.

Alison hesitated. No, she had nothing to "sell." She even debated with herself whether to tell Michelle what she increasingly wanted to. All she knew was how that night...how the Hive...had affected her. Who knew how many others it had touched, wittingly or not?

Alison breathed again. "This is getting off-topic. The short version is, meekness is something you can overcome."

"Okay. And?"

"I'll back up. Define 'downswing.'"

"Huh?"

"You said you and Brian were in a downswing. Elaborate."

"Well, work's been keeping me late," Michelle said. "And he can be OCD and always wants to cook together. Dinner, I mean. Which I get. It's what we do often. He just misses the routine."

"All right. How does he express his disappointment?"

Michelle looked down, then, with an almost robotic motion, turned and grabbed her bag and stood.

"Where're you going?"

"I know what you're talking about," she said. "And it's not fair. He's gotten much better."

"How much does he drink these days?" Alison took a breath, held it. "And sit down. Please."

They met eyes. Michelle seemed to be wavering, then, as Teri the waitress returned with the cappuccino and water, she softened and sunk back into her seat. They thanked her and she moved away, flashing a smile at Michelle and saving little of it for Alison.

"Brian doesn't really drink anymore, no," Michelle said, "and do you *see* any bruises or anything?" She shrank back a little, lowering her gaze.

"That's a fucking low bar."

Sighing, Michelle said, "Alison, I made the *commitment*—"

"All I hear is resignation. And powerlessness. I didn't say much the first time I started picking up on all this, I know, and that's on me. But I was still my old self and wanted to just laugh it off with you, when you'd tell me shit like Brian 'has a good arm' when he hurled the toaster oven across the room when he lost his old job, or when you said you needed to 'go easy' on him with videogames because he might disappear again for the night. I mean, what? Do you hear this?"

"Overspills," Michelle muttered.

"Huh?"

"I think I've told you before. It was my mom's word. Some people have an excess in them. Energy. Passion. Call it what you will. And it spills over into other areas."

"That's a terrible excuse."

"Whatever. It just is. It's the trade-off. I'm attracted to the Everest climber, and Everest climbers can be crazy. I would never climb Everest myself, but at the same time finding someone like me seems so...*vanilla*, so boring. I couldn't stand it."

This stung. Alison tightened her lips, stared unblinking at Michelle. *Was I that boring?* she wanted to ask.

Yet how much had collected in her over the years, oozing together— memories with thoughts, thoughts with assumptions, assumptions with urges, all festering in places even she'd not been able to reach? That is, until she'd nearly collided with that car and pulled squealing to a stop, engine rumbling, her vision blurred and that terrible, heavy buzz of *something* accosting her, like a possessing spirit, trembling her deepest recesses. Her Core.

The Hive looked like nothing: a normal street intersection. But that was the mask it wore.

"Okay, I'll shut up about this," Alison said. "For now. But first I'm going to tell you something."

"Uh oh. What?"

Just then, Teri reappeared, notepad in hand. "Aaand, are we ready?"

▭

Nowadays, Michelle was pretty much always up at this hour, so wakefulness was not the issue. It was breaking the Routine, or, more specifically, Brian's Routine. *Haven't eaten together in three nights now.* Why was *that* so catastrophic? And plus, how different was your spouse at any given dinner? At least the whisky had turned to wine, three glasses being the limit—though there were the "Fuck It" nights when he barreled ahead through the whole bottle.

But tonight, her husband's indulgence served her well. Brian had been out cold for several hours, Michelle just staring at him for what felt like the same amount of time before deciding to just *go*, to check out this place that had tickled her curiosity—according to Google, just a random intersection in the Yumela foothills—all the while not really knowing why.

She supposed it was the subtle rebellion: the twin thrills of sneaking-out—which she'd never experienced as a goody-goody teenager, still pretending to be totally straight—and the fact that it was connected to Alison, who Brian had never liked, calling her everything from a pompous hipster to "that ostrich."

You were her first taste of pussy, Shelly, Brian said once. *And she's probably not gotten over you. You know that, right?*

Driving, Michelle shuddered any time she imagined Brian waking to see she wasn't there. Talk about a break in Routine. She was risking all of next week on this, she knew, a storm of paranoia, put-downs, of prickly discomfort. A physical strike here and there, though those had gotten far less frequent.

She tightened her grip on the steering wheel. Her lower back and stomach muscles ached from her taut posture. Dark neighborhoods rolled by, empty though they still felt busy, as if shadow-children were romping in their own summer play.

Alison, she thought, *what am I doing?*

"It's not exactly...real," Alison had said at the café the other day.

Apparently, this "hive," as she called it, could be better "felt" without distraction, and with time: "like acclimating to a temperature," she'd said. Though she'd been quick to add that that was an imperfect analogy.

"I don't know what it is," Alison went on. "I researched it and didn't find anything specifically unusual about the area itself. I did come across a message board where an ex-Yumela cop mentioned the police nickname for the intersection—the 'Crashpoint.' Because of higher rates of accidents there. I didn't verify this, but I don't doubt it."

Of course, Michelle had pressed with the follow-up of *Why?*, until something appeared in Alison's eyes: a sudden awareness. A flood of conscience that only drove Michelle's curiosity.

"Nevermind," Alison said. "I'm gonna stop. I'm sorry I even brought it up."

Michelle crossed her arms. "No, wait, you can't just *not* tell me. After all that."

Alison shook her head. She glanced furtively away, appearing to avoid further eye contact—potential weakness to exploit.

"It's irresponsible of me," Alison muttered.

"What is?"

"Telling you."

Anger flickered, deep within. "Telling me *what?*"

Alison sat forward. "Please. I don't want you getting hurt." Then, sitting back, she added: "Or anyone."

Anyone—like Brian?

If only to salvage anything good in that catch-up, Michelle dropped the subject, and the two had wound down their decidedly awkward lunch, punctuated by half the same hug that had begun it.

But Michelle had gotten enough: "Crashpoint." Yumela foothills. And in the dead of that night, she'd Googled it alongside certain keywords. She'd found the message board, on Reddit. The intersection in question, as far as she could tell, was Drummer Street and Baul Canyon Boulevard, about forty minutes from her with traffic.

Without traffic, she discovered, it was about twenty minutes.

She was now on Baul Canyon, ascending slowly toward the black moon-traced mountains. This area was more rustic. More trees, greater spaces between the houses. No other cars.

Then, the lonely traffic lights at Drummer and Baul Canyon greeted her with a bright green eye. Approaching, she slowed to a crawl before coming to idle in the center of the intersection.

Okay.

Michelle breathed.

Now what?

▭

In fact, the call didn't wake her. Alison was already up, draining what she hoped was the last of that night's beer. She was scrolling her newsfeed when she started at the buzz, and the insistent unknown number now demanding attention.

Four rings in, she answered. "Hello?"

"She's left." The voice was tired, restrained, but cutting. She recognized it right away.

"Brian?"

"Yes." There was a distant, rushing quality to his voice, as if he were outside—or driving. "You know it's me."

The anger rose in Alison, a distant chorus of harsh, wordless voices. She could almost feel the dilation of every vessel. The brightening pulse of that radioactive Core.

"How do you have my number?" she said. "You force Michelle to give it to you?"

"Fuck you. Listen, this is fucking *serious*. She was here this evening. She got into bed with me. But then I wake up and the fucking bed is fucking *empty*."

Alison gritted her teeth, tried to calm herself. He wasn't asking where she went. Maybe because he already knew.

"You guys hung out a few days ago," he continued. "She's been weirdly distant since then. I mean, she's been distant anyway 'cause she's always fucking 'working,' but this has been different."

Possibilities paraded across her mind. She'd stopped herself that day, telling Michelle about the Hive. It struck her as patently irresponsible to spread information about something she really knew nothing about, something that might represent a breach of the unknowable into the known.

It's sticky. That's what Alison remembered about the place. It was sticky, yes. And it caught the debris that passed through it.

Debris like—

"Well?" Brian snapped. "What you got to say? What did you do to her?'"

Do?

"She's not here," Alison said. *Does Brian know my address, too?*

"I know she's not there," he said, with all the terrible confidence Alison needed to figure he *did* know where she was. That maybe he'd picked up intel somewhere else, or, God, somehow installed spyware on her phone to track her movements, which she'd heard of people doing.

In a swell of defiance that twitched her hand and tensed her neck muscles till they ached, Alison said, "Fuck off. I don't owe you anything."

She hung up and, without flushing the toilet, hurried to dress. She had told Michelle about the Reddit board. Gave her, maybe, just enough to ignite her curiosity, to get snooping, to fan whatever embers had to be flitting around her friend's own heated depths.

Alison was out the door, but not before retrieving the gun from her nightstand, and making sure it had a full chamber.

▭

The journey to the intersection was so blurry Alison considered it may not have been too different from driving drunk. She thought constantly about Michelle, about what kind of emotional chain reaction that one catch-up lunch might've triggered. *Not your fault*, a voice tried to tell her. After all, that Michelle would even follow up on Alison's scant babbles about the Hive just proved how trapped the woman felt. How powerless.

How desperate.

Driving faster than she ever had, Alison did notice one thing: the seemingly total absence of other cars, strange even for 3:00 a.m. She'd expected at least one or two other lonely headlights. But rather, it felt like she had entered some dead alternate dimension.

Several blocks into Baul Canyon Boulevard, and she spotted the car up ahead, parked in the middle of the intersection with Drummer. Though the car faced away from her, she could see the headlights were on, the faint plumes of exhaust wisping up into the night. Closing in, she made out the bumper sticker—CO-EXIST.

No sign of Brian that she could see. Good. She'd beat him here.

Hopefully.

Alison parked, killed her ignition and jumped out.

"Michelle?" she called. "Is that you?"

Of course it's her. The windows were all black. Maybe tinted? Nonetheless, she thought she could *feel* Michelle, even hear her in a bizarre way, like a fine, comforting hum.

Yet what she couldn't feel or hear were the Noises and the Voices she'd encountered before, the angry, wasp-buzzing that had led her to call this area the Hive in the first place. It was quiet now. But, at the same time, there was something palpably off.

She looked into the driver's side window. Michelle was there, pale, face tilted toward her. Gone from her eyes was the Gilded Glaze—this was a fucking *Zombie* Gaze. A Dead Gaze.

"Michelle!"

Alison rapped on the glass, then yanked open the door. Something made her stop—and it wasn't the new pair of arriving headlights.

She stared into the car, dumbstruck.

Nearby, a car door slammed. "Hey!"

Brian. The rapid patter of footsteps approaching. Alison didn't acknowledge him, still fixated as she was on the sight before her, that almost made her wet herself.

It was as if the inside of Michelle's car had been filled with black sand, or some dark soot had been pumped into the car. She could see nothing of the dashboard, the steering wheel, the clutch, the windows... nor could she even make out much of Michelle's lower half, like it had been partially consumed by shadow. By some void.

"*Hey!*"

Brian came close enough to glimpse Michelle. Alison managed to wrangle enough presence of mind to anticipate the reaction, to ready her hand on the gun in her jacket pocket.

"Shelly? *Shelly?*" Instantly Brian whipped around toward Alison. He hadn't changed much—he looked thicker, redder in complexion and less hair. "The *fuck* is going on here? What happened to her?"

Brian advanced. Alison drew the gun and pointed.

"*Don't,*" Alison said. "Do. *Not.*"

He stuttered to a stop. His fingers danced at his sides, like windchimes in the gust of so many harried thoughts about what to do next.

Then, just behind Brian, it rose—a motion of pure shadow, like a black sheet billowing up.

Pale arms lashed out, seized Brian's throat and pulled him back. Michelle: groaning, heaving, animated by some mania beyond words and which the atrophied athlete in Brian could not resist. In one hand she squeezed his throat and with the other dug her thumb into Brian's eye—"Ahhhhoooww *FUCK what the F*—?" before Michelle slammed him to the ground, hard enough the man's head bounced twice on the pavement and Alison thought she heard a grotesque *crack* and a pathetic pained moan.

Though Brian looked stunned, his motions that much clumsier, he still appeared conscious as Michelle drove her teeth upon her husband's face and, like some ravenous ghoul, began wrenching and tearing away strips of flesh, the blood-spray hardly making it as far as the screams unleashed to the darkness.

Alison watched, gun trembling in her hand, though in that second she was a million miles from it, arrested by the vision there of a giant shadow-figure hovering around Michelle, long arms and legs and all writhing as she writhed, moving as she moved. Like the thing had some symbiotic connection with her. Like it wore Michelle as a pair of physical teeth.

Using her, Alison thought, to rip its way into this world.

Brian kept screaming. Michelle's motions became almost bird-like, a vulture stringing up tissue in its beak. Brian's legs spasmed.

Nearby houselights began blinking on.

Alison's senses came rushing back to her. "Michelle!" she cried. "*Stop!* Get *off! Get off!*"

But even as those words left her mouth, they carried with them a scent of falsity, like she was some B-actor, reciting the script of her conscience, ignoring the deeper satisfaction she felt in that pulsing Core in her.

Yet when the blood pooled and pulped and Brian's screams died down, and when Michelle turned and looked at her with that beard of gore and those busy-yet-vacant eyes, hovering over the chalice of mush once Brian's face, Alison knew she had to do it. That if she didn't, she might be next.

"Michelle—"

Her friend cocked her head, almost like a listening dog, then moved toward her, eyes somehow emptier by the second, all of Michelle imploding, collapsing into bottoms beneath bottoms.

"Stop please—!"

The Michelle-thing lunged. And so the streams of Duty and Delirium met at Alison's index finger—and she pulled the trigger.

It was a straight shot, the few rounds at the range compensating for her shaking. The gunshot thundered down the canyon and the bullet plowed into Michelle's temple, crumpling her almost intimately over Brian's body.

Alison just stood, queasy and quivering. Michelle lay there, blown apart and motionless. Never to move again. Never to speak. The sheer *finality* of it—

More activity stirred in the neighborhood. Sirens rang in the distance.

She heard them now: the Noises and the Voices were growing again, rising to refill this space. They swarmed about, wasp-buzzing, homeless once more. She didn't exactly know what the "stickiness" was here, what the Hive actually *was*. By whatever eye she could perceive it, much of it remained obscured beyond the blizzard of human refuse... the scraps of rage and revulsion whipping about it, all emptied from so many, over God knew how many years.

Overspills.

She knew, though, that *it* knew. That it was a patchwork intelligence. Some formless form. A living coil of emotional flypaper.

The Noises and Voices grew closer. Constricting. Descending on her. An assault against which the gun in her hand was now a lump of useless metal.

A haze darkened over her. That Core pulsed. Brighter.

She thought she saw Brian's leg twitch—*he still alive?*

One thing was for certain: the sirens were growing closer.

More meat.

About the Author

Born and raised in Los Angeles, **MIKE ROBINSON** is the award-winning author of ten books, including the literary horror trilogy *Enigma of Twilight Falls* and *The Prince of Earth*, a Maxy Award Finalist. He is also a freelance book editor, and an active screenwriter and producer. In between, he hikes—preferably with his two dogs—swims, draws and tries to learn the didgeridoo.

S[P]LASH!
ANNA TABORSKA

Marina had been exploring the reef ever since she could remember and knew every coral colony and every tentacled anemone by heart. She knew the crevices in which the octopuses hid, and under which rocks to find the tastiest crabs. She loved drifting with the tide and diving into the crystal depths. But things had been changing lately. The water was warmer than it used to be, and the corals were blanching and dying. Gone were the delicate damselfish, the graceful angelfish and the hundreds of other dazzling fish species that had once formed part of this complex ecosystem. The coral reef was silent. The crabs that had fed on the fish were gone.

Marina had little choice but to move to one of the other islands. Problem was, the other islands were busier, which meant noise and dirt, pollution and trouble. She dawdled and pondered, and took her time getting to the nearest island. Much of it was littered with ugly little houses and a couple of even uglier administrative shacks.

By the time she'd had a good look around and found a quiet cove, away from prying eyes, it was late afternoon. She rested a while, then dived to inspect the reef. The sight that greeted her shook her deeply. The ghostly, ossified corpses of corals protruded from the sand like broken teeth. A solitary wrasse hung listlessly in the water like a lost soul. A quick inspection of the sandy floor revealed that the crabs, too, had left or perished. Marina drifted for a while, wondering what to do next.

"Hey!" The voice broke through her troubled thoughts, frightening her and sending her diving out of sight. "Hey, where you going?!"

Marina swam fast, disappearing behind a cluster of rocks. She could hear the man calling out to her to come back. Cautiously, she peered out from her hiding place. She could see the man approaching the water, searching for her.

He was like no one she'd ever seen before. Tall, slim, muscular. With brown hair and golden, sun-kissed skin. There was an air of confidence and sophistication about the man which the hard-working, tired-looking locals lacked. Marina wondered where he'd come from and what had brought him to the islands. His voice was low and strangely soothing, despite the touch of agitation with which he called out after her. Her fear subsided, and Marina observed with curiosity and growing interest as the man stood and scoured the cove for her. As he craned his head, Marina watched in fascination as a little blood vessel pulsed in the man's neck. After a while he turned and walked away. Marina felt a pang of disappointment then, and a strange and unfamiliar longing in the pit of her stomach.

▭

That night the man couldn't sleep. He kept thinking about the girl he'd seen in the cove. She couldn't have been much older than sixteen or seventeen. He'd only caught a momentary glimpse of her before she swam away, but he was hooked. There was something irresistible about her pale, radiant beauty, and he knew he had to have her.

The man turned from side to side in his bed, fighting his demons. He'd told himself time and time again: no more women. Not for a while, at least. Not while the police were still actively looking for him. He'd made a mistake before, got careless. Not taken enough time to plan his last conquest; not buried her deep enough. Acted on impulse.

That's why he'd had to go off the grid; why he was having to hide out on this godforsaken island. And he'd been doing okay—relaxing, lying low, chilling out, taking it easy. Until the girl. Until she'd triggered that familiar longing in the pit of his stomach. Now all he could think about was the feel of her skin giving way beneath his blade, splitting open like a tender fruit, her life erupting then draining from her with each crimson slash.

The man lost his battle with himself and left the fisherman's hut he'd rented as soon as dawn broke. He spent the morning wandering around the village, looking for the girl, but there was no sign of her. The hungry feeling in his guts was growing, and he had to satiate it. Tired and frustrated, he headed for the secluded cove, intending to settle down on the warm sand and wait.

Marina had been swimming beyond the outlying rock formation, occasionally diving to search fruitlessly for crabs or glancing towards the beach. She knew instinctively that the man was coming back, and the feeling of anticipation tinged with yearning was almost unbearable. She was feeling lightheaded and increasingly desperate.

Just when she thought she couldn't wait any longer, she spied the man approaching from a distance. As she observed from her hiding place, he looked around the small beach, then headed towards the water. He stopped a little way from the waterline, and scanned the cove. Marina watched intently; the little artery in the man's neck started to throb, betraying his own tension.

Slowly Marina pushed herself away from the rocks and swam out towards the shore.

"Hey!" The man had spotted her and was waving. "Hey, over here!" He beckoned to Marina. He looked relieved and excited at the same time.

Marina could smell a predatory scent emanating from him and hesitated for the briefest moment. Then she swam towards him.

"Hi." The man smiled, showing a full mouth of healthy teeth. "What's your name?"

Marina smiled shyly, drifting just beyond the shallows.

"Why don't you come out and join me?" The man's velvet tones belied the predatory scent that was now coming off him in waves. Marina smiled again and moved a little way back out to sea. The man's smile faltered—just for a moment—then he was grinning again. "Okay," he called out. "You've twisted my arm, I'm coming in."

▭

The man stripped down to his bathing shorts. It had been far too long, and he couldn't wait any longer. He glanced over his shoulder, checking that they were alone in the cove. Reassured, he walked out into the water, wincing a little at the difference in temperature between it and the air. The thought of how the expression in her eyes would change when he wrapped his hands around her slender neck propelled him into the cool water. He would squeeze until she passed out, then drag her out of the water, into a sheltered spot he'd picked out earlier, resuscitate her, and start all over again. There was an innocence about the girl, and he would take his time robbing her of it—again and again. He waded out as far as he could, and when the water reached his chest, he started to swim towards the waiting girl.

▭

Marina welcomed the man with open arms. This close, his scent was sweet, intoxicating, and Marina finally understood the yearning she'd been feeling since she first laid eyes on him. As the man reached for Marina's neck, his aroma intensified and the blood vessel in his neck began to visibly pulse. Marina smiled again—this time a wide, open-mouthed smile—revealing two full, concentric sets of razor-sharp teeth. Then the throbbing artery, and much of the man's neck, disappeared in a vibrant fountain of bright red blood, and Marina knew that she'd never go hungry again. The crabs may have disappeared, along with her coral playground, but she realised they were only ever a poor substitute for the marrow she could chew out of men's bones.

Marina slashed and mauled, devoured and rejoiced in her new food source, consuming considerably more than her own bodyweight. When she was done, there was nothing left bar a pair of tattered swimming trunks and a large patch of crimson water. With a joyful flip of her glorious, glimmering aquamarine tail, and a resounding *splash!*, Marina sank happily into the depths.

About the Author

ANNA TABORSKA is a filmmaker, screenwriter, and British Fantasy Award- and Bram Stoker Award-nominated author of short story collections *For Those who Dream Monsters* (Mortbury Press, 2013, 2020), *Shadowcats* (Black Shuck Books, 2019) and *Bloody Britain* (Shadow Publishing, 2020). Her debut collection won the Dracula Society's Children of the Night Award. Anna has written and directed five films and worked on TV productions such as the BBC series "Auschwitz: the Nazis and 'The Final Solution'".

"I'M JUST so angry all the time," said Jane. "I'm hoping this will help, at least a little."

Michael nodded and tapped a few keys on his computer. "That's why we're here. Now, you were asking about our 'Beat the Shit Out of a Virtual Reality Simulation of the Politician of Your Choice With a Baseball Bat' package, right?"

Jane lowered her eyes. "Yes."

"You seem a bit uncomfortable. Don't be. Beating a politician to a pulp in real life is morally wrong, not to mention illegal, but there's nothing wrong with blowing off some steam in our simulation. Nobody actually gets hurt and you'll feel better afterward. Have you selected a politician?"

"I've narrowed it down. There are so many to choose from."

"If I might make a suggestion, we've just completed our Tod Crez simulation."

"Don't you mean—?"

"For our purposes here, I mean Tod Crez. We don't want lawyers getting rich off our little business, do we? Anyway, it took longer than the others because it was such an unpleasant task for our programmers.

Imagine having to look at images of him all day." Michael shuddered. "Our on-site psychological counsellor certainly put in some overtime."

"But it will actually feel like I'm beating the shit out of him with a baseball bat? I'm not interested in just playing a video game."

Michael smiled. "You'll feel like you're really there. Now, there are limits to what technology can accomplish. The sniveling and the punchability are fully intact. I cannot in good conscience say that our simulation completely captures his sheer wretchedness. I mean, it's ninety-five percent there, but there's this *blecch* factor to the man that doesn't quite transfer to the virtual environment. A repulsiveness that makes you cringe with every word that comes out of his grotesque mouth. Still, it's recognizably him, and we do guarantee that you'll be satisfied or your money back."

"Then let's do it!"

As Jane put on the VR headset, she was instantly transported into an alley. She looked all around and took a couple of steps forward—it felt like she was really there! She held a baseball bat and gave it a practice swing. It genuinely felt like swinging a real bat.

Tod Crez walked into the alley, chuckling.

Their eyes met.

"No! Don't hurt me!" he wailed. "Take my wife and daughters instead!"

He turned and fled. Jane hurried after him—

—and then was back in the real world.

"Sorry," said Michael. "We only designed the alley. Our programmers imbued the simulation with all of the qualities of the real man, which unfortunately includes the cowardice. We'll reset and try again. Back in three, two, one..."

Jane was back in the alley. Tod Crez sneered at her.

"Why are you so upset?" he asked. "Life is precious—well, I mean, before it's born, obviously—and we stole those Supreme Court seats for *you*. Now you don't have to make difficult decisions. You can smile and leave that part to us!"

Jane swung the baseball bat. It struck the simulation right in the face. Clear ooze splattered onto Jane's virtual shirt.

"What the hell?" she cried out. "He's *secreting!*"

"Exactly like the real Tod Crez!" the disembodied voice of Michael informed her.

"No, no, no, this is just gross. End session!"

Jane took off the headset.

Michael frowned. "I'm sorry. We try to make the experience as realistic as possible, and truthfully, there is no satisfying encounter when it comes to Tod Crez. The Brent Kavanogg simulation has our highest customer satisfaction score, and I'll be happy to give it to you for free."

Jane accepted the offer, and it was delightful.

About the Author

JEFF STRAND is the Bram Stoker and Splatterpunk Award-winning author of over fifty books, including *My Pretties, Autumn Bleeds Into Winter*, and *Clowns vs. Spiders*. He lives in Chattanooga with his wife and gigantic cat.

See his website, Gleefully Macabre, at:
https://jeffstrand.wordpress.com/.

Sam sat at the corner of the Watering Hole's back patio and peered out across the rolling hills of Butler, Tennessee, as daylight faded. He was already dehydrated from being out in the heat for most of the day, and the salted peanuts at his table had left his mouth as dry as a petrified hunk of wood. After several minutes alone with only Johnny Cash's "Hurt" echoing through the speakers to keep him company, he was relieved when a waitress stepped out of the air-conditioned bar and headed for his table. Wearing a bit too much makeup and a T-shirt that likely would have fit her better when she was twelve, she set a frosted mug of Tennessee-brewed IPA on his table and stepped back like a magician that had just made a dove appear from thin air. Sam took a pull from the glass and smiled as the ice-cold beer washed away the dry tickle at the back of his throat.

"Thanks, sweetheart." The words fell from his lips with just enough drawl to hopefully be charming. "Been a long day."

"Not to mention a hot one." The waitress's eyes shot left and right, taking in the otherwise empty patio. "I know we've got umbrellas out here and all, but it's still hotter than hell. You sure you don't want to come inside with the A/C?"

"A little claustrophobic in there tonight." Sam hoped he didn't sound antisocial or worse, like a wimp. "The game's got your little 'watering hole' pretty packed, and I've been around a good forty or fifty construction workers all day. Kind of enjoying the peace and quiet." He leaned in slyly. "Not to mention, the fine company."

The waitress shot him a flash of a smile, a twinkle in her sky-blue eyes. "Yeah. We're usually slow on Tuesdays. Like you, I'm guessing, a lot of out-of-towners like you who want to see the game."

"Out-of-towner?" Sam splayed his fingers across his chest. "What gave me away?"

"Butler is a tiny little flyspeck of a town. I may not know everyone by name, but people I've never seen before are few and far between." She grabbed a damp rag from the empty patio bar and wiped his table down though it wasn't the least bit dirty. "So, you here to work on the dam like all the rest?"

"Something like that." He rubbed his knuckles at the collar of his shirt. "I work for the company that's financing all the dam repairs."

"And you're here to inspect?"

"Like I said, something like that. Drove in from Knoxville yesterday and crashing at the Americourt Hotel for a few days till I'm all done." He crinkled his nose. "Not exactly five-star accommodations, but it'll do."

Her mouth quirked to one side. "A lot worse places than that you could have ended up. Heck, my cousin works night shift there on weekends."

Sam held his hands before him palms out in faux surrender. "Hey, any place where I can cook my own waffle in the morning is fine by me." He took a sip of his beer. "That's the thing about contract work, I guess. Sometimes it lands you in Memphis…"

"And sometimes it lands you in Butler." The waitress shot him a half-apologetic smile. "So, stranger. What's your name?"

"Sam," he said. "Sam Mabry."

"Donna." She glanced toward the door leading back into the bar. "So, Sam Mabry, how long are you in town?"

"Probably a couple more days." He cracked his neck. "Hoping to make it back to Knoxville by the weekend."

She cocked her head to one side and smiled. "Not feeling the whole Butler vibe?"

"It's not that," Sam said." Just miss my own bed."

"I get that." She raised an inquisitive brow. "Got a girl back in Knoxville you need to get back to as well?"

"Not at the moment." Sam took another pull from his beer. "Life's been a little on the busy side of late."

"A real shame." The sky continued to darken and the crescent moon, already high in the sky, appeared from behind a cloud. Donna visibly shivered, a worried look flashing across her features as if she'd just remembered she left the oven on.

"You okay?" Sam asked.

"I'm fine."

"You're shivering." He rested the back of his fingers on the back of her arm. "You have a fever or something?"

She pulled her arm away, maybe a little too fast. "I said I'm fine." Her perturbed expression shifted quickly into one of contrition. "Sorry. Just remembered something." She turned to go back inside, but stopped midstride to peek back at Sam. "Ummm...this may sound strange, but do yourself a favor and don't pick up any hitchhikers while you're in Butler."

"What, you have car jackers here or something?"

"Something like that. Just trust me. You see someone on the side of the road, just keep driving and don't look back. There are some around these parts that don't take too kindly to strangers."

"What about you, Miss Donna?" Sam inclined his head to one side and grinned playfully.

"What about me?"

"Do you take kindly to strangers?"

She bit her lip. "We've been talking a fair bit, Sam Mabry, so I don't know if we qualify as such anymore."

"I like the way you think."

"Good." The pink of her cheeks intensified. "I get off in a few minutes. Stick around and I'll buy you a drink."

Sam raised his glass. "I've already got a drink, courtesy of a lovely young lady I met earlier, but I'd be up for an after-dark tour of Butler, with the right tour guide, of course."

Donna crossed her arms and rolled her eyes playfully. "Why don't we just start with a drink and see what happens from there?"

Sam nodded and let out a quiet chuckle. "All right. A drink it is."

"Now, don't you go anywhere. I have to turn over a couple tables to the other server and need to settle up with management before I clock out. You good for a minute?"

Sam examined his mug, still half full, and swirled the frothy liquid inside. "This should hold me till you get back."

"All right." She took in a deep breath. "See you in a few."

As Donna disappeared back into the bar, a humid breeze played across the patio. The cheers of the crowd inside punctuated by the clink of bottles being pitched in the trash from inside warred with the cicadas and occasional bird call as the sky finally went dark. The Man in Black had been replaced by Ronnie Milsap's "Smoky Mountain Rain," a song Sam hadn't heard in a decade or two. Hints of jasmine and honeysuckle filled his senses, and he closed his eyes, finally enjoying for a moment a day that had otherwise been hot, sticky, and miserable as he awaited the return of the lovely Donna. He'd come out to the Watering Hole simply for a beer to drown his doldrums, but the evening was definitely looking up.

"Well, hello there, handsome."

Sam's eyes jerked open to find another woman standing at his table. Mid-thirties and slim, she was dressed in a green-and-white gingham housedress and flats. Her dark hair, pulled back from her face in a classy updo, stood in stark contrast to her pale complexion. Her overly blushed cheeks and lips painted crimson were at odds with the simplicity of her dress. Sam couldn't take his eyes off the mysterious woman. From her high cheekbones to those piercing green eyes to the cut of her collarbone, Sam found his eyes wandering down to her left hand.

The diamond on her ring finger wasn't much to look at, but it was there.

"My apologies," she whispered with something like a quiet snicker. "I didn't mean to frighten you."

"It's...all right," Sam stammered. "It's just... I didn't hear you come up."

"I was sitting by myself over in the corner." She bit her lip. "Wasn't trying to eavesdrop, but it's not that large a patio."

Large enough that I didn't notice you sitting ten feet away?

She drew a step closer. "Did I hear you say you're visiting our little town?" Another step. "A contractor for the folks working on the dam?"

"That's right." Sam motioned for her to join him at his high top. "This is so weird. You were out here the whole time? How did I possibly miss you?"

"You were talking to the nice waitress when I ventured out here." She pulled out a stool and took a seat. "Couldn't stand the smoke inside. Thought I'd get some fresh air."

"They're letting people smoke in there?" Sam craned his neck in the direction of the bar. "Thought they outlawed that years ago."

The woman shrugged, unconcerned. "What can I say? Butler isn't like everywhere else."

"Your hometown, I'm guessing."

"Yes and no," she said. "Been gone a while. Butler's not the same as I remember, but I find myself drawn back here from time to time."

"What's your name?" Sam asked.

"Elizabeth," she said, "but everybody around here calls me Lizzie."

"Lizzie it is, then." Sam took a sip of his beer and remembered that Donna, who seemed a pretty sure thing, was due back in just a few minutes.

Oh well, he considered. *Sometimes you just roll the dice.*

"So, is everyone in Butler this friendly?"

Lizzie smiled. "I've introduced myself to more than a few strangers over the years."

"I'm Sam," he offered, violating his usual rule of waiting for the woman to ask. "Only in town this week as far as I know. Hoping we can get everything with the dam repairs sorted so I can get home by Saturday. Not much else going on, though."

"Working on the *dam*." She said the last word as if it were in fact the curse word and not merely the sound-alike that made children giggle.

"Not too fond of the dam, huh?" Sam studied the woman, brow furrowed, his body pulling away instinctively from the woman, if only by a millimeter.

"They even moved the graves, you know." Her words sent a chill up Sam's spine. "Every last one."

"Graves?" Sam asked. "What are you talking about?"

"When they flooded Old Butler, back in '48 on this very night. You're here working on the dam. I just figured you'd have read up on the history of the town."

"I know a piece here and there, at least the pieces I need to know."

"Did you know they relocated the whole town? Over a hundred families, fifty or so businesses, churches, schools...and 1,281 graves." Lizzie's grim smile did nothing to quell the gnawing at the pit of Sam's stomach. "Joke used to be that they left no stone unturned."

"Over a thousand, huh?" Sam did his best to inject a bit of levity back into the conversation. "Sounds like the government really went out of its way to look out for the community."

Whatever vestige of a smile that remained on Lizzie's face vanished. "That's one way of looking at it, I suppose."

"Now that I think about it, at the beginning of our brief, they did say that Old Butler flooded every few years anyway. That's one of the reasons they decided to do what they did. The government moved everybody to safety, gave them a fresh start in a new place. What's wrong with that?"

"Oh, they didn't move everybody." Her expression bordering on disdain, Lizzie's eyes bored through him. "There was a man named Tom Roan, died in the flash flood of 1940 when the creek that bore his name rose up and came a-lookin' for him."

"Wouldn't he have been one of the graves they moved?" Sam asked.

Lizzie's lips grew tight. "Tom had no grave. They never found his body, you see. Wherever he ended up after the flood, they just left him there to rot at the bottom of their lake, all in the name of progress."

"But that was eight years before." Hair rose on Sam's neck and his scalp crawled like he was covered in ants. "Like you said, they didn't flood the town till 1948."

Her eyes narrowed. "Eight years. Eight minutes. It's all the same."

"All the same? To who?"

Lizzie rose from the table and paced along the edge of the patio. "The people around here say his widow went a little crazy after he died. Refused to leave the house Tom built even years after he disappeared. Locked herself inside and raised a 12-gauge at anyone who dared peek in the windows. When the waters came in '48, that was it for her." She let out a quiet sigh. "At least that's how the story goes after all these years."

"Is the story true?" Sam asked.

"Folks around here think so. Lizzie is a legend in Butler. She even has a bridge named after her down on Roan Creek."

"Wait. Her name is Lizzie? Like yours?"

"Mom named me Elizabeth." Lizzie shot Sam a half-amused glance. "But thanks to my dad, I've been called Lizzie since the day I was born."

"And it doesn't creep you out that you're named after the town's legendary crazy chick?"

"The question is..." The slowly returning amusement in her gaze evaporated. "Does it creep *you* out, Sam?"

He backed up and punted, the only course of action that made any sense. "Honestly, she sounds like quite the devoted wife." Sam eyed the door to the bar and wondered how much longer Donna was going to be. "Not to mention, grief does strange things to people, I hear."

"Till death do us part. Isn't that what we all stand up and say in our white dresses and dark suits in front of friends and family and God?"

"I suppose." Sam's eyes dropped just enough to notice the rise and fall of her chest, her breaths coming fast with emotion. "So, what are you doing here all by yourself at closing?"

"By myself?" She pursed her lips, her eyebrows rising in question. "I thought I was here with you." Her tone shifted subtly, and the adrenaline pumping through Sam's body dropped a notch or two. Suddenly, the strange woman was flirting with him, no bones about it. Donna was due back any minute, but there was just something about this Elizabeth that pushed all of his buttons at once. Fear and excitement and lust all warred for control of his thoughts. But in the end...

"I've got to tell you, Lizzie. I've been in a lot of bars and met a lot of women, but yours is the oddest pick up I've ever heard. Do you always lead with tales of flooded towns and drowned husbands?"

"Just figured it would interest you, you know, considering why you're here." Her lips turned up in a perfect smile. "Plus, I prefer to be...unforgettable."

Sam's gaze drifted down her body. He found himself wondering what she might be hiding beneath the loose-fitting green-and-white gingham dress. "You are that." He noted again the sparkle on her left ring finger. "I've gotta ask."

She held up her hand and slipped the ring from her finger and dropped it into the pocket of her house dress. "Ancient history. That's been over for a long time." She looked away. "Still, I wear it to remember."

Sam rose, looking again at the door leading to the bar.

Last chance, Donna.

"You keep looking to the door for a woman when you already have one standing right in front of you." Her eyes slid closed, and the wafting jasmine and honeysuckle redoubled in Sam's mind. "Don't you like what you see?"

"Of course I do. It's just that—"

"Don't think so much, Sam. Just act."

"Act..." Sam pulled in a deep breath, the hypnotic fragrance coupled with Lizzie's unavoidable gaze driving out any thought beyond how to possess the mysterious woman. "You want to get out of here, then?'

"Not yet." She drew close to him, so close he could feel the warmth of her flesh. "I want you to kiss me."

Sam's brow furrowed. "Here?" His eyes threatened to return to the door leading inside, but her fingers at his chin brought his gaze back to hers.

"No." She pointed to her neck. "Here." She ran her fingers past her collarbone and rested her trembling fingertips at the hint of cleavage visible at the top of her dress. "Here." Her smoldering gaze filled his vision. "Everywhere."

Sam glanced left and right, confirmed they were alone, and then, without another moment's hesitation, pulled the woman into him. Uncontrolled lust overtook his body like a gasoline thrown on a fire. His mouth on hers, they explored each other with hands and fingers and lips and tongues. One moment they stood intertwined by the table he'd occupied for the last hour, and the next he pushed the strange woman in the gingham dress against the outside wall of the bar. Shivers traveled up and down his spine, the heat radiating off his body more than matched by the feverish warmth of her bare skin.

Sam was far from anyone's example of prudish, but such public passion lay far beyond anything that was his norm. Inescapable lust and desire ruled his every thought and action as the two of them wrestled as one, Lizzie playing his body like a virtuoso musician with a shiny new violin.

And then, just as their shared heat hit a literal fever pitch, Lizzie's body went suddenly...

Cold.

Sam's eyes opened to find Lizzie's flushed skin replaced by pale, colorless flesh, her beautiful baby blues with all but empty sockets, and her well-coiffed tresses with bedraggled hair filled with weeds and crawling insects. He pushed the bloated corpse away, struggling to break away from her suddenly cool lips, but she only pulled him in tighter, her sludge-covered tongue probing his mouth like a rotten strawberry covered in mold. He tried to scream, but his efforts only opened his throat to the rush of tepid water, muck, and silt that flowed past his vocal cords and filled his lungs with the turbid flow of Roan Creek. Caught in Elizabeth Roan's icy grip, the last thing Sam Mabry saw was the neon sign blinking ironically in the window of the bar.

"Ladies Night" in vibrant pink and cool blue burned onto his retina as the remainder of the world faded to black.

***

Donna returned to the patio with a pitcher of beer in one hand and a remote control for the house speakers in the other. Fixed up to the best of her ability, she glanced over at the table where the good-looking contractor named Sam Mabry had been sitting. She'd been gone less than fifteen minutes and had gotten the distinct impression she'd be spending the rest of the evening charming the pants off the handsome out-of-towner. In her few minutes away, she'd allowed her mind to wander down some familiar yet dangerous paths.

Would he have the first clue how to properly kiss a woman? Was he just looking for a fun night? Or maybe two? If she played her cards right, could he be her ticket out of Butler?

Hell, does he like kids?

Because little Jimmy starts kindergarten next year, and if kids are a no-go...

All that, and now, he was gone.

"Well, shit," she muttered. "Another one bites the dust."

She wandered over to the table to collect the half-empty mug and coaster from Sam Mabry's table. That's when she stepped in the puddle of muddy water by the empty barstool.

"Seriously?" she grunted. "Should have known. It's been another year." Donna rested the pitcher on the table, sat in Sam's recently vacated seat, still warm, and buried her face in her hands. "Dammit,

Lizzie, you usually stick to the roads at the edge of town." She raised her head and stared out into the trees where the crickets and cicadas chirped and whirred and screamed. "And of all nights, why did it have to be tonight? Dammit, this one was cute."

After another minute, she rose from the table, cleared away all evidence that Sam Mabry had ever been there, and mopped up the puddle of silty water before heading back inside to ask to change her schedule to close that night.

If there was a better alibi than a room full of men seeing you come and go all night and then getting in your car to head home, Donna couldn't think of it.

Just before she stepped back through the door, she again peered out into the darkening woods that surrounded the old bar and muttered, "You know, you could have at least waited till he paid his tab."

About the Author

DARIN KENNEDY, doctor-by-day and novelist-by-night, writes and practices medicine in Charlotte, NC. Works include his Fugue & Fable series: *The Mussorgsky Riddle*, *The Stravinsky Intrigue*, and *The Tchaikovsky Finale*; his The Pawn Stratagem series: *Pawn's Gambit*, *Queen's Peril*, and *King's Crisis*; his YA novel, *Carol*; and *The April Sullivan Chronicles*. Find him online at darinkennedy.com.

THE PATRON SAINT
STEVEN VAN PATTEN

THEY SAT across from one another on opposite ends of the center island counter. Five feet of glass mosaic tile stood between them. They sat in silence, eyes downcast, each of them absorbed in their own flavor of shame. An ex-husband who had failed to protect his daughter. An ex-wife who had fallen for a smooth-talking opportunist.

"I'm sorry," Cathy said.

"You're sorry?" Keith mocked. "What exactly are you sorry for? I feel like we have that conversation a lot."

In that moment, his mind flashed back through their sordid history. Their torrid college romance, her initial inability to choose between him and a bad boy drug dealer, a rivalry that ended with the dealer's incarceration and Cathy settling for him.

"You don't understand," Cathy sobbed. "Our baby has a gift."

"A lot of people can fucking sing, Cathy." He was seething. "Some of those people become recording stars. Some of those people become fixtures at their local karaoke spot. So far, to my knowledge, only one has been kidnapped by a record producer who, thanks to current events, is now a wanted pedophile. That particular distinction unfortunately falls to my only daughter, who thanks to her star-fucker mother will probably be dead in a few hours."

"The police said they have leads! She'll probably be fine!"

"After years of therapy and an HBO special about how her mother sold her into sex slavery!" His angry eyes narrowed to slits as he leaned closer to her. "Let me ask you something. Parent to really bad parent. How many times do you think this man has already done things to our child?"

Tears welled up in her eyes. "We had a lifestyle to maintain, and she wanted to be a famous singer. It's all she ever wanted. And you weren't any help! You and your damn restaurant. How is anyone supposed to become famous with you as a father!"

"Only the greatest narcissist in the world would rehash an adolescent insult of how boring my life choices have been while their daughter is probably somewhere being raped!"

"Didn't you hear what I told the police? They're in love!"

"Like he was in love with Cynthia Bradford, that traumatized girl we just watched on the news? Are you serious?"

"I know that bitch, Cynthia! She's just looking for a payday!"

"Get the fuck out of my house!"

"But the police said they'll call you..."

"They're going to call me because after talking to us, they realized that emotionally speaking I'm an adult and you're an evil ten-year-old. But if you don't leave, they won't have to call me because I'll be in holding for finally murdering your ignorant ass! Now get out!"

She sniffed away her sadness as indignation set in. "I don't know who you think you're talking to. I still have people I can call—"

"I still have the restraining order on your brothers and I'm a gun owner with no criminal record, so if you want to lose those jackasses one way or the other, be my guest! Now get out!" Keith stormed out of the kitchen, across his living room, past several shelved 'Best Baker' trophies.

After a moment, she shoved her clutch under her arm and followed him to the front door. "You shouldn't have called the police, Keith. Now, if those cops kill Manuel, you will have just sent another great black man to his grave. And when it happens, I'm gonna get on Twitter and let his fans know about your snitch ass."

"Listening to you is like listening to cancer speak. If I hear anything from the police, I'll text you. Now go." He raised his eyes just enough to see her shadow pass to the other side of the door. Frustrated tears stung his eyes as the door closed.

He took a deep breath and walked back to the kitchen, his haven now that he was a nearly famous Michelin chef and not the insecure twenty-something that he was years ago. Back then, he'd been made to feel lucky that the beautiful brash paramour chose him over much faster and flashier men. Now, he knew the truth: he should have let her go at the first sign of her insatiable materialism and lack of interest in anything outside of social climbing.

As he sat down, his mind began to flash through several significant moments of his child's life. Her first day on Earth at the hospital. Her first word, which oddly enough was 'shoe.' Her first steps. Her first performance in a musical, the brainchild of a rather ambitious fifth-grade teacher. Her first television appearance.

All of these memories were rendered bittersweet for him by Cathy in one way or another. The baby's delivery was a maelstrom of chaos, thanks to Cathy's brothers, who nearly got them all kicked out of the hospital by being drunk and belligerent and openly smoking weed. Her first word was 'shoe' because her mother, devoid of any other intellectual pursuits, spoke of footwear more than anything else. The standing ovation at the end of Kimberly's brilliant fifth-grade performance would serve as the catalyst that would spur Cathy on to pimp their child out in order to make her a famous R&B singer. He actually hadn't been invited to her first TV appearance but caught it at home.

A tremor of hope seemed to shoot through him when the cellphone went off. That hope would morph into fresh anxiety as he looked at the phone before answering. He had ended an argument with a woman who was the worst mistake of his life, only to now have a conversation with the woman who would never forget the worst mistake of his life.

"Mom."

"Keith! Oh my God! Are you okay?"

"I'm not the one who's kidnapped, Mom!"

"Well, I know that! No need to be snippy with me! I told you not to have children with that tramp!" His mother sounded her usual high-strung self. "Are the police there?"

"They just left. They seem to think Manuel has crossed state lines with her, which officially makes it a federal beef. The FBI called while the police were here and said they're doing everything humanly possible to find the two of them."

"Did you speak to that woman?"

"I did. She was here. She's gone now."

"I'd like to slap her across the face. The worst mother I've ever heard of, and I'm stuck with her."

"You're stuck with her?"

"Okay, *we're* stuck with her, but only because you couldn't see it. When she seemed to be picking between you and that criminal, I said to let her go. She's only going to hold you back and make you unhappy. I tried to warn you."

He rolled his eyes. This much was true. He had dismissed his mother's warnings over and over because she was his mother, and today, another bill for his naiveté had come due in the form of a kidnapped daughter.

"Oh, if only that judge would have given Kimberly to you and not this uncouth chicken-head girl. If only you had fought a little harder."

"I was much younger, mother," he explained. "It's not that I didn't want to, I just didn't know how to express it. And at the time, she had a little piece of a job and a new dude. I was still in school."

"I understand that, baby, but now look at us. And for the record, you knew that woman wasn't fit to be someone's mother. What's my grandbaby supposed to learn from a self-centered tramp like that except how to be just as ignorant as she is?"

"Your granddaughter is still a great girl," Keith snapped. "She just got caught up. It's okay. The police are on it."

"Well, there is no telling what that nasty man is doing to that baby. But it's okay. I'm on it."

The sudden manifestation of enthusiasm in his mother's voice made him momentarily question her faculties. "What does that mean?"

"It means, I'm going to pray on it. I'll call back in a few."

When he heard his own voice, it sounded like surrender. "Okay."

"I know I didn't do a very good job of instilling faith in you and that woman probably beat what little glimmer of hope you ever had—"

"You do remember I'm remarried, and my current wife loves me, right?"

"I know, but there's been damage. You know it and I know it."

Keith sighed. This was not a conversation he wanted to have.

A moment later, she finally seemed to sense his discomfort. "Well, I'm going to pray for us both. Now, when you feel the blessings coming, don't block it. You accept it and thank the universe. I love you, son."

He wanted to tell her to spare him the spiritual mumbo jumbo and wait for him to call her when he had some news. He knew that he really didn't have it in him to handle any more rambling about faith and mistakes. He could feel his soul ripping apart over all of it. However, "I love you, too," was all he could muster before he finally ended the call.

Despondent, he sat for a moment looking straight ahead, the kitchen filled with pressure cookers, food processors, high-end cutlery, and pots and pans. His current wife, Emily, who he'd met while pursuing his culinary career, was holding things down at their restaurant while he stayed home to deal with this family crisis. He may not have had faith in a higher power, but he did believe in her. He'd have to call Emily and update her on this fiasco at some point, but for the next few minutes, he would hold his head in his hands and cry the tears of a guilt-ridden father. There would be no real solace in his sanctuary tonight, as the demons born of his regrets would take up any extra space the impressively equipped kitchen had to offer.

High on the list of things New Orleans native Eleanor Babineaux never had a chance to share with her son Keith was her deep understanding of the Yoruba and voodoo religions. In her earlier years, her husband Rick, a very traditional southern Baptist who she loved and respected despite his close-mindedness, had forbidden any such practices around their son. However, his father's determination that Keith be a garden variety, off to church every Sunday protestant would not take hold. After experiencing too many incidents involving so-called Christians being less than Christian-like, Keith became disillusioned with organized religion. After the death of her husband, Eleanor tried to introduce Keith to the 'true religion of their ancestors' only to be rebuked, thanks in no small part to Hollywood's bastardized portrayals of the culture. Now, as far as she was concerned, Keith was spiritually rudderless and voiceless in the face of the ancestors and the loas. She had failed him. If she'd had her way, Keith would be the one kneeling before an altar filled with offerings to the ancestors, praying for Kimberly's safe return from the clutches of a statutory rapist. But tonight, that responsibility would fall to her.

Her makeshift altar was really a Lazy Susan that sat on a red 4x4 square of rug in the far end of her living room. A gold satin cloth covered the Lazy Susan. On top of that stood an assortment of green, white and red candles, bowls of various sizes, and a cauldron. A portrait of a beautiful black woman with caring eyes, wearing a flowing blue dress and smoking a pipe dominated the center of the arrangement. An afro framed the woman's face like a halo and topped it as a crown would.

Eleanor started by lighting all of the white and orange candles only, then went into a quick prayer to the four corners: North, South, East, and West.

"I pray to the ancestors and to Yemaya, patron saint of women! Hear me, loving orisha! My granddaughter, doomed by having a less than intelligent mother and a father who has given up on his faith! I beseech you! Hear my prayer! Return her safely."

From her pocket, she pulled out a news clipping that contained a picture of Manuel Hightower posing in front of the Grammy Award's Step and Repeat two years ago with deceased rapper $onavabitch. She placed it in the cauldron and struck a match, only for a sudden breeze to blow the match out.

Eleanor's head whipped left. The window she'd left open *could* explain the sudden gust. Only, as her eyes adjusted, she realized that she hadn't. Meanwhile, the article in the cauldron caught fire on its own.

Startled, Eleanor turned back and watched as the flames rose into a hot blueish-white ball. The lip of the cast iron cauldron began to melt as she scrambled backward and to her feet. Then, just as quickly as it had started, the fire extinguished by itself. A pillar of white smoke remained, but as another burst of wind hit it, instead of dissipating, the smoke solidified and changed color until standing over the cauldron...

"Yemaya!"

Eleanor fell back to her knees. Fear engulfed her as she stared up at the beautiful but stoic face. "Yemaya, I have prayed to you more than the other orishas for I know you are the patron saint of women. I *am* a simple woman. A grandmother praying for the safe return of a grandchild."

Yemaya took a long drag from her pipe, then let the pearl white smoke drift out of her mouth before she spoke with a mild West Indian accent. "I come to you aware of your predicament, but I am not here to intervene in these matters. I am here to tell you that there is one, a being cursed by other gods, who has commiserated with me over the woes that women suffer at the hands of weak men. She is willing and able to avenge for your benefit. All you have to do is submit to that judgment."

"Her judgment? I don't understand. Do we get the child back or not?"

"That will be up to her." She pointed a finger at Eleanor. "You have to answer."

"Why am I being helped? What does this other being want in return?"

"She only wants your permission."

"Who is this? An orisha. A loa or some other deity? What is her name?"

"In the underworld, we don't use each other's names, but if you saw her, you would know her. Her descendants don't pray to her, nor give tribute. She sustains herself on revenge, which is why she is willing to help you. Now, give me an answer!"

"Can I see her?"

Yemaya's eyes widened. "She cannot appear before you! Because she is cursed, her face is an abomination! Your soul would be seared! And your body would be no more than an empty shell!"

"But I still don't understand—"

"It is not for you to understand!" Yemaya held her hand high as she seemed to grow larger. "Do you want the child rescued or not?"

"Yes, but—"

"Then say the words!"

Something didn't feel right, but what could she do? In all of Eleanor's decades of prayers and burnt offerings, this was the first time an orisha had given her more than a whisper or simply bequeathed her with some faith-based inner strength. In fact, this was the first vision she'd experienced after losing her virginity to Keith's father. The anxiety and uncertainty brought tears to her eyes. "I submit to the judgment of the one whose face I cannot see."

"Very good." Yemaya nodded solemnly as she began to disappear into the wall. "Prepare to receive your granddaughter and teach her the ways of the ancestors."

Eleanor bowed in reverence. "I will. I will show her the way, oh great Yemaya."

As the apparition dissolved into an ethereal mist, a gust of wind burst through the room and extinguished the candles.

Eleanor remained bowed before the altar, ever pious even in the dark.

———

"You're my motherfucking lawyer! You're supposed to make this kind of shit go away! As much money as I made the label last year! Y'all got me hiding in this hotel room like some kind of fugitive! This is some bullshit!"

Sitting at the edge of the super king-sized hotel room bed wearing only a bathing suit, Kimberly stared absently at the TV on the wall in front of her. This was in stark contrast to fully clothed Manuel's animated pacing back and forth across the room as he screamed into his cellphone. She thought about turning the TV on so she wouldn't have to listen but figured in his agitated state that she would only get yelled at or worse.

"Seriously! What the fuck am I paying you for?"

She couldn't hear the lawyer's side of the conversation but could tell that the lawyer was asking uncomfortable questions.

"What? No, she's fine! She loves me and she loves Vegas. You sound like that punk ass cop that left a message a few minutes ago."

Another pause.

"What? Her father? I don't care about him. Fuck him! If he was a real nigga, he'd call me himself. Going to the damn cops like a little bitch!"

No matter what you hear or see, do not turn around. Do not face me, child!

Kimberly's breath stopped as her mind struggled to process where a disembodied voice could possibly be coming from.

"Sam? Sam! I know this motherfucker didn't just hang up on me…"

If he hadn't been in such an angry state, Manuel might have noticed the growing shadow moving behind him as the form of a curvaceous, statuesque woman with undulating hair drifted off the wall and into the room.

Manuel threw the cellphone on the bed, just behind Kimberly. "I'm so fucking mad right now. I need to fuck you again just to calm my ass down. Take them damn clothes off, girl!"

He began to unbuckle his pants.

Kimberly neither moved nor gave any indication that she heard him.

"Bitch, perhaps you didn't hear Daddy! I said..."

Then he heard the hissing. He turned around.

"What the fu—"

The entity grabbed Manuel by the shoulders, accosting him as if he were a small child, with a strength that dwarfed his. The ten snakes in the apparition's hair lunged forward, each of the mouths burying fangs into his flesh. His chocolate brown skin turned a marble-like grey as the poisons filled his body. He screamed for only a few seconds as the toxins quickly petrified his vocal cords.

Kimberly peripherally caught a split second of Manuel's agonized last moments before she closed her eyes. The monster must have sensed that Kimberly had peeked because she heard the voice again.

DO NOT LOOK AT ME!

A moment later, Manuel's lifeless body crashed down to the floor with a 'thud' in front of Kimberly. Her eyes drifted down. Whatever had been injected into him was toxic enough to literally melt him. Flesh and muscles bubbled into a jelly. Bones disintegrated to ash trapped inside the jelly. Hours from now, a large black stain on the carpet would be all that remained. She closed her eyes but couldn't escape the image of the mess on the floor.

Go to your grandmother, that she might teach you the ways of your ancestors and not the way of the idolaters that brought your people here in bondage.

"My grandmother? Who are you?"

I am the one who was defiled by one of my gods, made an abomination by another, and rejected and vilified by my own kind. It was only in the underworld that I found the orishas and loa and ascended ones of Africa. Like me, they want actual justice meted out in this world and the next. I am Medusa, The Accursed One! Evil men feared me hundreds of years ago and they shall fear me again!

The shadow drifted back towards the wall from where it had entered and disappeared. Sensing that the gorgon had left, Kimberly opened her eyes and looked again at what was left of Manuel. Recoiled on the bed, she suppressed a scream and cried quietly for a few minutes.

It would take her some time, but she eventually found the strength to get dressed, grab her things, and leave the hotel.

"This motherfucker is gonna act all indignant, like he was parent of the decade! Fucking dream-slaying, hating-ass Negro!"

Cathy drove her white BMW M4 Coupé as fast as New York City's FDR Drive would allow, which during rush hour on a Wednesday wasn't nearly as fast as she preferred. Before her girlfriend Nicole called, Cathy had been cursing up a storm as she cut off more cautious drivers with signal-free lane changes and flipped them her middle finger whenever they dared honk their horns in protest.

"So he's blaming you?" Nicole's voice blared over the car's speakers. Nicole, like Cathy, was a dedicated party girl, enabler, and equal opportunity narcissist. She was the shoulder to cry on, the friend who took Cathy's side no matter how horrible she'd acted or how ridiculous her course of action. "Him and his damn cupcakes! Fuck him! Y'all are doing the right thing! Manuel is going to make your baby a star. He told me so!"

"That's right. And so what if she lost her virginity to him? Shit, that's Manuel Hightower! The motherfuckers we lost our virginity to wasn't even close to that stature!"

"Child! I know that's right!"

Betrayer of women! Betrayer of your own child! You gave your child's innocence and honor away for nothing!

"Bitch! What you said?"

"I said, 'child, I know that's right.' What you thought I said?"

Cathy's eyes caught a flash of the gorgon's red gaze in her rearview mirror. The hair snakes' fangs found Cathy's ears, neck, and skull. The last thing Cathy saw was her milk chocolate complexion turning greenish grey as the car swerved out of control, bounced off an Acura RDX, then slammed straight into a guardrail. Despite the damage to the car, Nicole's voice could still be heard asking if her friend was okay.

Until the gas tank exploded.

⸻

"Dad?"

"Son? Are you okay?"

"No. I lost Kimberly...and I lost you, now that I think of it."

They were sitting in Keith's father's favorite coffee shop. The same coffee shop that had a carrot cake that Keith Sr. loved so much. Keith Jr. tried to replicate it once to surprise his father when he was fourteen.

He noticed that his father looked much younger than he did when they last saw each other. Thirty years younger. The face behind many a grounding and spanking. The coffee and carrot cake were on the table, but everything was the wrong color.

"You lost me? Oh son! You can never lose me. And don't worry. Kimberly will be home soon."

"She will?"

"Yes. Your mother put some things in motion. Powerful woman, your mother. I think I impeded that power during my time with her. That may have been wrong. Now son, I need to warn you."

"Warn me?"

"Yes! You see, you're getting a second chance. Now, your mother is going to be stepping in to mentor a little more than she'd been allowed to up 'til now, but I need you to be strong. Be protective. Be the father I know you can be."

"I can. I will."

As his father smiled, Keith saw two women walking up behind him. One was a stunning African beauty with a large shining mane of an Afro. The other woman's eyes glowed red and her hair seemed to slither. A tongue flickered.

His father's face turned angry. *"DO NOT LOOK AT HER!"*

Keith woke up gasping for breath. As reality took hold, he realized two things: he had fallen asleep in the kitchen, and his wife was coming through the front door.

He managed to get to the middle of the living room at the same time she did. Emily's hair was slicked back and her make-up was mostly sweated away, clear indications that she'd put in a full day. Her black dress jeans, jacket, and blouse had a few flour stains, but she still somehow managed to look great.

Seeing the distress on her husband's face, Emily threw her purse on the couch and ran to him. "Oh my God! Are you okay?"

He embraced her. "Yeah, I'm okay. Just sitting here. I fell asleep after dealing with the cops and Cathy."

Emily's eyes widened. "Fell asleep? Wait. You don't know."

"Know what?"

"It was on the news. Cathy is dead. Lost control of her car on the FDR. There was a fire and a massive pile-up. Traffic is backed up all the way to Yankee Stadium."

He reeled as if about to faint. Emily snatched at his arms and steadied him just as his cellphone rang behind him. He walked back to the kitchen and answered.

"Hi Mom. I know about Cathy."

"Hello, son. You should also know you can pick my granddaughter up at the airport in about seven hours."

"Y-y-you spoke to Kimberly?"

"She called me when she couldn't get either of her parents on the phone. Yes, she's coming home, baby. Now, you be sure to bring her by this weekend."

He hung up with his mother and sat back down at the kitchen table. Emily eventually sat down across from him.

"What are you thinking?" she finally asked.

"I'm thinking things are going to be okay." He gave her a weak smile.

"Good. I heard your mother through the phone. I guess we'll be driving to JFK in a few hours."

He nodded. "I suddenly have a craving for carrot cake."

"That's funny. Me too."

About the Author

STEVEN VAN PATTEN is a Brooklyn-based horror writer known for the *Brookwater's Curse* vampire trilogy, the two- soon-to-be three-part *Killer Genius* series, and the *Raise Some Hell* horror anthology series he's written with fellow HWA members Marc L. Abbott and Kirk Johnson.

SVP's short story works appear in numerous anthologies, including *Tales from The Canyons of The Damned*, the Bram Stoker nominated *Under Twin Suns*, and *Even in The Grave*.

Check out www.laughingblackvampire for more.

Esharra-hammat knew that there was something wrong in her domain when she awoke that evening. The ripples were coming from a metaphorical stone thrown into the MagniZent Strip Club, bringing more-than-metaphorical ache to her bones. Thus, it was no surprise when she stepped through the door and there was a girl crying, huddled with several others.

As Esharra's heels tapped against the floor, the girls looked up, the new one trying to hide her tears. Ava—that was her name—with a penchant for blue hair dye and playful jokes behind the curtain. The others stayed around her, bristling like mother hens at her approach. Esharra hid a smile. They *would* take it the wrong way, still unlearning lessons from terrible bosses.

The only one with relief on her face was Heitiare, wild hair simply pulled back. She had given up taming it with straightener and bleach, and simply let it be, taunting those who admired it with threats to break loose any moment. Esharra was proud to see that she no longer wore bandages over her hands, the scars healing from Heitere's own wildness lashing out. Her self-harm had not stopped at her hair.

"I'm sorry," Ava choked, swallowing a sob. "It's my fault..."

"What is it?" Esharra asked, placing a gentle hand on Ava's head.

A sob tore through Ava's throat, and Esharra was unsure if it was from the trouble or from the kindness.

Heitiare took over. "I was going to call you. Ava has a man who's been bothering her. She told him to fuck off and told the rest of us he should fuck off. But he managed to get past the bouncers. Ava's set is next." She paused. "He's carrying."

"What are we going to do?" Manju whispered, as if the man could hear through the walls and the antsy audience outside. "He's already acting squirrely, and his hand is right next to it. I don't know what he will do once he sees her. Or doesn't."

Esharra read all of her fears in one glance. The panicked crowd trampling each other as booms rang out, muffling the screams of the wounded and dying. Those who thought they were safe slumping over as bullets tore through plywood walls and fake satin chairs.

And if she did survive—sitting in cold interrogation rooms, feeling naked under the fluorescent lamps as they kept asking, "Who are you? Where are you from?" And that's if they weren't stuck under the equally cold fluorescent lamp as the doctors monotonously explained how much the damage was, both in flesh and cash.

"I will take Ava's shift. Go and lie down. Try to breathe. I will be by later with tea."

Ava looked at her with disbelieving puppy dog eyes. "But—"

"No buts. I'm the owner after all." She let a dagger slip into her voice, and the rest backed away, not asking how this petite woman with gray hair was going to entertain the crowds. One who creaked as she stepped away from them.

"What music do you want?" Heitiare asked as she broke away from the group, her posture straight and voice calm despite the worry rippling around her.

"Your choice, you know my tastes, even if you probably don't have anything with a santur."

"Well, actually, I have one song that has something close." Heitiare's calm composure broke into embarrassment. "It was hard to find something with a dulcimer that wasn't too kiddie or too stuffy, but I found one. I've been practicing a new routine…"

The adoration she projected was like that of an acolyte. *She is one, isn't she?* Esharra asked herself, feeling far from home.

"Good. One song is all I need." A single nod, and Heitiare was gone to prepare the stage. Esharra walked over to one of the changing dressers, gingerly removing her coat and dress. The fabric that felt thin between her fingers grew heavy as she pulled it off. Heavy as time and age.

She felt their stares as her back straightened. Esharra ran her hands down her spine, smoothing the skin, then removed the pins and shook out her hair, the gray quickly overwhelmed by thick black. She threw her underwear down, letting the air caress her body, fully feeling herself expand into the space. It felt good, like slipping back into a loose robe after wearing a tight leather catsuit in the hot sun. Esharra looked into the brightly lit mirror and saw her own face staring back, the first time in weeks. Months. Years?

The girls let her pass in a silent hush, not one of them objecting to her using their table, or how she didn't touch any makeup, or how full nudity would bring the wrong kind of legal attention. She gave a playful wink as Heitiare rushed in and watched as the poor girl nearly melted into a puddle. Esharra breathlessly whispered, "Someday you, too," as she walked out onto the stage.

The metal beats of hammer against dulcimer sang through the air. So close and yet so far, the steel of the dulcimer not as warm as the bronze she had trained with back when she was young. The sterile recording removed the small currents of air agitated by the instrument, the faint splash of sweat that only the imitated would catch. The men had been joking and grumbling, a few yelling at the stage about what was taking so long. Only a few, not too dulled by drink, were puzzling over the music, the sudden shift in the air that their animal instincts noticed.

All movement froze as she stepped forward with a single hip thrust, gliding to the pole. One leg up against the pole, and her arms pulled her forward. She spun, first lazily and then more quickly with each rotation. The stage fell away from her, the artificial lights fell away from her, the roof fell away from her and finally the pole. Still she spun, the momentum too great to stop now.

The beat was pounding, drums from her past joining. As hand beat against hide, her own feet beat against the sunbaked brick, falling down on her knees with a shimmy. The men were still there, underneath the tall trees cultivated by diverted streams, fed by the great river. With snake-like flexibility she emerged back into the air, heavy with flowers from the courtyard, not sweat and cheap cologne.

She looked down at the men, the full moon behind her. Not a single murmur or gasp disrupted the music, so held they were by her. Their eyes followed her every movement as she scanned the crowd. Drinking it in, begging for more—no longer demanding like they had before she stepped out. She could've ordered anything from them—their gold, their lives—all for just a touch of the goddess residing in her.

Her eyes settled on one. His hand was frozen on the waistband of his torn jeans. She could see the outline of the gun, handle jamming into his side. His sandy hair was unbrushed, his clothes unwashed. He had been driving himself to the brink, preoccupied with what he thought he should have. Giving himself to the demons that wandered the wasteland beyond her beautiful city.

The drums rang out with a powerful blow, and the dulcimer rang down the scale as she took her first step on the stairs. The statue-adorned temple stairs or the flimsy stage ones, they were both the same now as the crowd stood still. She weaved through the masculine mass before alighting upon the man that tormented Ava and the others.

No one rejected raised an objection. For what weight would the lioness give to the words of a gazelle?

She felt his breath hitch as she sat in his lap. Her hips rolled forward and back as she placed a hand against his chest. The rest of the men watched her hips, but he watched her hand as it sank down into his chest, wrapping around his heart.

She felt it all then. His anger as girls laughed, as they looked through him. As the men came home with the girl in all the movies yet, when he tried, they refused. That when he cornered them in hallways, instead of falling into his arms, they pushed him away. Said no. Even if they said yes to others. Others who weren't good. Who weren't nice, like him. That he was no different from the men in the movies, and yet —nothing. That this loneliness was a personal affront, the pain in his chest was all those bitches' fault, that it would be like that in the past and the future.

He begged her with his eyes. To take this pain, this beast from him. For was it not the sacred prostitutes that tamed Enkidu, the beast-man, transforming him into monster-slaying king protector? His beast would be nothing to her kind.

She could pacify it, let him leave light and free. Let him return to live properly, at home in the world. But he didn't approach her with the pain clawing in his chest. He was here to cage Ava, to make her live in fear, to take what was not given.

Esharra reached another hand in and grabbed deeper. His eyes opened wider, as she held all of his wildness. Not just the fang and claws that tore. But the coiled muscle that drove him to wake every morning, that pulsing blood that he rarely felt outside his game controller, taunting friends for their weakness as he sprung upon them in the digital arena. That part that prowled his apartment at night and let him dream of a life outside those four small walls.

His eyes pled for not this, for her to simply take his heart and let him die here and now.

But she had no mercy to give as she pulled all of his wildness from his chest. His head bobbed down, he wanted to sob like Ava had only minutes ago. But he couldn't, the same way that you couldn't draw water from a dry well. With a graceful sway, she dismounted, climbing out of their reach as she devoured a blood red meal.

Enough to sustain her for another dance.

About the Author

ELIZABETH DAVIS is a second generation writer living in Dayton, Ohio. They live there with their spouse and two cats—neither of which have been lost to ravenous corn mazes or sleeping serpent gods. They can be found at deadfishbooks.com when they aren't busy creating beautiful nightmares and bizarre adventures. Their work can be found in *After the Gold Rush*, *Eternal Haunted Summer*, and *Illumen*.

JUSTICE
CRISTEL ORRAND

Statue-still, beatific,
Her gaze held aloft,
Unlike any mother
I had ever known.

The roadside shrines
Prettily carved of stone,
Depicted less strength
Than her flesh and bone.

They called her Lady,
And Mother, ignoring,
Her weighted scales,
Equal and imploring.

But still they came,
To play the penitent,
To touch her water
And absolve their sin.

As if Woman would
Forgive their hands
Upon her sisters'
Hearts and wombs.

The old judge came,
Begging blessings
So long he'd grizzled
And grown white.

Chanting devotions,
Praying for favor,
But she had grown
Tired of man's ministry.

The statue said,
"Aye, and Ave,
But it is your last—
Decide, and let it be just."

It was for his wife.
He wanted it badly,
More even than he
Ever had wanted her.

Full, as though he'd
Siphoned the statues'
Power, drunk on it,
Enraptured by control—

He presented it.
"Beautiful chains!"
he exclaimed.
"For your protection."

His wife smiled, beatific,
Gaze soft and aloft,
Unlike any woman
I had ever seen.

Ecstatic now,
He laid the chains
About her wrists,
Locking her in place.

But the spirit
Was upon her
And she asked
Him to take her

To Mother's grave.
There, she rose,
Sweetly, singing love,
Arms, embracing—

Hands about his neck,
In manacled torsion,
Wrought hard with
Incontrovertible truth.

Rolling his sick, slack
Form into the grave—
"You offered me chains
For my own protection."

Laughing her way out,
She kissed the statue
Whose eyes did alight,
Her scales, now upright.

About the Author

CRISTEL ORRAND is the author of two novels, *The Amalgamist* and *Khayal*, the "Heartwood" poetry collection, the novelette *M.O.U.T.H. Piece* in the "Objectified" anthology, and is working on a southern gothic series, and her poetry. She is a mom, consultant, bibliophile, advocate, gardener, storyteller, cancer survivor, scavenger, and a pugilist, of all sorts. Cristel lives in Raleigh, NC, with her artist husband, kids, and dogs, doing anything they can dream up and cram into a day.

THE GIFT
RAVYN CRESCENT

ELISA KEPT HER BACK STRAIGHT, her head up. She would stay professional. No matter what happened, she would stay strong. Seconds ticked by as the Zoom meeting opened and she saw the two men who she'd been waiting to meet. Their eager eyes and exciting smiles came up in the little boxes containing them, and just as soon as they arrived, she saw their eyes dart to the top of the screen where her image appeared on their screens, and then their smiles faded.

"Hello, I'm Elisa Hanta," she introduced herself. "It's wonderful to meet you both face to face."

Mark Roven, the man she had spoken with over the past week as he offered her a job, leaned back in his chair as if desperate to put distance between the two of them, forgetting they weren't even in the same state despite the night sky in the window behind her. "I'm not sure you're who I'm supposed to be meeting today. Let me ask my office manager."

"You sent me an email twenty minutes ago confirming our meeting. E. Hanta, that's me. See? It's in the bottom left under my camera feed."

She could see the eye roll he tried to hide by rubbing his nose. "I was expecting someone else for this position."

Elisa felt the shiver roll across her skin. Her jaw tightened and an all-too-familiar headache struck her just above the eyes. A whisper sounded in her mind, a voice that wasn't hers, but shared the same thought. *They were expecting a man.*

She shook her head, trying to force the other voices away, and brought up their email interactions, sharing her screen, even as her chest tightened. "Oh, no, you were expecting me. These are our conversations, remember? You told me this call was just a formality that HR required, and I should consider the position mine already."

"I'm just going to come out and say it, all right?" Mark made a pyramid with his fingertips, still leaning back in his chair. "I find it very unprofessional that you hid your identity in your application."

"I didn't hide anything," Elisa insisted.

"Your name."

The headache grew worse. "I used my initials and my full surname. I provided references, my full and honest resume, even copies of my certifications."

He drummed his fingers together, looking around the room. "You've made this an uncomfortable situation and I don't appreciate it. You and I both know that you hid your name for a reason, right?"

"All right," she said. "I will remember to include my full name from now on."

He blew out a puff of air in an aggressive sigh. "That's not the point —you're not the type of person I'm looking for, and I don't want this to become a fight. You know you're not, or you wouldn't have hidden your name."

The other man, Jim T. according to his screen name, cleared his throat to get their attention and gave an exaggerated nod. "I can agree with Mark on this; it's unprofessional to hide details, and our company is looking for a manager we can trust and count on for years to come. We've acquired a lot of properties and we have a strict way we want them done, so we need someone who can be around for the long haul."

"I agree." Elisa nodded. "I'm looking for a company I can stay and grow with as it grows."

Jim shifted some papers on his desk. Why did he even have so many papers? He had to be on the computer anyway for this call; why not just have them in another tab? "It's just that we're seeking a low-risk candidate. We'd prefer someone who we know won't need to take any time off."

Elisa's torso spasmed as a jolt like lightning raced from the base of her neck, down through her, her hands curling into talons as she fought to regain control. This was an increasing occurrence, same with the voices; her doctors couldn't determine the reason, saying it was anxiety, perhaps a panic attack, and she needed to try and relax. Not an easy thing when this was her fifth interview after sending out over two hundred job applications, always ending the same way. She got more responses when she stopped including a photo or her first name, but as soon as they saw her, they lost all interest.

Jim's eyebrows went up. He typed something, but even after he hit "Enter," no message popped up—at least not one she could see, though she noticed Mark's eyes drift to the side.

"I won't need time off," she said. "I'm perfectly capable of the job, and my references can assure you of that."

Mark gave a sly smile. "Well, we don't know that... What if you meet someone?"

"It won't be a problem." She forced a pleasant smile, praying they would just drop the topic. *They won't. This is all they really care about.*

"How do you know?" Jim asked. "We don't mean to imply you're not already with someone, what we're saying is you just don't know that you won't end up needing to go on maternity leave."

"No. I won't."

In an instant, both men looked at her, their eyes sharp. "How do you know?"

This was the dangerous part. Elisa had seen people end up blacklisted for answering wrong. She'd lost her last job because of a co-worker who had thought they were doing her a favor by outing her. They likely had, but the outcome was going to be the same regardless. As soon as the office conversation turned to birth control, she'd known her time there was running out.

Mark and Jim stared at her, ready to judge in an instant. They were like vipers, coiled and ready to strike if they heard what they expected. She had to make a quick decision. Insisting it would not be a problem alone hadn't worked; they would keep pressing or decide on her own. Her only chance was to get ahead of it this time before the rumors began. She hated having to out herself without an actual ability to choose when and how... It put a knot in her throat she feared she'd choke on.

"I'm asexual."

Jim looked back at his papers, but Mark's expression flashed to one of disgust before he, once again, rubbed his nose. The man couldn't keep his hands off his face. "We don't need to know about what you do —or *don't* do—behind closed doors, but I was looking for someone I knew would be around a long time. Maybe a family man, someone who would stick around because they have others to support."

That's rich! A group of voices sang in her head, a choir in perfect harmony. Elisa tensed, her eye twitching as she heard them. Another "side effect" of her rising stress levels, her doctor had suggested. It had never been so loud before. *They want a trademark family man, but don't want anyone who might need paternity leave.*

"I have to support myself."

"Well, you don't have to, you could get—"

Jim cleared his throat loudly before he sent another hidden message.

Elisa took a slow breath, trying to calm the muscle spasms that ran through her entire body. She leaned forward, staring Mark dead in the eye. "Look...this job posting has been listed for three months. You have properties that need to be managed, and you're losing money by the day having them sit vacant. I've got a CPM, a CRM, and a CPS. I even just got my CFM. I'm already trained and experienced, I'm ready for the job."

Silence passed—seconds ticking by as Jim scanned her resume and Mark met her determined stare with a bored gaze.

"Fine. We can write up something and start you off at thirty-five annually."

"That's well under standard."

They know, the voices whispered, anger evident in their tone. Anger she herself was struggling to hide.

"I thought you wanted the job?" Mark asked, shaking his head. "We're taking a risk here, and you said you were passionate about the work."

"But it's nine grand below minimum. I have ten years of experience."

"Take it or leave it."

"I'll...need to think about it." That's how all the interviews went. Elisa clicked the exit icon and closed the meeting before she screamed into the void. Cursing the company and the world itself. She tried so hard, got the certifications, she battled through harsh situations to get the experience—everything they said she was supposed to do—and they *still* treated her like an object!

She'd always heard that women were weaker, growing up. She'd been determined to prove them wrong; she'd believed that if she showed the world she was strong, that she was equal, eventually they'd treat her that way. But instead...

They don't want you the way you are. You aren't worthy in their twisted vision. You're not the same as them, you're a lesser being...inhuman.

She snarled, an animalistic noise she'd never made before. Her teeth sharpened into fangs, causing her to bleed as her tongue got in the way. She brought her hand to her mouth as another spasm rocketed through her body. Her hands curled, but this time the pain continued down them, feeling as if something were jammed under her nails, prying them off.

Elisa's anger turned to agony and fear. She stared at her hands, shaking as the nails fell off like loose teeth, replaced by massive, sharp claws.

She choked on a scream as her body spasmed again. Her legs gave out, and she dropped to her knees. Elisa dug her claws into the cheap carpet below her, the muscles in her stomach tightening so strongly she tried to vomit but nothing came up. She felt a cramp in her feet that was the worst she'd ever felt. She grabbed one of them, trying to use pressure to soothe the pain when she felt the bones crack. Her toenails suffered the same fate as her fingernails; her entire foot seemed to be reforming itself.

Elisa tried to stand, to get to her phone on her desk—anything, but her muscles convulsed and rippled against will. She was a hostage to her own body and the pain was overwhelming.

The choir voices spoke again. *Change hurts... This is a gift.*

"I don't want it!" she screamed.

Accept...or don't... You decide.

Images flashed before her. Every time she was told to accept being bullied because it meant the boy liked her, every time she was told she was too emotional rather than having her abuse acknowledged...why had they always treated her like she was the one at fault?

The pain turned to burning rage that seared her from the inside out as she latched onto the memories. Teachers telling her how lucky she was that her father was willing to come get her when she missed the bus, ignoring that she'd missed it because someone had stolen her backpack, ignoring how she begged and pleaded with them not to call him. She remembered how the principal sneered at her, telling her she couldn't attend her junior high graduation because she'd finally told the police about what happened at her father's home and "ruined that poor man's reputation."

She saw images from the lowest points in her life. When her math teacher told her he was going to pass her only because he would teach her class the next semester, and if he didn't pass her, it would put her as a burden on another teacher. The boy in sixth grade who grudgingly asked her out while others snickered around them and one of her only friends rushing over afterward just to insist she wasn't a part of daring him to ask her out.

Elisa threw herself onto her back, struggling to catch her breath. As the images flooded her head, she got angrier. She'd thought that the trouble she'd been having as of late was new...but no, it was something she'd not let herself notice for a long while. She still felt terrified of the world around her. When she walked down the street, she hated how nervous she felt. She hated how she flinched if someone shouted at her; she hated being told she was the one over-reacting when she'd been quiet.

With a scream of rage and anger, the entire apartment shook around her. Her body let out a pulse of energy. Lightbulbs exploded; her computer flickered and then turned off as smoke started to pour out of it. The windows around her shattered and broke; parts of the ceiling rained down around her.

Wings burst from her back, a spaded tail sprouted from the base of her spine, but a feeling of power overwhelmed any of the pain she'd felt. A power that had been there her whole life, any time she'd taken pride in something, stood up for herself, felt determined and triumphed. A comforting energy that had been deep inside of her, but one she'd never imagined could be so physically strong.

When the changes stopped, she heard footsteps in the hall, voices talking about the blackout and arguing its possible cause, infuriated shouts about broken electronics and surge protectors having failed. Elisa got up and found she was taller now...no, not exactly taller. Her feet had reshaped themselves; she was walking on the balls of her feet which had spread out. She lifted one and saw it curled, making itself smaller like a bird's talons but expanding again as she set it down.

This will make you faster.

She walked to the bathroom and realized she should be afraid of the reflection she saw, but...she wasn't. She looked strong, powerful. Wicked and strange, just as they treated her.

Power corrupts, Elisa reminded herself. That corruption was evident all around her, wasn't it? This world was full of corruption and greed. The planet was dying because of that greed, their world set to collapse because too many in power were being paid off by the people profiting from the problems.

"What is this?" she asked aloud.

A gift.

"I don't want to be a monster." Elisa surprised even herself with how calm her voice was. How calm she felt. The energy around her felt like home.

Not *a monster*.

"I look like a devil. I don't want to be evil." Tears formed in her eyes. "Is this really what I am, deep down? I'm evil?"

Do you feel evil?

"I look—!"

Do you feel joy in the suffering of others? Feel superior and look down on those less fortunate? Mock people in fear? Do you feel evil? Why would appearance matter?

Elisa blinked. She examined herself in the mirror. "No, I feel like... myself. Stronger, a stronger version of me, but so what? A lot of cruel people are certain they're good."

How true. But this is a gift. What do you want?

What did she want? Such a complex question. To pay the rent on time, to be able to afford to eat something other than macaroni or ramen every day, to not live in terror of the people in power...or who might come next.

What have you always wanted?

"Justice." She spoke the word without a thought. A complex question suddenly became so clear. "Vengeance! For everything they've taken from me, for all the pain they've caused."

There was no reply. She was left alone, staring into the mirror, wondering what her next move was. She'd always felt somewhat alone, but now? How was she supposed to even attempt to fit in? How was she going to get justice alone? Even as powerful as she felt, would she be strong enough? There was so much corruption; she knew now her purpose was to eliminate it.

There was a shriek in the hall. Elisa walked to her door and peered out the peephole. People shouted to each other about the grid going down. How could that be? It was a clear evening, no storms. Nothing should have caused a blackout. But as she looked behind her, out the window—chaos. Lights bursting, streetlights shattering and raining down glass and sparks, windows breaking. Houses, apartments, businesses.

Elisa walked to her window and peered out, pushing away some of the shattered glass onto the street below. She leaned out into the cool night air, noticing that her eyesight was much sharper than it had been. Her eyes locked on the apartment complex across from hers, at the person inside who was on their hands and knees as wings sprouted from their back and a burst of energy erupted from them so powerful it shoved their furniture into the walls.

Sirens wailed in the distance, car horns and alarms going off in every direction. Screams of terror and confusion echoed through the streets, growing louder. Elisa could smell smoke in the air. Shadows of figures moved in the sky, flitting out of crashed cars, peering around from rooftops.

Elisa smiled with the revelation that she wasn't alone. There were a lot of victims in this world, a lot of people told they were abominations, that they were wrong for things they could not control; for how they were born. If the world wasn't going to accept them as they were, then they'd become what their situation forced...

...and they would dance to the sirens.

About the Author

RAVYN CRESCENT has been writing since she was little, using it as an empowering outlet to express and confront her greatest fears. She turns on a murder podcast to relax and spends most of her free time reading about serial killers and all things paranormal, all of which creeps out her family but led to her meeting her husband, who is just as creepy as she is.

THE END OF DAYS
CARINA BISSETT

The signs were there
from the beginning:
we burned bras,
demanded rights, our lives
sacred, vigils
against violence,
silence broken,
vehement in the vindication
for all women.

In an instant, you
tore it down,
turned back time,
declaration sealed,
ears plugged against our cries
and those of our daughters
and yours suffering
under the commandments
of righteous men.

And so, we march,
a monstrous regiment
dressed in white,
trumpets blaring,
winged justice,
talons sharp as knives.

Harpies, hags, harridans,
you chant, reality refused.
A temporary setback,
we settle in the trees,
gathering winds in our feathers,
a tempestuous promise
for those determined
to shackle women
to their wombs.

And then it happens—
the stain, the slight against
your family name,
shame locked away in a tower,
and you think you've escaped.
But our ears and eyes are open,
and we offer a rescue, a shield,
flight to a garden, an apothecary
seeded with cures against creation.

We wait for the full moon,
gather to guard her choice,
her salvation, sanctified,
surrounded by the safety of sisters,
as she bleeds your blessing
into the ground, and she
no longer belongs to you,
but to herself and a future
free from evil eyes.

She grows talons and claws,
wings glorious as she soars
unchecked, and our flock grows.
The new night witches, we bomb
accusations, women's wisdom gathered,
stored and shared
to our daughters and yours,
the ways to nourish life and those
to ease the way, an ending.

We nest together, hatch plans,
the Furies reborn, curses personified.
Feminazi, bitch, cunt, you claim.
Our tears turn to dust, as
we scry for solutions, divine
retribution, and we rise furious,
prepared to release our wrath,
to wreak vengeance on those
who dare to deny us.

The end of days comes
unheeded: the blood moon,
locusts unleashed, darkness
falling, storms summoned,
fire and brimstone
raining down.

And as the waters rise,
wash away the wicked,
we rouse, spread our wings,
fall from the sky to pluck out
your eyes, tear out your tongues,
leaving only your ears perfect,
pure and whole, untouched
so that you may finally hear
truths spoken, words
other than your own.

About the Author

CARINA BISSETT is a writer and poet working primarily in the fields of dark fiction and fabulism. Her work has been published in multiple journals and anthologies including *Upon a Twice Time, Bitter Distillations: An Anthology of Poisonous Tales,* and *Arterial Bloom.* Her poetry has been nominated for the Pushcart Prize and the Sundress Publications Best of the Net and can be found in the *HWA Poetry Showcase* and *NonBinary Review.* She is also the co-editor of the award-winning anthology *Shadow Atlas: Dark Landscapes of the Americas.* Links to her work can be found at http://carinabissett.com.

*AN INTERVIEW WITH LYNNE HANSEN,
COVER ARTIST*

When Rachel and Carol were first envisioning this project, we started talking about where we would find exactly the right cover—especially challenging given the time frame of the project! Luckily, Rachel is a faithful subscriber to Lynne's newsletter and let's just say that the pre-made cover image for that month was meant to be. We wanted to to know a little more about the story behind the art, and so we invited Lynne to share some more information about her work and the cover for *A Woman Unbecoming*.

Q (Crone Girls Press): Welcome to Crone Girls Press! We are so excited to have your art as the cover for this anthology. Can you share a little bit about yourself and your art?

A (Lynne Hansen): I've been a cover artist for 12 years now, and I specialize in horror book covers. If I can combine creepy, clever, and beautiful in a single piece, I'm happy. If I can use my art to connect the right readers with amazing authors they'll love, I'm even happier.

Q: You have an impressive portfolio of artwork and cover art. Did you always want to do cover commissions? How did you get into this particular field?

A: Before I was a cover artist, I was an author. I used to teach marketing and promotion to authors all over the country. My day job at that time was working in marketing at a historic theater. I used to create ads and newsletters—stuff like that. I got started creating covers because my husband, Bram Stoker Award-winning author Jeff Strand, needed a book cover. His novel *Wolf Hunt* was due to come out from a big publisher in two months—and then the publisher terminated their horror line. I volunteered to do a cover for him so he could self-publish. It was WAY harder than I ever thought it would be, and it took me forever! But we put in tiny little print on the copyright page: "Cover art by Lynne Hansen, www.LynneHansenArt.com" and people noticed. I started getting commissions for books that weren't written by my husband. And then I got hired by New York Times bestselling author Christopher Golden to help resurrect his backlist. I did 38 covers for him over several years. It's really helped me grow as an artist. All of the work I've ever gotten has been through word of mouth. I'm so grateful.

Q: For this cover, what inspired the story?

A: So the Supreme Court overturning Roe V Wade is what inspired this piece. I felt so lost and betrayed, and I wanted to create art that spoke to my personal dread of what the future might hold. But I didn't want to create something super political. I'm not the kind of artist who likes to hit you over the head with something. So I channeled my emotions and created a woman in bed, terrified of the sound she hears off to the side when the real danger is right there in the room with her. I brought in these bright neon colors to give this feeling of a disconnect from reality. And when I was done, I realized that the hands that were reaching through the walls were like the hands of all those people who want to reach in and violate the personal rights of women. I didn't start out to create a political piece, but in the end, that's what happened. The subject was just too heavy on my mind not to. When Rachel and Carol told me about this anthology, I knew that I had made this art for them, and all the amazing stories they curated.

Q: On your site, you talk about wanting your art to tell a story, which is something we've always admired about your artwork—all the details that, combined, offer the viewer a story that works on a number of levels. What are some of the details you'd love the viewer to know more about?

A: I always want a book cover to pop when it's small, and then when folks get up close, they discover details they hadn't noticed before. So in *A Woman Unbecoming*, I want you to see a woman scared in bed when it's small. But when you look closer, I want you to notice that she's looking off to the side when the danger is behind her. And she isn't just sitting up, she had her arms wrapped around her knees. She's been that way a long time. and when you slide to the spine, you'll see the alarm clock on her nightstand reads almost 3:00. It's the middle of the night. And when you look closer still, you'll notice the glowing flares coming off the letters in the title—like a knife slicing through. You don't notice all of these things at once, but the more you look, the more you see. And the more you engage with a cover, the more likely you are to be interested enough to read the back cover details and maybe give it a try.

Q: In your artist statement, you write that you "...bring a stylized real-world sensibility to the darkest humanity has to offer, while somehow managing to make the most twisted nightmares beautiful." We definitely agree that your art does that! What draws you to the darker side of humanity? What about the horror genre appeals to you as an artist?

A: I think the more connected you are to the darker side of life, the more you appreciate the light. One of my earliest memories as a child was watching late night creature features with my dad on one side and my big brother on the other. They taught me to love being scared, and that horror could be fun.

Q: In addition to the amazing pre-mades you send out in your newsletter, what are you working on next?

A: I've just started designing dresses featuring my art, which are so fun to wear! Bats and books and ouija boards and lots and lots of skulls. lol I'm currently test driving them at conventions and trying to get everything just perfect. This fall I'll be opening my very first online store—Positively Creepy.

Q: Anything to add?

A: If folks like my art, I'd love to stay in touch. I have a newsletter and each month I send out a new Creepy Calendar for my list subscribers. It can be printed out, or used as wallpaper for your computer. And sometimes I turn that art into a premade book cover that folks can get at a discount. I also share behind-the-scenes pics and videos of my work and periodic marketing tips for authors. But the best part is that folks actually write me back when I write them. It's such a great way to stay connected in these busy times!

About the Artist

LYNNE HANSEN is a horror artist who specializes in book covers. She loves creating art that tells a story and that helps connect publishers, authors and readers. Her art has appeared on the cover of the legendary *Weird Tales Magazine*, and she was selected by the Bram Stoker estate to create the cover for the 125th Anniversary Edition of *Dracula*. Her clients include Valancourt Books, Cemetery Dance Publications, Thunderstorm Books and Raw Dog Screaming Press. She has illustrated works by New York Times bestselling authors including Jonathan Maberry, Brian Keene, and Christopher Golden. Her art has been commissioned and collected throughout the United States and overseas. For more information, visit LynneHansenArt.com.

To learn more visit her at:
COMMISSIONS: www.LynneHansenArt.com
INSTAGRAM: www.instagram.com/lynnehansenart/
TWITTER: www.twitter.com/LynneHansenArt
FACEBOOK: www.facebook.com/LynneHansenArt/

Faculty and alumnae of Bryn Mawr College presented a webinar discussion of "Reproductive Rights After Roe" on July 26, 2022. Panelists Sue Frietsche, Mindy J. McGrath, Tamarah Moss, Sharon Ullman, and Linda Wharton offered suggested readings on the topic, listed below.

The college's write-up of the event from August 2, 2022, "The Overturning of Roe: How We Got Here, What to Do Now, and What Comes Next" is available online at https://www.brynmawr.edu/news/overturning-roe-how-we-got-here-what-do-now-what-comes-next/ and includes links to many of the sources.

SUGGESTED READINGS

Nicola Beisel and Tamara Kay, "Abortion, Race, and Gender in Nineteenth-Century America," *American Sociological Review*, Vol. 69, No. 4 (Aug., 2004), pp. 498-518.

Janet Farrell Brodie, *Contraception and Abortion in Nineteenth-Century America*. Cornell University Press, 1994.

Marlene Gerber Fried, ed., *From Abortion to Reproductive Freedom: Transforming a Movement*. South End Press, 1990.

Marlene Gerber Fried, Elena R. Gutiérrez, Loretta Ross, and Jael Siliman, *Undivided Rights: Women of Color Organize for Reproductive Rights*. South End Press, 2004.

Michele Goodwin, *Policing the Womb: Invisible Women and the Criminalization of Motherhood*. Cambridge University Press, 2020.

Carol Joffe, *Doctors of Conscience: The Struggle to Provide Abortion Before and After Roe v. Wade*. Boston: Beacon Press, 1995.

Laura Kaplan, *The Story of Jane: The Legendary Underground Feminist Abortion Service*. The University of Chicago Press, 1995.

Mikki Kendall, *Hood Feminism: Notes from the Women that a Movement Forgot*. Penguin Books, 2021.

Sara Matthiesen, *Reproduction Reconceived: Family Making and the Limits of Choice After Roe v. Wade*. Vol. 5. Univ of California Press, 2021.

Leslie J. Reagan, *When Abortion Was a Crime: Women, Medicine, and Law in the United States, 1867-1973*. Univ. of California Press, 1997.

Dorothy Roberts, *Killing the Black Body: Race, Reproductive and the Meaning of Liberty*. Vintage, 1998.

Loretta Ross and Rickie Solinger. *Reproductive Justice: An Introduction. Vol. 1*. Univ. of California Press, 2017.

Johanna Schoen, *Abortion after Roe*. University of North Carolina Press, 2016

Rickie Solinger, *Pregnancy and Power: A Short History of Reproductive Politics in America*. NYU Press, 2005; 2019.

Rickie Solinger, ed., *Abortion Wars: A Half Century of Struggle, 1950–2000*. University of California Press, 1998.

Andrea Tone, *Device and Desires: The History of Contraceptives in America*. Hill and Wang, 2002.

Mary Ziegler, *After Roe: The Lost History of the Abortion Debate*. Harvard University Press, 2015.

Marlene Gerber Fried, Elena R. Gutiérrez, Loretta Ross, and Jael Siliman, *Undivided Rights: Women of Color Organize for Reproductive Rights*. South End Press, 2004.

Mary Ziegler, *Dollars for Life: The Antiabortion Movement and the Fall of the Republican Establishment*. Yale University Press 2022.

Crone Girls Press originally began as a Facebook group for fans of speculative fiction, hosted by speculative fiction author and writing coach Rachel A. Brune. As the idea took hold to publish an anthology of horror fiction in honor of her favorite fall holiday, Rachel began soliciting stories of dread, despair, and doom, all of which made for some uplifting reading. Upon receiving some truly terrifying—and excellent—material, she decided to go for broke and start working on an anthology series that would feature work by established and debut authors...from the darker side of speculative fiction.

We've now published four full-length anthologies and are always adding to our series of three-novella mini-anthologies, Midnight Bites. *A Woman Unbecoming* represents the latest publication in our efforts to publish chilling horror from the widest variety of voices that we can include in our pages. Enjoy—but don't stay up *too* late past midnight...

Thank you, Fiends!

We so hope you enjoyed your stay with us. If the sights you have seen and the dreams you have escaped stay with you after closing these pages, wouldn't you do us the favor of warning others of what they might encounter, should they happen to open these covers?
Share your thoughts, whether they be the careful, measured words of the diligent reader, or the sobbing cry from the asylum, on Goodreads or Amazon!
We'll be seeing you soon.

Our list of other titles is always growing. To stay in touch, join us on Facebook, follow us on Twitter, and sign up for the Crone Girls Press newsletter: http://eepurl.com/gPT5s1.